Cassie
and the
Spectral
Shade

Book One
The Chronicles of Eridul

DANIEL NICHOLS

Cassie
and the
Spectral
Shade

Dedication

Sara Awen Nichols
1993 - 2003

Of a palm against the sky; I hear a whisper
As vassals beat their mats with rattan canes;

I hear the urgent cries from stilted towers,
The peal of auburn metal: Come in. Come in,

Hark the silted sands as passage narrows;
A flash of red that breaks the chronic din,

It tunes the waxing notes, in lilting prelude
Like a wanderer, like a light on distant hill

A breeze so fresh it lifts the shackled spirits
I Attend the whispered strains that lie
within.

THE GOVERNOR`S SCHOOL

One

The small white bus jostled its way through the towering columns of buildings, heading east to the one part of town the driver was certain the little bus had never visited before. Bright reflective glass was soon replaced by graffiti-covered plywood and pristine sidewalks with a crumbling urban landscape, further marred by the scent of despair.

Into this jarring scene, the pristine little white bus sailed, with its deep-blue, emblazoned lettering announcing it to be the property of the **Governor's School for the Arts at Walnut Grove**. Its destination? Building fourteen, South Kettle Lane.

Pulling up at last to the half circle at the front of the towering public apartment building, the little white bus was greeted by a trio of figures, which appeared to be a mother and her two daughters. The slightly taller of the two young girls was beaming and did a little hop when the driver pulled the crank on the bus door and leaned out toward them with a quizzical look on his round, bearded face.

"Cassandra? Cassandra Cole?" the driver intoned, looking directly at the pretty, young girl who stood next to a shabby-looking suitcase. She clutched a black art portfolio under one arm and held her younger sister's hand with the other.

"Yes, that's me!" the girl beamed, releasing her hold on the younger girl, whose face soured immediately. But there was no stopping the excitement in her voice and carriage of her step as she bobbed up to the driver and presented him with a neatly folded sheet of paper. The girl had deep-green eyes and light-ginger hair that tumbled loosely about her shoulders and whisked about in the brisk breeze. She had a bright smile and a winsome dimple on one cheek as she gazed at the driver expectantly.

Dutifully, the driver took the sheet of paper and checked its contents against the clipboard he carried with him from the bus. "Indeed it is. A pleasure to meet you, Miss Cole. My name is Bentley... yes, like the car... no, I have never owned one, but there are certainly plenty of them to be seen at the school." The old man smiled as he offered a hand to Cassie, who took it and returned a firm shake before twirling around toward her sister, whose frown had only grown deeper.

"Now, Charlie, you and I have a deal. I'll be back for Christmas, which isn't that long from now, and YOU are going to make new friends and help Aunt Nonie." Cassie delivered this with the sternness only a loving sister could muster, including the hands on hips pose that seemed to come with the job of elder sibling.

Charlie's little head drooped, but Cassie was having none of it as she wrapped her up in a hug that lifted her little sister from the ground, swinging her around until Charlie was laughing and squealing to be let go.

"I presume that you must be Joan Williard-Stewart, the child's..." The driver hesitated, not quite sure what to make of the difference in last names.

Joan took the driver's hand in a cordial shake while nodding.

"Yes, I'm Joan. These are my sister's girls, but the adoption has finally gone through." In saying this, a tremulous smile broke across her face as her eyes misted.

"Congratulations then. I suppose I'll get things loaded up, and we'll be on our way," replied the driver with a courteous nod toward Joan before taking the suitcase in one large hand and carrying it to the back of the bus, where he busied himself depositing it in the back compartment.

While the driver loaded Cassie's lone suitcase, Cassie gave Charlie one last spin before swinging her in front of her and dropping to a knee. "Charlie. I know that this makes you sad, and I know that you're sad because you love me..." Cassie pulled Charlie into a tight embrace, whispering, "I love you too. Truly, I won't be gone long, and Aunt Nonie needs your help. Promise me you'll be helpful... promise me?"

Charlie sniffed in a tear as she hugged her sister tight, burying her face in her sister's shoulder and nodding.

With tears in both of their eyes, they turned toward Joan, who waved a hand in front of her own face and laughed while biting her lip. "Oh, now look at what you've done. You're such a big, beautiful girl. Your mother would be so proud."

Cassie straightened and walked swiftly up to her aunt, wrapping her in a tight farewell embrace. "You ARE my mother, Nonie," she whispered into Joan's blouse.

Not wishing to be left out, Charlie completed the circle, and all three took a moment to laugh and cry together before breaking apart as Joan took Charlie's hand and smiled back at Cassie, who turned and made her way to the little white bus.

"You may have your choice of seats, my dear," offered Bentley as he leaned over to give the door mechanism a quick pull once Cassie had climbed aboard.

Having picked up its precious cargo, the little white bus roared to life and with a double honk pulled out of the semi-circle drive in front of the apartment towers to begin the long trip back to the rolling campus at Walnut Grove.

Noting after a quick inspection that the bus looked empty, Cassie settled herself in the front seat opposite the driver, scooting to the window and waving furiously back at her aunt and sister as the bus pulled away.

As the tower receded from view, and graffiti was at last replaced with the pristine glass storefronts of the city, Cassie absently began humming a small tune.

"Ah, a musician then?"

"I'm sorry? What did you say?" The bus driver had remained so silent that Cassie had forgotten about him.

"Your humming there, figured you must be a musician? Everyone's got a specialty at Walgrove's..." Bentley replied in a jovial tone as he turned the bus toward a large highway entry ramp and pressed on the accelerator.

"Walgroves?" repeated Cassie, though she felt like a bit of a heel repeating things. And her confusion this early on didn't bode well for what was to come.

"Sure. Walgrove, or Walgroves... it's what everyone calls the school. You can't very well go around saying the *Governor's School for the Arts at Walnut Grove*. It's quite a mouthful, after all. So, everyone just calls it Walgrove's or Walgrove's Academy, if you like."

"I see. Not a very attractive name, but I suppose that makes sense." Cassie shrugged as she peered out the window toward the landscape that sped by. Having visited once for her interview, she knew that the school campus was enormous, situated on nearly 6,800 acres of rolling hills that abutted one of the foremost climbing surfaces in the area. That last bit of detail she had picked up from the brochure she had read so many times that the staples had fallen out.

"So, music, then, is it?" queried the driver once again. "You'll like the music department, I think, though it may depend on if you are an instrumentalist or vocalist, I suppose."

"Oh... no... no, I'm not a musician at all, neither instruments nor vocals, though I do enjoy singing. But, no, I'm here for painting, sculpting... that sort of thing," Cassie replied as she fingered the black portfolio she had carried with her onto the bus.

"Of course, of course, I should have known. That must be your portfolio there with you. Well, you'll have to show me some of your work once you get settled in. I do love a good drawing or painting." The driver looked back briefly to smile at Cassie before turning his eyes toward the road.

"So, you mentioned that I'd enjoy the music department... Do you know anything about the visual arts program?" Cassie was interested in learning anything and everything she could. Her interview process had included a number of faculty, but as school had not been in session, there'd been no students on campus to meet, and the tour had been limited to the immediate grounds.

"Oh, sure. They're a fine group. Pretty quiet. Usually keep to themselves. The visual arts seem to be a bit of an individual thing, if you know what I mean." Bentley began to slow the vehicle down as he turned the small bus off the expressway and down the exit ramp. "Won't be long now, and you'll get to see for yourself!" Tilting his head back toward the road, Bentley turned the bus left and under the overpass. The city was little more than a silhouette along the skyline now.

"It's not a very large group. These days, everyone is into the digital arts: websites, games, and whatchamacallits. All the other programs have been struggling for new students. But I'll take the good old-fashioned stroke of a brush any day."

Cassie frowned at this. She appreciated his sentiment but knew exactly what he was talking about. Painting, drawing, and sculpting were all wonderful things that no one seemed to appreciate anymore. Most of her fellow students from the city school had access to computers and tablets at home with an amazing array of tools that could render art that would take Cassie months to replicate with a brush. Trying to keep up was what helped to push her skill far enough to gain the notice of the scholarship committee.

"Don't you worry, young Cassie," assured the driver as he pulled the small white bus through an enormous wrought iron gate that framed the main entry into the school. "Normal people like you and me don't need all the fancy trappings. Creativity, after all, comes from the heart, and if I can tell anything at all about a person, it's how big their heart is." This he said as he pulled the bus to a stop beneath a large, stone portico that arched over the drive. The lights of the towering structure were lit, as the day was beginning to fade, casting a cheery glow to the building's beautiful facade. After shifting the bus into park and setting the brake, the driver turned in his seat to face Cassie. His dark eyes sparkled with sincerity as he finished the thought, "Always follow your heart, Cassie, and don't let anyone take it from you."

"Yes, well she's too much of a chatterbox for that, if you ask me," quipped a voice from the back of the bus.

Cassie gasped and turned quickly to see a slight young man who was only now sitting up from where he had apparently been reclining in the back seat.

"Don't let that one bother you, he's as frightened as you but too proud to ask anyone for help," retorted Bentley as he reached for the door lever one last time and pulled it toward him with a loud creak. "Everyone out, then. It should be just about time for the evening meal if you hurry."

"Hey, if you're not going to move, do you mind scooting in so that I can get by?" remarked the young man, who had quickly slid to his feet and was now standing over Cassie.

"I'm sorry," replied Cassie, still blinking in surprise and confusion as she slid back into her seat to let the young man pass.

"I'm certain that you are. All you mudders are the same, head half in the clouds and the rest of you covered in some sort of paint." The young man pushed past and out of the bus without another word, leaving Cassie gaping at his rudeness.

"That's Ludwig. He'll be with the writer's group, part of the digital arts society now... most of them lack... people skills, I think," explained the bus driver as he shook his head and exited the bus through his own door. "Don't worry about your bags, they'll be taken to your room, and I can carry the portfolio as well if you like," Bentley added while peering back at her through the open driver's side door.

"No, that's okay, I'll just hang on to this for now," Cassie responded as she stood at last, picked up her portfolio, and stepped down and out of the bus.

The scene that spread before her was even more beautiful than she remembered. The evening sky painted the tall glass of the front atrium in gorgeous shades of vermillion and sapphire. Constructed of pale sandstone, the main building rose two or three stories in height, with dark slate tile along the roof and an entryway that was framed by a long, covered archway featuring pillars of glossy black river stones and a mosaic walkway of the most intricate design.

"Well, you didn't think a school for the arts would be ugly, did you?" blurted the voice of the young man who had not yet ventured into the building. "You can call me Ludo if you like... it's a lot easier for people to wrap their tongue around than Ludwig. And apologies for my rudeness back there. It turns out that you're quite pretty, and I figure it wouldn't hurt for people to see me walking in with you." His wry grin and sardonic tone hinted at his attempt at making a joke, but Cassie was having none of it.

"From the looks of you, I don't think it would help me at all to be seen walking in with you. So, if my reputation is based on the company I keep, I suppose I'm better off heading in on my own." With a flip of her hair, Cassie left him standing flat footed as she strode down the walkway and through the open doors, head held high. She couldn't help but smile at the sound of his hurried footsteps as he attempted to catch up with her before she reached the entryway, portfolio tucked neatly beneath her arm.

Two

"Fair and worn lone traveler. Come. Rest. That I, your wounds, may bind."

"Would that you could spare me a mortal's fate, for eagerly would I come. But there, across the sea my prize awaits."

"None but lady death awaits on Mortis Isle. Be still. Be calm, and stay awhile. When the morning comes, your prize will be there still."

"Detain me not, fair queen of light. While comely thy visage be, yonder lies the prize for me."

The pair of students moved smoothly across the stage, transitioning into a haunting duet cut short by a shrill shout from the back of the auditorium.

"Cut! Cut! Ghastly. Terrible! Again... go through it again, this time with... I don't know... anything at all. The two of you look like you've forgotten absolutely everything you learned over the last three seasons. Start from the top and at least TRY to make me feel something this time around." Bale Adonis lounged against the theater chair as he watched his senior performers move slowly back to their places for the start of the scene. Last year's season's ending show had been brilliant, perhaps the best that had ever been performed in the school's long and awarded history. He hated having to lose such an incredibly talented cohort, and while he held some hope for this year's crop of third and fourth year scholars, this muckety display suggested that he perhaps should retire early.

"Adi... Adi... if you push them too hard this early, you'll break them all. Come now, let the children enjoy the opening week before the thrashing begins." The voice of reason drifted down to Professor Adonis, who reluctantly rose to his feet and clapped his hands. "They're merely seventeen, after all, don't you remember what it was like to be seventeen?"

"Very well, very well. We're done for the evening. Alright, everyone, you're free to go for now. Go look at the evening meal, but don't touch anything that isn't leafy and green. I'm not casting any chubby characters this year." Master Adonis sighed as he turned to greet his fellow master and sometimes muse. "Ah, my dear Cressida, right as always." Bale turned dramatically to face his colleague fully and greeted her with a faint kiss to either cheek. "How did I ever think that these wriggling worms would magically metamorph on their own. I can't believe a new year is upon us so soon."

"You'll have them in top shape in time. I believe in you, Adi... you always pull through." Mistress Cressida McClaine, the professor of choreography, smiled demurely as she held out a gloved hand in expectation that Bale take it. "Now, I need you to come with me beyond prying eyes, as something of greater importance has come to my attention involving the new crop of scholars that has just arrived."

"I can only assume they are all bow-legged, crooked, and raspy, with interest only in computers. And let me guess, there are neither mudders nor scribblers this year." Adonis lifted his hand with a dismissive wave that matched the dramatic scowl on his face. Nevertheless, he took Cressida's hand and began to walk with her toward the back of the stately auditorium, which was dark save for the lights that illuminated the stage below.

"Adi, you know that you shouldn't be encouraging those biased terms. The visual arts may lack relevance in the digital world, but they are still exceedingly important for... other things." Cressida looked cautiously about as the two professors walked hand in hand up the aisle to the doors in the back, pushing through them to the hallway beyond.

Willem winced at the cutting tones of the receding faculty, but their success in preparing students for the big stage was difficult to ignore. Both masters were celebrated in the most important circles... the school's board would have accepted nothing less. This, he knew, as his father was one of the directors and made certain that he was reminded often how much of their fortune was being invested to ensure his place here. But with Bale Adonis, there were no free rides. No matter how important his father may be, Willem needed to earn his place like everyone else.

Once he was certain that the professors had departed, Willem sagged and nodded to Janice, who also wore a look of abject rejection. "You did well, Janice. We'll get this, don't worry."

"He changes his mind constantly. How can I possibly reach a point that moves every time I look at it?" Exasperated, Janice pulled a set of earpods from the pocket of a light, hooded sweatshirt she was wearing and turned toward the back of the stage.

As the other students departed eagerly for the aforementioned reception dinner, Willem remained, mulling over the night's events and the professor's sharp critique as he picked up a broom from off-stage and began to clean the floor in slow steady strokes.

Having spent the entire last season and the summer memorizing lines and rehearsing scenes, it was more than a letdown to feel as though he were starting everything from scratch. As he watched Janice disappear behind the curtain, he felt that all of his work had been for naught. He needed to earn the lead for this season's show. His father, Willem S Marshall III, had demanded as much.

"The family reputation is at stake, son!" Willem remembered his father shouting with the dramatic flair that only an actor of his father's caliber could muster on command, or in this case at the dinner table. "We haven't invested five years in your education for you to play supporting roles your entire life. If you can't land the lead in even a single play, how can you expect to be accepted into Remauld?"

The Remauld School of Performing Arts was easily the most prestigious university for traditional theater, and in Willem's father's mind—the path to glory. Nearly every actor of any note first passed through the winnowing Remauld mold before launching into the international celebrity that Willem's father so deeply craved his son to attain.

Walgrove was just a steppingstone, but Willem had to admit, if he couldn't succeed here, how did he expect to take the next step?

Soaking in the emotion of the moment, Willem added this to his repertoire, internally recording the feeling in his gut, the strain in his arms and legs, and the fixture of his countenance for a later moment. He continued to push the broom in short strokes across the stage floor, seeking out other emotions within which to bathe. He must succeed this year.

Having walked alone backstage, Janice Tremaine climbed atop one of the unfinished set pieces and adjusted the earpods in her ears as she settled into a cross-legged sitting position.

"You're all hopeless," she mocked as she recalled Master Adonis' words. She knew well that success in this field required a thick skin and a short memory, but sometimes she wondered if she would ever have those in the right order.

Janice listened intently to a particularly challenging stretch of a flute solo. While she didn't actually play the flute, as instruments were never her thing, she was, like most of the Performing Arts students, minoring in vocals and found the cascading trills and arpeggios that the instrument could attain quite helpful in improving her own art. As a rising third year student, she was 'embracing the draff,' which was to say—coming to the realization that being good at anything required an immense amount of dedication and arduous work.

She'd had quite a bit of fun her first and second year, as most scholars did, exploring all that Walgrove had to offer, from curriculum to events and activities of every kind. Her overall class standing had not suffered too badly, for which she was thankful, but her in-focus standing was well below where she wished it to be, having only secured a supporting character and a couple minor solos in last season's arts festival that the school put on to highlight the talent it had accumulated within its ranks.

It wasn't really the performance she was interested in, for she had happened upon something that was far more interesting—and she was certain that this flute solo was the key. Having committed the part to memory, Janice remained seated but straightened her back and opened her chest. The platform situated her about ten feet above the black floor below. Closing her eyes, she let her arms fall loosely to her side before rolling her shoulders back gently.

"Here goes nothing..." she whispered softly. And then she began to sing the phrase. In reality, the phrase was a simple arpeggio; in practice, however, hitting the odd intervals in succession was no small feat. After a few runs through the lines, she opened her eyes. Nothing.

With a small frown, Janice closed her eyes again, calming her breathing as she did, before beginning once again. This time, she started slowly and softly, the notes rising from her chest like a gentle breeze. She imagined herself seated in the ancient land from which the verses came. Over and over, she sang the brief musical phrase, taking in each note and filling it with every fleeting emotion she could muster. Fear rolled past and was pushed into the arpeggio, shame too, along with self-loathing, but also hope and envy, accompanied by a small spark of childish joy. She was like a careless scientist, blasting her beaker of sound with bursts of random compounds in the faint hope of discovering a miracle cure.

Exhausted at last, and utterly spent, Janice sagged, her breath coming in ragged gasps. She lifted a hand to her head to tug the light earpods from her ears... and felt only air. Blinking open her eyes, she squealed in delight as she watched her breath float away like a misty cloud.

"I'm cold! It's cold!... I can't believe I did it!" She clapped her hands together and sprang to her feet, feeling in her pocket for the ever present phone. She needed to tell Maxine immediately... but the pocket was empty. It was then that Janice noted the tufts of snow on the ground and soft, flittering flakes that cascaded through the air all around her.

Fear began to overtake her joy. She had reached the other side, but now what?

"Hello? Hello? Is anyone there?" Janice called into the darkness as she wrapped her arms about herself and shivered.

Willem paused in his sweeping as the voice began to rise from backstage. "Must be Janice," he murmured as he focused his attention on the lilting tones. It was beautiful, mysterious... there was so much pain, yet the simple, repeated notes were not in themselves sorrowful. Quite frankly, it was some of the best singing he had heard, but not part of the repertoire or this season's show. "Perhaps an early start on her senior project..." he muttered as he resumed pushing the broom. But after another moment, his interest piqued and mind unable to focus on his task any longer, Willem walked lightly to the edge of the stage and set the broom against the wall before navigating through the series of overlapping curtains along the wings that lead toward the back.

The song was beginning to crescendo as the singer repeated the musical phrase over and over, each time with greater fervency, as if willing Willem to find her. Yet as he pushed the last curtain aside, the song came to a sudden and abrupt end... the voice ringing in the empty auditorium, followed by a clatter like the sound of someone dropping their phone. Willem scanned the open space backstage but saw no one. The floor was clear, the lighting and ballast ropes neatly secured to their pegs along the back wall. Nothing seemed to be out of place, and there was no sign of the mysterious source of the voice. "Janice..." Willem offered tenuously. "I'm sorry if I startled you, please continue... I just... I wanted to say that it was... it was really quite good."

Receiving no reply, Willem walked across the blackened floor to the back wall where he knew he would find the overhead light switches. With a click and a hum, the room brightened immediately under the dim fluorescence of the working lights.

Once again, Willem scanned the room, holding his breath to listen for something... anything. But there was no one—there was nothing. Then his eye caught sight of something dangling from the top of one of the makeshift platforms. On further inspection, he recognized the looping wire belonged to a pair of earpods, and as he climbed lightly to the top of the platform, he discovered a mobile phone lying face up on the top of the platform, the screen unlocked and glowing.

Three

"Welcome… both of you. You are the final two to arrive. Please join your fellow first years in the Great Hall, where the staff and faculty have prepared a lovely reception for you." The speaker greeting Cassie—and she could only assume by the hasty footsteps behind her that Ludo had also arrived—was an extremely tall, stately woman with horn-rimmed spectacles, through which she was peering down at the newly arrived scholars. Her name tag identified her as Mistress Audrey Maude, mistress to the women's dormitory.

"Given that I have only two name badges remaining, I'll assume that you, my dear, are Cassandra, and this hasty young man must be Mister Ludwig." The woman offered a prim smile as she handed each of them an embossed name badge sporting their full names along with a small, colored circle in the upper right corner.

"In order to help simplify your transition to the Governor's school here at Walnut Grove, we organize all of our scholars into societies and within societies by your designated year of acceptance. As both of you are first year scholars, you will be seated with your fellow 'first years' at the far end of your society's table."

"So... Scribblers are red?" Ludo asked quizzically as he took his name tag and eyed it before slipping the magnet off the back and clipping it over the pocket of his rumpled blazer. His face wore an open display of distaste for the recent inclusion of writing scholars into the newly formed Digital Arts Society. Cassie assumed he wanted to write, not hack, and the very notion that writing was now considered a 'Digital Art' seemed to anger him to no end.

"Such an astute but unnecessary observation, Mister Ludwig. And there are no 'scribblers' here, there are only digital arts scholars. Now, please hurry in, as the reception is about to begin." With a graceful wave of her arm, Mistress Maude directed Cassie and Ludo down a short hallway that ended in an ornately framed double set of doors that towered above them on either side like ancient wooden sentinels.

"Well, Miss Cassandra, I guess I'll see you around," quipped the young man as they entered the enormous hall. Immediately, Ludo slouched and slowed his pace, casting a bored expression on his face as he moved off to the table on the far right that was clearly marked with vibrant red signage.

Cassie, however, paused in the opening to the Great Room and gaped in wonder at the marvelous spectacle before her. She had never seen a room so large with ceilings so tall. Great, darkly stained wooden beams framed the arching roof that stretched at least forty feet above her. Laid out across the hall were four long tables that ran nearly the length of the room, each crowded with a group of well-dressed students, who in turn wore some small color declaring their society.

"It's amazing," Cassie admired, not aware that she had spoken aloud.

"Indeed it is. Quite the marvel. But... your seat, please, Miss Cole," commanded a calm voice from just behind her. Turning slowly, Cassie blanched in shock as she gazed up at an ornately dressed woman, her long, academic robes brushing the floor and brilliant white hair pulled back in a thick bun. In her hand, she held a ceremonial scepter, and behind her stood a long line of masters and professors, also dressed in full academic robes, waiting for Cassie to take her seat so that the procession could begin.

With color rising rapidly to her cheeks, Cassie bowed her head apologetically and stepped quickly to the side while scanning the table for her society's matching color: gamboge. A small part of her mind knew that she would have appreciated the uniqueness of the semi-translucent yellow pigment derived from the Cambodian tree of the same name, but the larger part of her mind was panic stricken as a thousand eyes stared at her from all angles. Fortunately, the students had the courtesy not to laugh at her expense, though no small few were hastily covering wicked grins.

"What a dreadful way to start..." Cassie murmured as she slid onto the bench at the far end of her designated table.

"It's not the best but also not the worst," consoled the voice of a fellow first year sitting across from her. The speaker, a wonderfully pretty girl, Cassie noted absently, was dressed in the appropriate school uniform for the occasion, with a pretty yellow scarf tied neatly and loosely around her neck. "Last year, one of the new screechers started playing some bawdy tune with his trumpet... someone pranked him into believing that he was supposed to herald the arrival of the faculty." The girl giggled and smiled warmly at Cassie, stretching a hand across the table. "Sarah... Sarah Dawson. I'm new as well, but my older brother is a prefect in his final year, so..." she shrugged to indicate that she was therefore naturally familiar with the happenings in the school.

"Screechers?" asked Cassie as she shook the other girl's hand.

"Oh... all the societies have nicknames, even the sub societies like choreography and writing. The masters hate it, but there's no stopping it. We're known as mudders... cause, well..."

"We make quite a mess..." concluded Cassie coyly.

Sarah smiled and nodded. "Exactly. You'll fit in here just fine," she said with a wink as she turned her attention to the front of the hall where the headmistress was stepping to the podium to begin the ceremony.

Her embarrassment fading, Cassie took a moment to look once more about the room, "So, this is my new home..." she whispered with a deep sense of satisfaction, turning as well toward the front as Headmistress Floquet began her address.

"Welcome, scholars, new and returning. Your faculty, staff, and I have been working diligently this summer to prepare what we believe to be an exceptional season of experiences and opportunities for you all. Please join me in welcoming back our society deans." A smattering of applause started and died off as the headmistress introduced the primary professors for each discipline.

"Returning this year as Dean of Performing Arts is our very own Master Bale Adonis. The city is still talking about your incredible year-end performance, Bale, and we look forward to what you have in store for us this year." Master Bale Adonis stood and bowed theatrically to raucous applause and shouts from his society scholars.

"Master Grimpen Galleon returns for his sixteenth year as Dean of Musical Arts." Once again, applause, but this time accompanied by an obviously rehearsed chorus that echoed brilliantly through the great hall and was accompanied by a booming percussive beat as the Musical Arts Society students hammered the table in unison. Cassie couldn't help but smile at the enthusiasm and display of skill that was already evident.

"Returning for her eighteenth year, the one and only Mistress Shileen Beckett, Dean of Writing. If you have not picked up her latest novel, please ensure that you do, as it is a marvelous piece of literature and an instant classic to be sure." Mistress Beckett, a short and stout woman with graying hair, wore a winsome smile as she nodded demurely toward the headmistress, then once again toward the remnants of her society, who now were seated at the far end of the table in their newly assigned red. Many, however, continued to wear the original green, which gave a holiday feel to the table as each of the writing-focused scholars pounded the table with heavy books, making a thunderous racket that echoed about the hall.

"Joining us for the first time this year as a newly appointed society master is Master Ignus Radcliff, who will serve as our very first Dean of Digital Arts." This statement was followed by raucous and disorganized laughter and jeering. Cassie could see why there might be some animosity toward the new discipline.

"And last but certainly not least, the newly appointed Mistress Cynthia Zeltrix, who joins us from her prior appointment at the esteemed Portico College of Arts as Dean of Visual Arts."

Cassie blinked in amazement at the mention of Portico College and could only wonder why someone would ever leave the most prestigious visual arts college in the country for a position at a boarding school, even one with Walgrove's reputation. Yet she found herself standing, applauding, and cheering with the rest of her society—many of whom had fashioned banners and flags of all sorts so that their display of support was clearly the most colorful celebration of all.

Waving the students to quiet, the headmistress spread her hands in a broad, welcoming gesture as she continued.

"The Governor's School of Arts at Walnut Grove was founded in 1794, but the roots of our school are much deeper and much older than the foundations of these buildings. Our tradition of excellence spans generations and continents, for we stand upon the shoulders of great men and women as far back as the illustrious Sumerian empire. All of you, my young scholars, are now part of that long and proud tradition. Future generations will look to the example you set this season. The world expects greatness... and we will deliver."

The room erupted into cheers and applause that continued for several moments before the headmistress leaned into the podium, her face growing a shade more serious.

"Leadership begins with each one of you. Do not look to your prefects or your masters to set an example. Each one of you must embody the excellence you expect to see in those around you. You are not here to merely mark the time, you are here to confront every challenge head on... and to overcome." This phrase was marked with a resounding boom as the headmistress struck the stone floor with her staff, and as she did so, the floor in front of the podium split open, and up from the opening arose a large, gleaming chalice that sparkled in the fire-lit room.

"Behold, the Governor's Cup!" cried the headmistress as she thrust a hand toward the sparkling trophy that stood at least four feet high, with huge handles on either side that were covered in colorful ribbons matching the assigned colors of each of the participating academies of art that comprised the Governor's Pantheon, as it was called. Cassie noticed immediately the overwhelming shade of purple, marking Walgrove's academy as the most represented among the thick tapestry of ribbons, but her nose wrinkled as she noted that each ribbon tip was a different color—primarily a deep blue that corresponded with the colors of the Performing Arts Society.

Sarah interjected as though anticipating her thoughts, "Yeah...

sorry to say, but we mudders aren't really the prize of the school." Cassie turned to see Sarah looking at her and shrugging. "Dillies and divas, that's the performing arts—actors and dancers—are the only ones the academy cares about... but who knows? With a new and celebrated society mistress like Madame Zeltrix, perhaps our lot is looking up this year."

Cassie completely missed what the headmistress was saying about the Governor's Cup, she presumed it had to do with how a school went about winning the contest but figured she could just ask someone after the reception. Indeed, her head was so full at this point, she found it difficult to focus on anything further. There was something about a schedule change and a special event later in the fall, but for the most part, the remainder of the evening whisked by so swiftly that Cassie was surprised to find herself walking at the back of a column of her fellow society members as they returned to their dormitories.

Happily, upon arriving at her room, she discovered that Sarah had been assigned as her roommate, as each society space was split between men and women's quarters and the first years were all assigned to doubles at the very back of the long hallway. For the Society of Visual Arts, or "mudders," that meant a climb down a flight of stairs to the basement, which smelled of clay, paint, and yes... mud. Sarah had already reached their room and unpacked earlier in the day, claiming the lower of the bunked beds as her own.

"I hope you don't mind if I take the lower bunk, I'm not very good with heights." Sarah shrugged as she plopped herself down on the firm mattress, which was covered by a yellow blanket and a soft, gray comforter.

"I'm just glad you're my roommate, I'm sure the other first years are fine, but you... well you seem like the kind of person I'd enjoy getting to know." Cassie smiled brightly and on a whim walked up to Sarah and gave her a warm hug, receiving one in return. "And you can call me Cassie. Cassie Cole. Sorry I didn't mention that earlier."

"Oh good, Cassandra sounds a bit formal, and the feeling is mutual... Cassie." Sarah smiled brightly in response before adding, "Well, I hear that you're a year ahead in age, so I hope that you don't mind rooming with a true first year." Sarah's reply came with a hint of hesitation, as she seemed uncertain about how to broach the subject of Cassie's entry to the school in what should be her second or possibly third year. While not uncommon, it was well known that only public scholarship students were admitted at the age of sixteen, which meant that Cassie was not likely from a wealthy family. Cassie had surmised that this might be an issue and was relieved for it to be out in the open from the start.

"I suppose there's some dreadful term for me, then, isn't there?" she prodded, hoping beyond hope that she wouldn't be saddled with a second derogatory title on her first day.

"Sorry about that but, you'll find that Walgrove has a thing for dreadful terms. But I suppose it would be best to know going into it. While other schools like ours place students into years by age group, here, first years are first years no matter how old you are. And, unfortunately, all older first years are called 'Judy,' boys and girls alike."

"Judy?" Cassie asked with a tilt of her head. She supposed that it could be worse, but having grown up in a public school, she knew how inflection could alter even the most innocent term.

"It has to do with one of the founders or the founders' child or likely something much worse than that. Truth is, no one really knows anymore, but if you get called Judy, you'll be expected to respond... and Judies get ripped and popped more than a normal first year, which is quite a lot." Again, Sarah shrugged. By now, she had doffed her academic attire and tossed on a comfortable sweatshirt emblazoned with the school seal and its adorable looking dragon as she plopped down on her bed.

"Ripped, popped? This is an awful lot to keep in mind. Good thing I have you to help me navigate things. I hope at some point that I can just get back to painting again." Cassie tried to lighten her tone, but her head was truly spinning now, and she was both exhausted and far too awake to fall asleep. Nevertheless, she finished unpacking the few belongings that remained in her suitcase, slipped on a new nightgown, and clambered up the ladder to the top bunk, where she crawled beneath the covers.

"Good night, Sarah."

"Good night, Judy."

They both laughed.

Four

Cassie smiled contentedly as she snuggled back against the pillow in the upper bunk. The day had been neither a complete disaster nor a complete success. And, for a bonus, her roommate was friendly, knowledgeable, and didn't snore. The last thing she needed to check, she couldn't do while awake, and so Cassie closed her eyes, breathed deeply, and wished herself into another world.

A biting chill to the air informed her that she had indeed arrived, and upon opening her eyes, she clapped her hands, partly to warm herself but mostly because she had really been hoping that these lucid dreams would continue after she started school. And indeed, her dream world was just as she had left it. But most importantly, there, resting next to her against the dark rocky wall, was her black portfolio.

The greatest mystery she had yet to uncover was how the drawings she made in her dreams ended up in her actual portfolio. For that matter, how was her portfolio was able to join her in both worlds? When the dreams first started, Cassie had performed all sorts of clandestine experiments. She'd discovered with great interest that electronic devices beyond simple things like lamps would never transfer to her dream, but her portfolio, pencils, brushes, and paints moved back and forth with her as long as she went to sleep and woke up in this same secluded spot.

"Let's see what you have in store for me today," she whispered as she peered about the small rocky enclosure. Cassie wondered if she ever mumbled in her sleep when she spoke in this place. She would have invited her sister Charlie into her experiments, but Charlie was just... "Charlie is just too practical." This she noted while scooping up her satchel of colored pencils and the portfolio before crawling easily outside of the den, pausing as she usually did to check for tracks in the new snow that always covered the ledge in front of her little nook.

"Nothing stirring today." Usually, she would find the tracks of a bird or other small creature. A slight shiver ran down her spine as she recalled the enormous paw print she had seen on one occasion. "I'm glad that you haven't been back," she said as she stood and stretched before pulling herself one ledge up, brushing the snow aside before sitting on the cold rock and pulling her portfolio into her lap. "Nothing but fog..." Cassie noted with dissatisfaction, shaking her head as she pulled her feet beneath her and stood up once again. "I wish I could get one day with a little sunshine. You'd think that if I could dream the same thing over and over, eventually I'd figure out how to control it better than this. Well, I really don't want to be awake too much longer today... I just wanted to check... wait... What is that?"

Cassie halted, straining to determine if the odd sound she had just heard would repeat itself. And there it was again. "Is that... another person?" She carefully set her portfolio down before lightly dancing up the ledge toward the snow-covered top of the rocky alcove.

"Help! Is anyone there? Please... Anyone?!"

The voice was faint, but it was most definitely a voice. "Well, this is new... and interesting. I must really have been overstimulated today to conjure up a voice." She looked around at the world of crisp white. "It sounded like it came from down there..." Cassie was poised at the top of the outcrop and often thought it funny how she had no fear of heights in the dream—though it was just a dream after all and she'd never been hurt here before. Still, she had read about people being injured in their dreams, so she had never tried anything truly crazy.

Slipping expertly down the craggy side of the cliff face, Cassie found a wide enough ledge upon which to drop, pausing as she did to await the call again.

After several tense moments with no further sound, Cassie took a few more steps along the ledge and peered over the side into a gaping gorge, at the bottom of which ran a deep and very cold looking river. "If you're all the way down there, you'll just have to help yourself," Cassie muttered before turning around and making her way back to her own cozy alcove.

Just before ducking in, she remembered her portfolio and clambered back up, grabbing it before shimmying down and sliding back into the cave. She had once dropped her portfolio in the dream and discovered when she woke up that she had misplaced it in real life. She assumed that she had merely dreamt about losing it because she had actually lost it in the real world, but once again, "You can never be too careful." Clutching the portfolio tightly, Cassie closed her eyes and drifted off to sleep... real sleep this time.

The new day dawned with a brilliant sun that shone brightly through the small window set in the top of the stone wall of their tiny, shared room. Sarah had already awoken and dressed by the time Cassie opened her eyes.

Cheerily thumping the side of the bed, Sarah beamed up at her, "Come along, Cassie. If you're late for the first session, you'll be called much worse than Judy. I'm going to run on ahead and see if I can find my brother."

"I'll be there, don't worry," Cassie responded as she sat up lazily in the bed, watching Sarah bound out the door. Cassie made quick work of getting ready, rather pleased to discover upon opening her wardrobe that it was stocked with all her uniforms and even a few bits of color for her society. From what she'd read in the manual, students, or scholars as they called them here, had four sets of uniforms: formal, scholar, athletic, and laboratory. Since all morning classes were reserved for general academic curricula, only scholarly wear was permitted.

To Cassie, whose family had never been able to afford a stitch of clothing more than was absolutely necessary, this wardrobe was an absolute bounty. In fact, Cassie lost track of time as she pawed through the varying offerings, being alerted of the impending hour only by the chime of a bell that rang through the stony hallway. With a shriek, Cassie threw on her new uniform, hastily gathered her book satchel, and whisked herself out the door and down the hall at a run.

"We do not run in the hallway," a stern voice commanded as Cassie rounded the corner and nearly collided with another student, just barely managing to keep hold of her books. "Look, Judy, you're not late yet. We set the chimes early for the first week so that you first years don't cost the society points."

Cassie blinked and looked behind her, recalling a fraction late what Sarah had said about being called Judy.

"Yes, I'm referring to you... Judy. Just because you're older doesn't mean you get to skip initiation. Many have tried, all have failed." The speaker stood a few inches shorter than Cassie, and she was not known for her height. Nevertheless, the stern look on the other girl's face was enough to elicit a meek nod from Cassie in acquiescence.

"Scholars do not merely nod. We speak truth to power." The other girl, with her fiery red hair crossed her arms as if waiting for Cassie to say something.

"I'm sorry... uh..."

"You're uh... uh... what, Judy?" the girl pressed. "Not very impressive, that's for certain." The girl squared her shoulders and affixed a sneer to her face as she continued, "Let me help you. Captain O'Dine... I'm sorry, Captain O'Dine, for prancing about the hall like a silly little girl..."

Cassie blanched and blinked, having not been treated like this by even the worst of the students at her public school.

"Come now, Captain, don't be too hard on the poor girl on her first day." Mistress Audrey Maude strode down the hall with a practiced grace, tilting her head to look down at the pair of girls through her horn-rimmed glasses. "Cassie, I was just looking for you. I noticed you were missing and thought I'd come and ensure that you were able to find your way since you were unable to join the tour group yesterday."

"My deepest apologies, Dorm Mistress, I had forgotten that Judy... err... Cassandra, had not been given a formal review of our society's expectations. I will be certain to catch up with her after sessions today to take care of that... personally." Captain Molly O'Dine tilted her head gracefully before excusing herself and exiting up the stairs.

"Don't let Molly frighten you, Cassie, she's new to the role of senior prefect, but she is both trustworthy and fair, otherwise your society would not have appointed her to the post."

"It's all... just a bit much, Mistress Maude, but I'll do better tomorrow. I don't want to let anyone down," Cassie responded as the color came back to her cheeks after the unexpected encounter. Taking her leave as well, Cassie leapt up the stairs, nearly tripping as she made her way out of Wolfmeck House to the top of the stairs and into the adjoining Adicus Lounge, which connected the Great Hall in the center to the masters' offices on the far wing and ultimately to the academic classrooms. Adicus Lounge was a shared lounge for scholars, and as might be expected on the first day of a new season, this scholars' lounge was awash with students, greeting one another after the long summer holiday. And as Cassie surmised from the leering she was receiving, it was well deserving of its nickname "the wolf meet," as no small number of the male scholars were sitting about, watching the archway from which each woman must emerge.

Someone made a catcall and a shout as Cassie appeared in the frame, "A ginger! Pay up, boys, I told you there was a ginger this year!" Ducking her head as though she could hide her strawberry curls, Cassie bravely entered the room, feeling every eye like a prickling needle on her skin.

It wasn't that Cassie was unused to the attention, she had attended a fairly disreputable public high school after all, it was the sheer brazen gaping that caused her free hand to ball into a fist in response to her desire to hit the nearest boy just on principle. As it happened, Mistress Maude appeared a few steps behind, and the presence of the tall dorm mistress sent the young men scurrying to their classrooms.

"No one will mind at all if you decide to slug one of them next time ... in fact, you might earn some points for your society if you do," Mistress Maude commented to Cassie while passing her, a slight smile curling on her lips.

Cassie relaxed the fist she had unconsciously been holding and smiled before moving along with the flow of fellow scholars through the long hallways to her first block, which was what they called the academic classes.

The room was beginning to fill as Cassie entered, but given the small class sizes, she was easily able to find her way to a place near the window, where she sat neatly, laying her satchel on the top of the table and withdrawing a notepad and a handful of pencils.

"Surely you aren't going to take notes like that, are you?" A young and all too familiar presence plopped down on the seat next to her, spinning a shiny new tablet computer on the shared desk and flipping it open while attaching a flexible keyboard at the base.

"Oh... it's you," Cassie muttered with a frown as she looked over at Ludo.

"Hey now, I apologized already. You have to forgive me... it's against the spirit of Walgrove to harbor such enmity against a fellow scholar." Ludo leaned an arm on the desk and looked over at her with a smile that some girl before must have let him get away with.

Cassie, however, was not that girl. Spying an open seat a row up, she slipped quickly up and into that seat, settling in right as the last student was rushing through the door.

"Aw, come on, you can't do that to me... we were just becoming friends!" exclaimed Ludo with a shake of his head as the newcomer, a rather sweaty boy, plopped himself down in the seat that Cassie had just vacated.

In reply, Cassie flashed a smile and fluttered her eyelashes in feigned innocence. "I can see the board better from here," she said softly before turning her smile to the girl who was sitting in the adjacent seat.

"Good for you, Judy ..." Captain O'Dine muttered in a droll voice before popping a pair of earpods in and increasing the volume on her digital player. Cassie frowned as Ludo chuckled overly-loudly behind her. By then, the professor was walking into the classroom, and without a word of introduction launched into his lecture on ancient civilizations.

TROUBLE FITTING IN

Five

"Another scholar is missing," informed Master Galleon as he sat in the wooden chair opposite the desk of Headmistress Floquet in her ornately adorned receiving room. The headmistress' manor stood across the lane from the entry to the school. The masters' manor was a beautiful structure, built in stone like the rest of the buildings but surrounded by an immaculately manicured garden in the old French style that extended several yards in every direction around the manor and nearly half an acre in front.

"This time it was one of our most promising students, Janice, and counting last year, that makes eight. Eight in less than a year. What are we to tell the families?" Master Galleon was a slight man with nervous hands that were far better suited to the ethereal trills he could achieve on the flute, his primary instrument, than any amount of manual labor. It was no coincidence he had earned the nickname "Mouse," for he indeed looked very much like one.

"Patience, Grimpen. We will get to the bottom of this. Do you have any further information? Are there any similarities to the other students that have gone missing?" The headmistress sat with her arms folded neatly across her legs, wearing a comfortable turtleneck sweater and soft, woolen, tailored pants. Her white hair fell loosely about her shoulders in astonishingly full curls.

"There is a digital file that the two in my society both checked-out before their disappearances. It's just a sample tape of old arias and arpeggios the scholars use for warmups. There's nothing to it really, but I have it for you." Grimpen offered a slim metal audio player to the headmistress with a proffered hand. "I didn't get much from questioning the other masters, but it appears that two students so far have gone missing from the Musical Arts Society, two from performing arts, and two each from visual arts and the written arts, or what was the written arts. I suppose the broader Digital Arts Society is too new to be affected by this sort of thing, but I've spoken with Ignus to alert him."

"You've done well, Grimpen... really." Mistress Floquet accepted the device and set it on a small wooden table that was standing next to her chair. "I will handle this as I have the others. Until we know more, we can only assume that the student has run off... which is why we've brought on Alistair and his security team."

Grimpen shuddered at the mention of the new security officer's name. "That man... that man is disturbing. Don't you think we'd be better off getting the police involved?"

Headmistress Floquet rose smoothly from her chair, hands held loosely together in front of her. "You and I both know the answer to that. The directors would never consent to bringing public authorities into campus matters. We have a long history of managing our own problems quietly and internally... and I do not intend to break that tradition."

Taking this as his cue, Master Galleon rose to his feet, offering a slight bow to the headmistress. "I'm aware, Headmistress... I just don't like it... not at all." He turned slowly then, hands trembling slightly at his sides as he walked toward the exit and past the row of headmaster portraits before proceeding out of the manor and into the surrounding garden.

"Grandmaster Caius would have known what to do..." This he said only after he was outside with the door closed safely behind him. While the new headmistress was both industrious and accomplished, the disappearances had begun shortly after her appointment. And Master Galleon could not help but connect the two.

As he crossed the lane and entered the side door to the Master's Hall, he paid no mind to a group of first year scholars who were walking together and chattering excitedly as they enjoyed their first half-holiday—a half-holiday was how the school described the Thursday and Saturday of each week, where there were no classes following lunch. On these days, scholars were permitted to pursue whatever they liked, often involving a sport or to put in additional work on their season project. While there were two half-holidays every week, the first half-holiday of each season was always celebrated with a field day full of competitions, food, and festivities.

Cassie had attempted to join the group that was jaunting down the lane toward the practice fields where the games were to be held, but to her chagrin, they politely ignored her, which left her awkwardly trailing behind, attempting to hold an enthusiastic smile on her face. After the group rounded the corner of Tripplett Hall, where math and science disciplines were taught, Cassie broke away along the path heading back toward the center of campus, her brow furrowed in frustration. A sudden motion drew her eyes from the path, and as she looked up, she found a handsome young man aiming a digital camera at her.

"Oh, don't stop now... that was absolutely brilliant! No, just ignore me, please. It's so hard to capture raw rejection like that."

Cassie blushed, her fist clenching as she halted, not wanting to run into him but also not wanting to turn tail and run. "Please put that thing down," she asked in as polite a voice as she could muster.

"But why?" countered the young man as he dropped his lens a tad and looked up from the viewfinder. "Don't you want to help me with my project? I'm doing a documentary on scholar experiences."

"Oh..." responded Cassie, not yet certain how to take this young man, who looked to be about her age or possibly a year older.

"The name's Jimmy... Jimmy Franks, but you can just call me 'Chopper' like everyone else." He didn't extend a hand, as he was holding the camera with the lens facing her, but offered a smile instead. "There, now, that smile is much better, though this next part is what I'm really after."

Cassie's eyes narrowed in response, "I see... and why is that?"

"Oh, wait, first your name... for the credits of course."

"It's Cassie... Cassie Cole," she responded cautiously.

"What? No, that's not right at all..." Jimmy responded as he began to circle around her, holding the camera steady to keep her face as the focal point. Chopper slid to her left until the practice field was at her back. "Your name's Judy, isn't it? That's why I need you for my documentary... the life and trials of Judy." The young man cackled delightedly as Cassie's face fell.

She couldn't believe this was happening to her. The next couple of moments slid by as if part of someone else's memory as she stepped up to the boy and his camera, grabbed the lens in a firm grip, and tore it from his grasp before smashing the camera into the walkway.

"Woooooowww... that was perfect!" exclaimed the boy, who was not at all ready for what came next as Cassie backhanded him across the face before grabbing the lapels of his jacket and pulling herself in, nose to nose.

When she spoke again, her voice was a violent rasping whisper. "Listen, you soggy little worm with your soft little hands, the next time you call anyone Judy, I want you to remember that we Judys come from some mean places that eat little worms like you for breakfast."

Shoving the boy away, Cassie kicked the camera and began walking swiftly away with no idea where she was heading, just knowing that she needed to get away from there as quickly as possible. In the background, she could hear the jeers and catcalls of a rowdy group of students who had undoubtedly watched the whole episode with delight and were now closing in on their wounded compatriot.

Letting her feet do the walking, Cassie ensured that she was well out of sight before picking up her pace, until she was running along the lane, glad that she had switched into her athletic uniform earlier in the day, as it would give her an excuse for jogging alone with all of the festivities going on. Tears streaming down her cheeks, however... those would not be so easy to explain away.

The lane wound around the outer edge of the campus, past the maintenance buildings and security office, until it curved down a shallow slope heading along the edge of a fenced meadow toward the towering forest line that framed the base of a rugged taprock mountain known locally as the Sleeping Turtle for its slumbering turtle-like shape. In many ways, this rugged basalt ridge resembled the landscape in her dreams, and it was reportedly a favorite among the students for free climbing or more casual climbing on some of the fixed gear routes.

While she climbed frequently in her dreams, Cassie had never taken the opportunity to see what it would be like in the real world.

"Well, I suppose that this is as good a time as any to give you a try," she murmured as she brushed her tears aside and jogged down the lane toward the forest and the towering rocky crags, lungs heaving more from emotion than the strain of physical exertion.

"Of course there would be a map. I suppose most of the climbing points have safety lines and nets too," Cassie muttered with no small amount of disgust as she drew up to a small path that led into the forest line. A wide wooden sign stood at the trailhead, highlighting a number of trails and giving names to various climbing surfaces, including their grading, the stiffest of them being a 5.12d called Turtle Face. Cassie had no idea what the number meant until she saw the handy key to the side, which indicated the climb to be in the middle-advanced range.

"Thinking of jumping already? Sorry, that was a bad joke in poor taste." A slim young woman around Cassie's age appeared from behind the sign, clutching a loop of rope that hung around her shoulder with a hand that was still whitened from climbing chalk. "Don't let them get to you this early... they really don't mean anything, it's just... you know... the thing to do."

"I don't know."

"Girlfriend, I can read your face like a book. New uni, fresh face, recently crying your eyes out, obviously not fourteen. Girls like you and I need to stick together. The name's Whittle, by the way. Whittle Apple." The slender but muscular girl held out a chalk-covered and callused hand, adding, "Yeah... it could be worse. You could have my name. Real funny prank by the 'rents, but that's what you get when you grow up where I did."

In spite of herself, or perhaps because of what she'd just gone through, Cassie barked out a laugh that was not at all ladylike before clamping a hand over her mouth in embarrassment and taking the girl's hand in a firm shake with the other. "Cassie. Cassie Cole. So, I guess you're a... a Judy as well?"

"Oh, I was happy when they called me Judy. Actually let people believe that was my name for the whole first season 'cause Whittle Apple...? Not so great. But then I got over it. But yes, I'm a Judy as well, from the Eastern Flats... Trident High."

"Oh my gosh! Same here," Cassie exclaimed in amazement and relief.

"You've got climber's hands, or the makings of them. Where on earth does a city girl like you get these kinds of calluses?" Whittle commented as she turned Cassie's hand over in her own grip.

"What? Oh, I don't know. I only climb in my dreams, I guess they're from the brushes or sculpting clay." Cassie shrugged in response.

"Well, if this is what sculpting clay does, count me in on that," quipped Whittle as she released Cassie's hand and clapped her on the shoulder. "Wow... shoulders too? Now you're going to tell me you're a swimmer or some other nonsense." Whittle lofted a brow with a smile. "No worries ... what happens in the Flats stays in the Flats, whatever your secret is, it's safe with me. Why don't you join me for lunch ... the rocks are getting wet now anyway, and I'm hungry and haven't seen anyone from the Flats since my first season."

Cassie was only too glad to have found someone with shared experiences and decided immediately to put off her exploration for another day.

And so, the pair turned and began to make their way back along the lane toward campus, the sounds of the festivities growing as they went.

Six

Drawing the long bowie knife against the whetstone in a smooth, continuous pull, Alistair Montrose, the new security chief of the Governor's School for the Arts, lifted the blade for one final inspection before tucking it neatly into the sheath on his right hip.

"Twenty years of special forces, including fifteen tours and eight special assignments, and all I get in the end is a post as a babysitter." Alistair wasn't fond of his new post. "You know, Garrot," he continued, "I took this as a favor, but if things get any quieter, you may as well just bury me out back." Alistair's colleague also looked like he'd spent a number of years in special assignments as he sprawled lazily on one of the gators the security team used to get around the campus.

"This is fine by me. You could do worse, you know. There's not a lot of options for old sheep dogs like us these days. I'm surprised they haven't replaced us entirely with drones at this point." The grizzled veteran spit a gritty mixture of tobacco and saliva on the cement floor of the garage before leaning further back and propping his booted feet over the steering wheel. "So, Ali... the missing kids, wha d'ya think about that?"

Lifting a hand to cup his chiseled jaw, the chief eyed the cork board and the lines of strings that connected student photos with various clippings over a map of the campus. "Frankly, I still don't see the point in these things. A bunch of strings is supposed to tell me what, exactly."

Garrot guffawed from his seat on the four-wheeler. "Well, why the heck did you put it together if you think it's useless?"

It was a fair question, one that Alistair didn't have an answer to. "They do it all the time on those shows, I figured there had to be something to it... but nope... it's just an idiotic jumble. Though Floquet was impressed when she came by the other day."

This revelation caused Garrot to sit up. "The old bat came all the way out here?"

"She's made of sterner stuff than you think," Alistair replied as he turned toward his lieutenant with a frown. "Don't underestimate her. You do realize she was covert? From what I hear, someone messed with her backstop and she was blown in the middle of an op."

"You're serious?" He had Garrot's full attention now as the other man was squeezing hard on the lump of tobacco in his mouth. "Well, that explains... not much, honestly... but it's good to know. Didn't feel like you needed to tell me earlier?"

"Would you have said 'No' if I had?"

"I might have done it for free."

The pair laughed at that while Alistair took a printed photo of the most recent missing student and pinned it beside the growing montage that surrounded the building labeled the *Jasper Lidicus Center for the Performing Arts*.

The Jasper Lidicus Center was home to the Performing Arts Society, situated on the far western end of campus between Marsh Field and Quibbley Hall, where senior seminars and projects were housed. Lovingly called "the Lid" by pretty much everyone—given the mouthful that was its formal name—the Jasper Lidicus Center had recently undergone extensive modernization to the tune of nearly a quarter billion dollars in renovations, if the rumors were true. The old stone exterior had been replaced by an expansive glass facade that stretched upward at an angle for the full height of the structure. The simple walkway in front had been replaced by an impeccably manicured French garden, with a fountain rising at its center. The school rag had printed an article on the renovations, referring to the prior state as, "pulchritudinous if not practical" and the new as a "bewitching and ostentatious pageant of benefaction." Such was how life was described on a campus with young writers.

As Cassie and Whittle walked past 'the Lid' on their way back to campus, Whittle paused, spreading her arms in a magnanimous gesture, with the towering crystalline structure glinting in the midday sun behind her.

"Behold! The jewel of Walgrove! The immaculate one from whose bosom shall flow all the greatness this fine institution has to offer the world!" Cassie shook her head, slightly embarrassed at the japing but enjoying the brief show nonetheless. "Oh, you of unbelief!" Whittle continued in a mock ceremonial voice, "You laugh in the face of greatness, for while you behold little, generations to come will know that you once stood upon the greatness from which the fourth civilization arose!" Whittle couldn't help herself at this point, laughing as she spun around, flinging the loops of climbing rope to the side.

"Seriously?" Cassie mocked along with her. "Tell me that those are not the lines from the ribbon cutting ceremony."

"My dear Judy. You have no idea what a steel trap this mind is," replied Whittle slyly before ducking over to her ropes and gathering them up. "Come with me, and let me give you a proper tour," she added conspiratorially, looking around as though expecting to be seen.

"Oh? Don't tell me there's a secret sublevel where the school is hosting strange experiments." Even as she spoke, Cassie followed her newfound friend as the pair made their way to a gated entryway to the grand French style garden that framed the entry to the great hall, making their way toward a large fountain at the garden's center.

"What? You heard already?" Whittle teased without further comment, skipping ahead to the fountain, where she slid to a seat on the edge and patted the spot next to her, indicating that Cassie should join her. As Cassie did so, Whittle leaned into her slightly while casting her eyes and a hand to the sweeping glass structure to their right. "The Jasper Lidicus Center... The Lid as we call it. Tell me, what do you see?"

Cassie sat confused for a moment, enjoying the closeness with her companion as her prior fears began to fade and thinking that this school might not be as atrocious as she first thought. "A very large, expensive building?"

Whittle tilted her head back toward Cassie, her eyebrows lowered in a furrow. "You are obviously not a scribbler, are you?"

"I paint."

"Paint, right. Stick to that," the older student responded cheekily before whipping her head back toward the Lid.

"And you?"

"Percussion. Don't ask."

"Noted."

"Where were we? Oh yes. This is no ordinary building. It is in fact a portal to an entirely new universe."

Cassie remained silent, waiting for the joke to continue, but when nothing came, she leaned back to better gauge Whittle's expression. Whittle returned Cassie's question with the addition of a smirk and a lofted brow, which Cassie had decided were the woman's most endearing features by far.

"I know you're joking, but... you're joking, right?"

"I have deduced this because I have no other explanation for the disappearances." This time, Whittle shifted her knees toward Cassie, her voice lowering as she continued, "Five students that I know of have gone missing in just the past eighteen months or so. And three of those have disappeared right here," Whittle pointed a thumb back toward the building for emphasis.

"Wait. You're serious?"

"Deadly."

"But why haven't they shut the school down then? Called the police? Is it even safe here?" Cassie's voice had risen, showing no small amount of concern.

"Quietly," Whittle rebuffed in an audible whisper, once again looking around before adding, "This place is filthy with cash... do you seriously think they would let public law enforcement into these matters? Half the parents of these students would be happy for a direct payout in return for a missing child, they'd see it as justified ROI."

"That's awful!" Cassie put a hand over her mouth, realizing how loudly she had just spoken. She was about to add something further, when the sounds of revelry grew louder as a group of students burst over the knoll that separated the Lid from Marsh Field.

"Well, this, my dear first year, is where I depart." Whittle had risen swiftly to her feet and was looking to make a quick exit.

"You're seriously going to abandon me to this... mob?" Cassie whined, though she knew well that she needed to at least try to get to know her classmates.

"Let's climb sometime... after all of... this," Whittle motioned toward the surging group of scholars, "has run its course and things settle down. And, hey. The smile you were just wearing is a much better look. You should wear it more often." With a wink, the upperclassman was trotting off, her climbing ropes slung back over her shoulder, hair jostling as she went.

By the time Whittle had exited the garden, the crowd of first year scholars was already making its way into the maze, stretching in single lines through each of the walkways and linking hands until the whole of the garden was filled.

Cassie reluctantly gathered herself to her feet and joined the circle of students that was forming around the fountain in the center. Each of the others had a colored streamer tied on some part of their body, leaving Cassie as the only one without one. The student to her left, a tall but portly young man with a bulbous nose and heavy chin, wore red, while the girl to her right wore pink. Cassie hadn't quite sorted out all the colors yet, but noted that the yellow of her house was thinly interspersed throughout.

Leaping up and onto the rim of the fountain that Cassie had just vacated was a strikingly dressed professor, his outfit a mashup of colors and textures as he drew himself into a dramatic pose— the very image of a royal jester, she imagined. Master Bale Adonis obviously enjoyed this part of the year, where his love for theatrics was on full display as he acted the part of the expositor, guiding new students through their first few weeks of orientation to academy life.

Lifting his arms, the surprisingly agile professor, who had once held an esteemed career in a big city acting troupe, spun about, his voice strong and musical, easily carrying across the garden as he opened the ritual with a few melodic lines:

> *Springing high hands aloft*
> *Spinning round smile soft*
> *Swinging by like a dream*
> *Singing golden memories*

> *Choosing sun's unwaning heat*
> *Chasing moon's elusive sleep*
> *Chilling though a choice may be*
> *Choosing is required of thee*

Following this pronouncement, the ornately dressed professor bent in theatrical aside with a hand to the corner of his mouth, adding, "Or for the less lyrical among us... Look to your left... look to your right! One of these scholars you must dance with tonight!"

Squeals and moans followed his translation as Cassie looked right toward the girl who was beaming up at a bespeckled but not uncomely young man. Clearly she was taken, leaving the hand to Cassie's left, whose grip had tightened considerably.

Cassie sighed and looked over at the boy whose large white nose pimple made focusing on any other feature exceedingly difficult. "This can't be happening," she murmured as the boy dropped the other hand he had been holding and turned toward her, leaning down to shout a reply in her ear over the din.

"Sorry! Didn't catch that?" The boy laughed, his fetid breath hot against her face, causing Cassie to turn her face to politely hide her disgust, but doing so didn't save her from the smell of sweat that rolled off him. Apparently he had been very... active in the games that morning.

Still, Cassie figured she should give him the benefit of the doubt; after all, treating others the way you would like to be treated had been hammered into both she and her sister since the time they were very young. "I said... when is the dance happening? I missed the first half of the day."

"Tonight after dinner!" was the overly enthusiastic reply. In so saying, he untied the ribbon from his leg and handed it to her with his name clearly scribbled down one side. "Bobby Franks... you can call me Beef... Gamer like my older brother, who's a third year here." The ribbon was soaked in sweat as he dangled it out to her. "Here, we're supposed to exchange these so we can find each other tonight at the masquerade."

Cassie couldn't believe her luck... getting matched with the younger brother of the upperclassman that she had just slapped earlier in the day. This was playing out like the worst kind of teen romance novel. Rather than taking the dripping ribbon, she patted at her hips and looked back up at him, feigning shock on her face. "Oh no! My ribbon must have fallen off! Wait here and let me go see if I can find it." Bobby "Beef" Franks was in the process of trying to tie his ribbon to her arm as she said this, which caused him to pause long enough for her to extricate herself with a turn toward the far side of the garden. "I think it fell off either somewhere in here or on the hill. Why don't you take that side, and I'll look on the other side."

Falling for her ruse, the rotund young man fortunately saw this as a chance to secure his prize, and so, swiftly agreeing, he moved off toward the far side of the garden as Cassie watched. Once he was out of sight within the throng, she ducked low and wove her way in the opposite direction, making it safely to the lane, where she picked up her pace, jogging back in the direction of the dormitory from which she had emerged this morning.

"Could it possibly get crazier than this?" she wondered aloud as she padded down the lane in the lengthening shadows of the waning daylight.

Seven

" I don't know why they didn't tell you about the masquerade!" Cassie's roommate Sarah looked absolutely stunning in her period-perfect dark, Victorian gown, replete with silk gloves and a gorgeous mask affixed to a stick—which she dangled loosely at her side as she stared crossly back at Cassie through her reflection in the room's lone mirror. "Just skip it if you prefer... you skipped everything else today, why start engaging now?"

The truth of the words stung, but Cassie's instinct in the moment was to defend herself. All she really wanted was for Sarah to listen, but deep down she knew this was her own fault. Right or wrong, surely she could expect her roommate to stick with her.

"Mistress Maude is already on my case, as is Captain O'Dine... that one will personally drag me to the dance or... whatever. I don't have a dress, I don't have a mask, I don't even have time to make them!" Cassie was ranting at the ceiling from her perch on the top bunk, one leg swinging freely over the side.

"Well, you'll not get any closer to a solution by lying around on your bed." Sarah's retort was sharp, followed by a growl as she flung an eye pencil at the mirror. "I don't need all of your stress too! I'll never finish this makeup... and then both of our nights will be ruined!" Sarah stomped away from the mirror and over to the bunk, her eyes brimming with emotion. "You know, when I first learned that I would be rooming with a... a JUDY... yes, that's right, I said it! I thought that I could handle it... make friends, help you through the tough first semester. But you have to WANT to be helped, Cassie, and YOU don't even want to be here!"

A sudden crack sounded in the room. Sarah, in her anger, had swept her fragile mask against the bedpost in a gesture, resulting in half of the mask remaining affixed to the stick as the other drifted to the floor. After a moment of tension filled silence, Sarah fled the room, bursting into tears and slamming the door in the process, leaving Cassie alone and bewildered on the top of her bunk.

As the minutes dragged by, she slipped down from the bed. Sarah's makeup box was strewn all over the room, along with a mix of costume pieces—silks, scarves, and the like. She spent a few moments straightening up the room, having nothing else to do. The broken mask lay in two pieces on the floor next to the bed.

"I guess this dance was really important to her..." Cassie stooped to retrieve the mask and looked at it for a moment. "Cheap, commercial junk," she muttered as she turned the mask over in an unconscious assessment.

"Well, it wasn't cheap, and yes, I've been looking forward to this dance since my brother told me about it his first year here."

Cassie hadn't heard the door latch and turned in embarrassment to face Sarah, gently setting the broken mask on Sarah's bed.

"Look," they both said in unison.

"No, you go..."

"No, this is my fault..."

Both of the girls sighed, and Sarah closed the door fully before walking over to her bed and sitting down heavily.

"How much time do we have before the dance?" Cassie asked quietly.

"It doesn't matter, it's ruined now, you have to wear a mask for a masquerade, and I don't have time to make one. I was going to use my own, and then I forgot it at home. It didn't arrive in this morning's mail, so I had to borrow one from one of the other girls. I'm supposed to be an artist, and..."

"You made that dress?" Cassie asked in growing admiration.

In response, Sarah looked down at the intricate garment. "Took me all summer," she smiled sheepishly. "I just wanted this week to be perfect... I guess I built it all up in my mind."

Cassie took a step closer and knelt down in front of Sarah, lifting her chin gently until their eyes met. "I'm sorry, Sarah. I had my own expectations too... and you're right, I should be enjoying this. But... listen, I can help you."

Sarah sighed and opened her eyes, staring at Cassie as a questioning look grew on her countenance.

"You may not have a physical mask, but you have something just as good."

Sarah frowned, her eyebrows burrowing down. "And what is that?"

"You have a Judy... and not just any Judy, you have a Judy who was scholarshipped here for her skill with a pencil and a brush, and if I'm not mistaken, that set of makeup you have over there is basically just brushes, pencils, and paints." Cassie stood, offering a hand to Sarah, who took it with a look of bewilderment mingled with a touch of hope blooming in her eyes.

"And, Sarah... with that dress and me as your makeup artist, you are going to be the most magnificent creature to grace these halls in the history of this frumpy institution."

"But what about you?" Sarah countered as she stood and allowed herself to be led to the mirror.

"Tonight is all about Sarah... and I'll just toss a few of these scraps together and go in as maid to your princess."

Sarah smiled at this and shook her head, tears of gratitude cresting in her eyes.

"Actually, I think I can use those tears..." and saying this, Cassie began to work.

The old bus driver swabbed at his forehead with the oily cloth he had been using to test the oil levels in the school's little white bus. As he did so, his old bones felt a subtle change to the pressure in the tidy garage, indicating that he was no longer alone. Without looking up, Bentley folded the rag and tucked it into a pocket in his coveralls. "Now, who would be wandering about a drafty old garage at this hour of the night..." His voice was calm, more a statement than a question.

A sighing response told him exactly who had dropped in to visit. "Ah, Willem... good to see you again, lad." Bentley turned around, placing his hands on his hips and leaning back to appraise the young man through the glasses that hung on the tip of his large nose.

"Janice disappeared, Bentley..." Willem's voice was tense as he hung back in the shadows.

"Come here, son." Bentley waved the boy toward him with a worn hand. "It's so dark in here I can hardly see you."

After a moment's hesitation, Willem stepped into the dome of light provided by one of the large overhead fixtures. "I'm sorry, I should have stopped by earlier, Bentley. We miss you back home."

Bentley chuckled at this. Having served as the Marshall family's motorpool director for more than three decades, he'd been unceremoniously dumped on the street by Willem's father two summers ago but managed to find work at the school, where his paternal friendship with young Willem had rekindled. "I highly doubt that I'm missed... but this isn't about you or I. Janice, you say? Are you sure?"

Willem pulled a mobile phone out of his pocket, tapped in a code, and offered the phone for Bentley's inspection. "I know I shouldn't have, but I found her phone, unlocked, in the back of the Lid's stage. She... there's no other explanation... she disappeared. I was performing with her only a few minutes before..." Willem trailed off as he watched Bentley's face furrow in disapproval. "You don't believe me, do you..."

"No, my boy, on the contrary, I do. Did she leave a message on this?" Bentley offered the phone back to Willem, who took it and nodded while swiping to the voice recorder before pressing on the most recent recording.

The voice that played back was unmistakably that of Janice Tremaine.

"I've finally found it... I found the recording everyone's been talking about. It's this weird flute melody... nothing special about it really. If I understand correctly, I can make the transition by just singing it correctly. Frankly, it seems like the worst kind of bad science fiction plotting, sing a melody to open a portal, but... here goes nothing."

Bentley stepped toward Willem and silenced the recording with the press of a large thumb to the screen. "Whatever you do, boy, don't try to follow her there. I may be an old man, but I know danger when I hear it."

"But what should I do? The headmistress would never believe me. Master Bale is… he's no help. My father would never believe me either"

"For now, son, let me think, let me think. But promise me that you won't repeat what she did."

Bentley watched as the young man nodded slowly, a faraway look cast across his eyes as he pocketed the phone and turned slowly to retreat back into the night.

As the door closed behind Willem, Bentley straightened and turned back toward the little white bus. "You know this garage has doors, Alistair."

The lean security chief sauntered around the bus and into the light, a smirk alighting on his face as his boots made only the softest sound on the concrete floor of the garage. "They said you were like a cat. Mind telling me what that was all about old man?"

"I've known the boy and his family for decades… just senior year jitters is all, Alistair, nothing more."

"Well, let's hope that's all it was, old man. Just know that I'll be watching you. All these disappearances, a strange old bus driver meeting students late at night in the garage. Things like this tend to add up."

"Ah… mathematics. I never took you for the sort, Alistair. I must say, your range of skills surprises me every day." Bentley smiled as he walked to the front of the bus, climbed the footstool, and closed the hood with a resonant thud.

Alistair frowned at the older man and spat on the spotless floor in response before exiting the garage through the same door through which Willem had exited.

With a little help from Sarah, Cassie pulled together an assort-
ment of silks and strips of cloth, and along with some of the feathers from the broken mask and with a little help from a flower
arrangement in the hallway, she had fashioned a maid's outfit,
replete with a basket of petals.

Walking ahead by several yards, Cassie began to lay a path of
flower petals along the floor, leading away from the archway that
joined Wolfmeck House, the women's dormitory, to Adicus Lounge,
which was lined with scholars, both men and women, who were
excited to see the spectacle. The first year men stood on the outer
edge on either side of the makeshift promenade, eager to join their
partners in the parade to the Great Room, where the masquerade
was to be held.

Cassie had to admit that the whole thing was impressive, if
not a bit sophomoric. The costumes of the upperclassmen were
amazing, their masks unique and intricate. She now wished she'd
had a chance to prepare her own costume rather than walking
in hunched over and hidden like this... but it was all part of her
design, and so she continued to shuffle forward, laying a path of
petals in her wake, wincing at the snickers that followed her but
eager to experience the reaction to her work.

A chill running down her neck informed her that Sarah was
about to step into the hall, and as they had rehearsed, Cassie
stopped and knelt to the floor to ensure that all eyes would be
primed with anticipation for Sarah's entrance.

But Cassie was not ready for what happened next.

Gasps of awe filled the room, but the gasps sounded strange
and warped, as if time itself were slowing down. Then, Sarah
appeared in the doorway, and as she stepped into the room,
everything seemed to freeze—though Sarah kept moving—one
foot set lightly on the ground as the other lifted in agonizingly

slow motion. The stunning layered dress undulated as if she were floating through deep water. Cassie gazed around the room from her crouched position. Globules of water shimmered in mid-air from a glass that was being lifted too quickly. Gaping tongues and wide eyes painted a menagerie of unnatural shapes and colors. The scene was amazing and grotesque—like a living Grünewald stretching all around her.

She could also see a shimmering, curving line, like the edge of an expanding bubble or sphere, speeding away from Sarah… it's touch oily and nauseating as it pulsed past her, rippling and expanding like a visible soundwave.

It was all over in a moment, as the "bubble" burst and time snapped back into a raucous cheer, glasses being tossed into the air, students collapsing in heaps as though passing out from the sheer magnitude of the display before them.

Cassie lifted her hands over her head, ducking to protect herself from what was turning from amazement into mania. She looked back toward Sarah, whose face was at first beaming but then registered shock beneath the sensational painting Cassie had created. In the blink of an eye, the entire lounge was in chaos and pandemonium, until a sudden clap of thunder stilled the room.

Cassie, still cowering on the floor, could see a counter sphere of force pushing the initial bubble back, and as it did so, the mania subsided as quickly as it had arisen—students caught midway through a leap stumbled as others blinked and looked around incredulously, and then a moment of hushed whispers was broken by the familiar voice of the headmistress.

"I think there is no question who wins the masquerade this year. Very well done, Ms. Dawson. Very well done indeed."

The calm voice of the headmistress seemed to release the lingering tension in the room, as the scholars all dropped their masks for a moment, many having to return to their feet as shocked gasps turned to thunderous applause that followed Sarah as she breathed a sigh and slowly but regally made her way toward the Great Room, Cassie forgotten as she crouched at the edge of the promenade isle.

A rough hand grasping Cassie's arm as she crept to the edge of the lounge informed her that she had not gone entirely without notice. Looking up, she saw the stern gaze of the headmistress bearing down on her, one hand grasping her arm, the other holding the ornamental scepter she had carried during the opening ceremony.

"You, Miss Cole, however, will come with me." The voice allowed no exception to this order, and thus Cassie found herself standing and meekly following the statuesque figure of Headmistress Floquet away from the hall and out into the night.

Passing silently across the lane, a lump of dread bubbled up in her stomach as Cassie surmised that they were heading toward the headmistress' quarters.

"You won't be needing that rag of a mask any longer." Floquet's voice drifted back to her, but the headmistress neither turned nor slowed, leading Cassie into the manor through the front door and then to the right, passing through a hall featuring portraits of prior school leaders before arriving at last at an ornate sitting room that featured a brace of cushioned chairs, a fireplace, and a small desk.

Motioning to one of two chairs that rested near the fireplace, the headmistress remained standing and waited for Cassie to take a seat before turning to gaze contemplatively into the fire. "Do you know what you did?"

Cassie slowly removed the mask from her face and blinked as she clasped the ragged strips of cloth in both hands on her lap.

"You obviously don't. Has anything like that happened to you before?" The headmistress had not yet turned to look at Cassie.

"I don't... I don't understand, Headmistress... what do you mean happened before?" Cassie knew full well what Floquet was referring to but didn't entirely believe that what had happened had actually occurred—or that she had anything to do with it.

Turning at last, Floquet's dark eyes focused intently on Cassie's face, her thin lips pursed in thought. "Tell me what you saw... and do not think to lie to me."

Cassie had never been very good at lying, but being truly confused, she answered honestly. "I don't really know. Sarah and I had rehearsed her entry. I was to be the maid and lay the flowers down. At ten paces, I was supposed to drop to my knees so that everyone would focus on her. I didn't really look up until I heard your voice... but it was... loud... people were cheering... it was unlike anything I've ever experienced. Everything here is."

Another tense moment passed as Floquet regarded her, and then she relaxed her shoulders and took a seat next to Cassie, sitting straight and tilting her head at a slight angle. "You look tired, Cassie. Adjusting to this school can be hard for anyone. A bit of advice as a former Walgrove scholar myself... don't try to go too quickly."

Cassie had no idea that Headmistress Floquet had once been a student here. It made sense but was a surprise all the same. "I'm trying to make some friends, but you are right, it is very different, there's a lot to take in."

Floquet nodded, seeming to accept Cassie's answer before languidly rising back to her feet. "We chose you, Cassie, because you are exceptionally talented. Many students come here because their parents pay us to take them. But we are paying you. You have immense potential, Cassie. More than any student I have seen since being here and more than many in decades. Take your time... make friends, enjoy the experience. There is plenty of time for you to make your statement as you learn."

Cassie nodded before replying, "Would it be alright if I skipped the dance this evening? I should have known to be prepared, but all I could do was pull together these scraps. I don't have a proper dress."

Floquet lofted a brow at her request but merely nodded, appearing to have already moved on in her mind.

Standing quickly, Cassie offered a half wave, as she didn't know what she was supposed to do in taking leave of the headmistress, and without further hesitation, she walked quickly down the short hallway and out into the night.

Headmistress Floquet watched the young girl go, waiting for her to be well gone before pressing a button on the underside of the mantle that overhung the fireplace. A light bell sounded, informing her that the communication link had been established. "The girl is far more powerful than we suspected. I want eyes on her constantly. And I think we need to orchestrate a distraction or two... the time is not yet right for her to discover the truth about who and what she is."

Eight

The day dawned bright, with a brilliant blue sky and a flock of geese alerting all below that they were heading south to bask in warmer climes. Cassie had risen earlier than usual, unable to remain in bed any longer, as today marked the first day of society blocks, and aside from the makeup, Cassie hadn't so much as handled a brush since coming to school... outside of her dreams, of course. The dreams, she happily discovered, continued each night as usual. There were no further incidents in the strange dream world, no shouts or sounds, just the normal scenery she had come to enjoy as a respite from the waking world.

She and Sarah were doing well once again. Sarah had collapsed on her bed around four in the morning after the masquerade, too exhausted to sleep but full of details of her wonderful night. She had begged Cassie to let her tell everyone who had painted the mask, but Cassie was adamant about keeping it a secret. For her own part, Cassie said nothing about her meeting with the headmistress, telling Sarah that she had felt ill and simply returned to her room, which was mostly true. In any case, Sarah's mind was so full of her wonderful experience as the Queen of the Masquerade that she hadn't probed Cassie any further.

These and other thoughts swam through her head as the last minutes of her mathematics class wound down and the bell finally announced the end of the academic period, marking a small break before her first society block was to begin. Pressing eagerly through the throng of students, Cassie completely missed the sight of another student crossing at an angle and collided roughly with what felt like the side of a tree, sending her and her portfolio sprawling through the hall in a shower of papers and pencils.

"Whoa, there, my apologies. Please, let me help you with that."

Cassie ignored the voice as she scrambled to collect several pages of notes and a few sketches that lay directly in the path of the ceaseless stream of feet. After gathering everything she could see, she crawled to the side of the hallway, pressing the mess of papers against her chest while looking for a place to set them down and sort them out.

"Here, hand those to me, and you can get them back in order, there's no good place to stop in this hallway." The voice now had a face to go with it, and a very handsome face at that. So much so that Cassie blinked and nearly dropped her papers again, instantly regretting feeling and acting like a stupid girl in a romance novel. But a quick look around revealed the truth to his words, and so, reluctantly, she handed the pile of papers to his outstretched arms.

"Sorry, I didn't see you... are you alright?" Cassie asked belatedly, realizing that this must be the tree she had plowed into.

"Pretty sure I'll have a bruise from that one. You should come out for the co-ed field team, we've got a spot for a bruiser like you for sure." While the words were harsh, the way he delivered them made her blush and feel like he'd just given her the most amazing compliment.

"I... guess?" she replied, having no idea what else to say.

"Here, why don't you let me fix those for you." Without waiting for a reply, the tall young man began to sort her bundle of papers until they lay in a neat stack in his hands, at which point he offered them to her with the kind of smile that was meant to melt the meanest arctic glacier.

The effect on Cassie was to leave her numbly accepting the stack of papers in silence, with her mouth slightly agape.

"Okay, then..." the young man added with a grin, graciously filling the silence. "And I'm serious about the offer. Co-ed teams begin practice this afternoon. We'll be on Field H at the Marsh. And don't worry, this is just the inter-society league, it's a good way to get to know scholars from across the campus."

Again, that brilliant smile, and then he paused as his gaze narrowed on a rough sketch that was sticking out of the messy pile... a sketch she had made during one of her dream episodes. "This... I think I've seen this before..." His voice trailed off as a thought skirted across his eyes.

It was Cassie's turn to interrupt as she quickly tucked the drawing back into the stack and shook the hand that was pointing haltingly toward the drawing. Abruptly, he turned and walked away, leaving Cassie standing flat-footed and hugging the mess of papers as the river of students trickled to a stream.

"He's out of your league, Judy," interrupted the voice of a passing student with a laugh. "Better close that jaw before you catch something."

"Seriously?" she muttered with a slight growl. This 'Judy' thing was really getting on her nerves. The comment, however, served to bring her back to the ground and what she was doing—which was heading toward her first society block, though it didn't seem quite as interesting now as it had that morning.

Society blocks were all held in their respective halls. In her case, she was required to walk to the eastern edge of the campus, just before reaching the tennis courts, to a small squat wing of a larger complex emblazoned with the building's name, Orkumb Gallery. The Visual Arts Society in recent years had been moved from their historic location in the larger adjoining Rezek Arts Center to make room for the Digital Arts Society.

While the two buildings shared an entryway, they could not have been more different. Having benefited from a recent alumni gift, the Rezek Arts Center had been expanded and retrofitted with a stunning array of technology in the form of digital walls, design labs, the best Wi-Fi on campus, and a number of additional improvements, like the beautiful windows and signage—a stark contrast to the essentially forgotten wing that now housed the Visual Arts Society.

As Cassie entered the main door and turned to the right, she found herself in a sparse show gallery with white walls, empty podiums, and frames that would eventually feature the work the scholars produced during the season. Open stairs led down to the lower level, where her block was scheduled to meet on this first day. And so, Cassie walked across the empty space and down the stairs, her steps echoing in the room until she found herself in a cozy mudroom below that took up nearly the entire lower level. Here, a handful of her society members had already arrived and were finding seats on a variety of stools, chairs, and overstuffed ottomans that had been hastily pulled into a semi-circle in front of a small podium. Mistress Cynthia Zeltrix was scheduled to address the society on this first day but had not yet arrived.

"Glad you found it... I was getting a little worried." Sarah was already sitting on a stool along the right side of the semi-circle amidst a handful of first year students that Cassie had regrettably not taken the time to get to know any better than a passing hello back in the dormitory.

"Oh, I managed to drop everything in the hallway on the way over... another minor disaster," Cassie responded in light tones, nodding at the other girls, who looked up at her arrival but offered no further comment beyond appropriate smiles. Like Cassie, they each carried a portfolio with them, most of which were in far better condition than her plain black case. In all, there were about twenty students present.

"So, I guess this first lecture is not for everyone?" Cassie had been hoping to meet the rest of her society today. According to what she had been told, there were fifty-four members in all, though many of those were upperclassmen.

"No, all of the third and fourth years met yesterday. Mistress Zeltrix wanted to divide the group early on," Sarah replied with a shrug and looked as though she intended to say more, but the inset double doors along the wall they were facing parted to reveal the statuesque figure of the mistress herself.

The storied Mistress Zeltrix was something of a celebrity in both academic and gallery circles. Her work had been displayed in elite galleries, from The Hole to the Thadeus Ropac Gallery and an extended "tour" of the Gagosian exhibit halls. Modernist to the extreme, Mistress Zeltrix rarely shied away from the controversial, which was in keeping with her participation in staged protests and flash art from the time she first appeared on the art scene. Her style was polarizing, and while Cassie tended to side with those who disagreed with her approach, there was no doubt that the woman was an impressively creative force.

"Excellent. You all have your portfolios with you. I want each of you to select one piece and present it to the group. Miss Idlewood, you may begin."

A slight gasp rippled through the group, as this was the last thing any of them were expecting. The gasp was followed by a rising rustle of papers and unsnapping of portfolios as those not named Idlewood frantically flipped through their sketches, Cassie among them.

Ignoring the presentation, Cassie frowned into the mess of papers and sketches that had once been a well-organized display of her work. Now it was a disaster, making finding the piece that she wanted all the more difficult.

"Thank you, Miss Idlewood. I'm surprised they even admitted you into the program. Your parents surely must have paid well to pass you off as an aspiring artist. You do know that, unlike the digital arts, you must have actual skill for this program?" The sharp voice of the mistress stunned the remaining chatter straight out of the room. One of the first year scholars to Cassie's right dropped the painting she had intended to show, as it was a similar still life drawing to what Miss Idlewood had just presented.

Two more students were called and dismissed with similarly harsh results, prompting the mistress to pause the proceedings as she addressed the group. "Does anyone here have something OTHER than a simplistic drawing or painting you made in middle school? Anyone?"

Faces all around turned to the floor as the mistress called for Sarah. "Miss Dawson, perhaps you have something for me. Last night I was told that you wore the most stunning mask... quite the spectacle, I believe... garnered you the designation of Queen of the Masquerade. I'm only too sorry that I missed it. Perhaps you have a sketch or two you could share with us?"

Cassie felt Sarah stiffen as she was called and cringed internally at her roommate's discomfort, and even more so at Sarah's reply. "I... I didn't create that design."

"No? An aspiring artist copied a design?" The disgust was thick in the mistress's throat.

"Oh no... a... friend did it for me." Sarah's reply was nearly inaudible as she glanced furtively toward Cassie, who stared back in wide-eyed horror, remembering all too well her conversation with the headmistress.

"That's even worse than pathetic. A woman in my society who is incapable of her own creativity... Dawson, is it? You have an older brother, I believe... perhaps a tennis court named after your family? Another spoiled little nit with a case of affluenza."

Cassie could take it no more, "I painted her makeup... I ruined the mask she had made and convinced her to let me make amends. She's very talented, she sewed her own dress, which was beautiful, much prettier than my design." Out of the corner of her eye, Cassie could see Sarah relax, though she couldn't tell if it was from relief at no longer being the target of the mistress's attention or because of the faint praise Sarah had tried to bestow.

"Ah... so now we have the truth. And you are... Cassandra Cole, I believe?" Zeltrix's voice was low and cutting. Cassie could only nod in reply as the tall, slender woman approached her, extending an open palm expectantly. "Let's see what you were going to show us."

Mechanically, Cassie handed over a simple charcoal sketch she had made. It was from one of the visions in her dream of a smooth rock wall with intricate patterns and symbols... a kind of parietal art or ancient pictograph. Cassie had picked it out as something that was at least different than what the students before her had offered.

Taking the sketch into her hand and lifting it for further inspection, the mistress gazed at it with narrowing eyes. "You should have presented a photo of your work from last night, Miss Cole. THAT would have been acceptable," she commented without looking back at Cassie. Rather than handing the drawing back, however, Mistress Zeltrix took it with her as she turned back to the podium, placing it there. Cassie hastily returned to her seat as the rest of the students sighed in relief, some of them looking at her and nodding appreciatively for having put the inquisition to an end.

"If there is one thing that you will learn while under my tutelage it is this—art—is magic. Make no mistake. The silly drivel you presented today is not art. I fear that perhaps only Miss Cole may ever even approach the true purpose of what art actually is."

Now, the looks on the faces of the students surrounding Cassie were turning to grim jealousy as the mistress positioned her against the others, never a good place to be as a new student.

"Many of you do not believe in magic, I'm sure, so let me define it for you. Magic is the force by which change is coerced. While physics and mathematics concern themselves with the manipulation of existing forces within a defined set of laws, magic is that which coerces a result that is unexpected... unnatural... but never unintended." The room grew silent as each of the students turned back to the mistress in rapt attention.

"Can you change a mood, evoke an emotion, spark a belief, alter a thought? This is magic in its simplest form. The tools that we use in the visual arts are NOT for expressing your deepest... feelings..." this word, Zeltrix emphasized disgustedly.

"Our skills, our tools, our *purpose* is to coerce the world to our design. The greatest practitioners have used their art to start wars, overthrow kingdoms, and even... kill." The room suddenly felt stifling as Cassie and the others shifted uneasily in their seats.

"From this day forward, you will bid farewell to all of your juvenile notions of what art is. If any of you are afraid, if any of you feel I am wrong, you are free to leave the program. But if you stay, you will dedicate every waking moment to this singular truth. Art... is... magic."

ART IS MAGIC

Nine

" I realize that your plan is for me to bring her along slowly, but the child knows something, or she has at least seen something. No one could come up with this on a whim." Mistress Zeltrix held out the sketch she had taken from Cassie earlier in the week, offering it to the headmistress as they sat casually on either side of the long table that featured prominently in the center of the ornate dining room of the headmistress' manor.

Taking the drawing and examining it, the headmistress set it on the table before responding. "She has an eye for detail, that is certain. But that doesn't answer how it was that she was able to enact a cupidatas with a bit of makeup."

"I thought dumb luck at first, but seeing this, she had to have been there, perhaps she picked something up... a brush..."

"A brush?"

"Don't patronize me, Pearl. I have no more of an answer than you."

"And yet, I brought you here to find answers, not offer excuses." The headmistress' voice leveled as her eyes bore into the Dean of Visual Arts. The lighting in the room dimmed as a frown appeared on Floquet's face, and suddenly Mistress Zeltrix was grabbing at her throat and making hoarse sounds as if struggling to breathe.

The tension held for a moment longer, then the headmistress relaxed back into her seat and lifted the sketch from the table to examine it once again.

Mistress Zeltrix coughed and drew a deep breath, the look on her face now of pure acquiescence and obedience. "Allow me to apologize, Imperator... I was out of place."

"You have served well in the field, where you have been free to act as you have seen fit. Your service has been remarkable, but another can take your place as easily if you find my leadership chafing." This, the headmistress said as she continued to regard the charcoal sketch, turning it around in her hand as she spoke. "And, you are not to use those terms while you are here. Headmistress will suffice."

"This is an honor, Headmistress. I am here to obey."

"You are here to help me finish the work that is so very near completion. I need every ounce of skill and artistry that you contain, not a mindless lapdog. I only ask that you show the respect of the office that I hold."

"Understood, Headmistress." Mistress Zeltrix bowed her head while remaining seated.

"Now, you said that you had a plan for the girl..."

The two powerful women spoke in hushed tones late into the night. When at last they both rose from the table, Mistress Zeltrix offered a brief bow before departing through the doors and out into the night, while the headmistress walked slowly to the fireplace, where she bent to feed Cassie's sketch to the flames.

"Alright, welcome, everyone, especially our first years. Many of you have played sports like football, soccer, lacrosse, field hockey, and the like. The fundamental rules of this game should be pretty familiar to you all. Basically, your aim is to score more and faster than the other team."

Cassie discovered earlier that the young man she had inadvertently bumped into in the hallway was named Willem Marshall IV and was the captain of not only the co-ed team but the school team as well. And, of course, he was in his senior season in the performing arts—a diva, as they were called. By all accounts, he was also the darling of every first and second year woman in the school. There was even a shared chatroom chronicling his every action and location, as well as several fake social media accounts. It was all a bit much for Cassie, who certainly found him attractive but not to the point of obsession.

Today he wore a purple top that did nothing to hide the muscle below, and he strode about in full command of his team and field.

"Perhaps obsession isn't such a bad thing," Cassie murmured softly before looking about quickly to ensure that no one had heard her. She noticed that some other members of the team were running a slow warmup circuit around the field, including Captain O'Dine, who cast warning glances at her with each circuit.

Assuming rightly that running would be involved, Cassie had selected her athletic wear, as that made the most sense, and discovered that she was not mistaken in her choice, though the other first year scholars also sported cleats and padding. From what she had learned from Sarah, the game was called Jalaw, the J pronounced with a soft "H" sound.

In Jalaw, two teams competed against each other, and the field resembled a rugby pitch or American football but didn't have to be as large as those, so it could be played almost anywhere as long as you had a designated safe zone and a pole or basket of some type. Each team was composed of twelve players, who were tasked with being the first to get twelve banners from their safe zone to the opposing team's safe zone. Getting a banner into the rival safe zone was called a scoring cross. Willem was getting into the details as she arrived.

"The game is played in two timed halves of twenty minutes each, but if there is a tie, the game continues with an untimed sudden death period. The longest game I've ever seen took two days to complete... so scoring is essential. And no, the masters don't stop classes, even for the Governor's Championship. Fortunately, this is just a friendly league, and so the game can end in a tie."

Heads nodded all around as if this were all well-known and obvious, leaving Cassie to think that perhaps she was the only one here who had never heard of this game before.

Captain O'Dine stepped up beside Willem as he motioned for her to continue the instruction, a role that Captain O'Dine took to naturally, like a shark to the hunt.

"There are two types of players," the diminutive but powerful woman noted as she strode in front of the line of newcomers. "Scampers and jammers. A scamper is an offensive player who wears the banner affixed to their waist and tries to make it to the opposing safe zone without having their banner pulled. A jammer is a defensive player, blocking for their scampers and pulling banners from opposing team scampers.

"A scamper can also pull an opposing team banner, but any team member who pulls a banner must immediately return that banner to their own safe zone before engaging any other player or attempting a scoring cross—doing so can be called for an interference penalty, where that player is sidelined for two to five minutes."

Captain O'Dine made her way to where Cassie stood, looking her up and down with a critical eye as she continued.

"When a scamper makes it into the opposing team's safe zone, they must place their banner on the scoring pole or basket before returning to their own safe zone. A returning scamper cannot touch or interfere with any other player on the field until both of their feet have crossed their own safe zone line."

"Once a scamper scores, however, they are able to freely retrieve any of their own banners that have been stolen and placed in the safe zone by the opposing team. They cannot pick these up and attempt to score with them until each banner has been taken back to their own safe zone. Jammers are only permitted to block and steal banners, they cannot score, and scampers are not permitted to block or impede any other player's progress."

"Finally, illegal moves include tackling, punching, kicking, or hitting of any kind, grabbing, tripping, grappling, and pulling. And that's the basics."

Cassie nodded with the others, as the game seemed to be simple enough. Then Willem stepped forward once again to add a final note.

"The strategy of the game comes in the designation of your players. Each team must assign who will be scampers and who will be jammers at the beginning of the game and then again at the half. You can play all scampers or all jammers if you wish, so understanding the opposing manager's playing style is critical. Okay then, let's have the first years run a few drills to see what you can do."

Willem took hold of the whistle that was slung around his neck and gave two quick blasts before turning and trotting to the center of the field. Cassie and the handful of other first years followed behind, with Cassie now fervently wishing that she had a set of cleats, as the grass was soft and slightly muddy.

Once they reached the center, Willem directed four of the seven to one half of the field designated for scamper practice and instructed Cassie and the two largest boys to head to the jammer side. As she jogged along with the young men, Cassie couldn't help but notice how physically outmatched she was with the two towering at least a head over her. Nor was it lost on her that one of the young men was Bobby Franks, who was leering at her.

"Oh, it's Judy. Come to play with the big boys. Funny how I didn't see you at the dance."

Cassie blanched and looked away, only too grateful for a familiar voice cutting in with further instruction.

"Alright... Willem says you three will make good jammers. I'm here to check his work." Looking away from the two hulking boys on either side of her, Cassie couldn't help but smile with relief as Whittle trotted up to them.

Whittle flashed a brief smile in return before covering her face in a mask of seriousness. "You two have the size, but do you have the feet? And you... agility doesn't always translate. So, step back, line up, and try to get around me."

The boys both chuckled as the three of them stepped back a few yards and formed a single file line.

"Are you sure? I mean, I was told not to hit girls, but don't worry, I'll go easy on you." Bobby chuckled as he said this, lowering himself for a charge, his pimply nose already glistening with sweat.

Dipping into a three-point stance, Bobby growled before rushing toward Whittle with his shoulder forward. At first, Cassie thought he was going to demolish Whittle, as he outweighed her by two to three times, but as he charged, Whittle simply waited for her moment, then ducked and dove at him with a forearm to his opposing hip as she planted a foot, sending him tumbling and spinning to the ground, where he landed with a wet thud.

The second boy's eyes flared at this, but he approached with a bit more caution. Lacking the ability to grab and grapple seemed to leave him in a confused state long enough for the quicker Whittle to glide in, feint a strike toward his upper body, which threw his balance before checking his hip and sending him reeling backward into the ground as well.

"Being a jammer is about gaining the advantage of balance. While brute force will work against an inexperienced opponent, you'll have to be sharp mentally. Alright, Cassie, let's see if you can get past me."

Having played several sports in school, Cassie was not entirely out of her element, but Whittle was clearly experienced at this game. Nevertheless, she began to trot toward the other woman, watching her hips and shoulders as she had been taught, and with a quick juke to the right followed by a spin, Cassie slipped just beyond Whittle's lightning quick strike, but having gotten a step beyond Whittle, she was not prepared for the hip check that eventually sent her sprawling into the sodden grass.

A hand reached down to her as Whittle offered to help her to her feet. "You show promise... I can see that you must have played for Coach Janice as well, if I'm not mistaken?"

Accepting the hand, Cassie sprang to her feet, replying, "Trident's strike thrice."

Whittle laughed and clapped her on the shoulder, "Looks like we have a new Jammer, though there are some tricks you'll need to pick up to account for your size. Who knows, maybe you'll make the school team someday."

Cassie blushed at the praise as she walked back to where the two larger boys were standing, their faces grim with determination.

"She took it easy on you, princess... just wait 'til we're in a real match," jawed Bobby before being interrupted by Whittle's next order.

"Alright. Now we test your stamina. Follow after me, scrubs," Whittle ordered before beginning a slow jog toward the edge of the field where a series of cones were set up in a variety of formations.

The remainder of practice was an exhausting string of jogging, sprints, calisthenics, and plyometric exercises that left the three first years, Cassie included, soaked in sweat, muddy, and heading toward a very sore tomorrow. But for Cassie, it was the first time that she began to feel like she was fitting in.

As she walked toward the shower house to clean up, Whittle caught up to her. "Well done out there, fellow Judy. If you're up for another history lesson, meet me by the fountain outside the Lid after curfew... there's something I think you'll find very interesting."

With a wink, Whittle spun away and back toward Willem, who was gathering his team captains in the center of the pitch for their assessments of the new prospects they had drilled during the day's practice.

"What a weird, wonderful place," Cassie commented to no one in particular before picking up her pace with the thought of being warm and clean driving her tired legs forward.

Ten

"So, Jalaw, then?"

Cassie was returning to her dorm after cleaning up, glad that she had been smart enough to bring the small duffle bag with a clean change of clothing, when the voice broke her wandering train of thought. Turning, she frowned, recognizing the slight young man as Ludo, the young scribbler who had arrived with her on the bus.

"Not even a smile for your oldest friend?" Ludo closed a notebook he had been writing in and rose to his feet as she drew near. "Come on, Cassie, right? You can't have made so many friends already that you couldn't use another."

"I guess you've pushed so many people away already that you're desperate for anyone to talk to," Cassie said with an overly pronounced huff, but didn't run him off.

"Oh... see, that was really good acting, perhaps you're in the wrong house after all. And you may have a point..." the younger man trailed off.

"If you didn't come on so strong, you might make some friends, Ludo. What were you writing there, anyway?" Cassie pointed to his notebook.

"We have to keep a daily journal. Part of our curriculum is to maintain a constant pace of writing, get us used to out-putting volume, I guess." Ludo shrugged but stepped up beside her to join her on her walk back toward campus, the fading noise of practices winding down mixing with birds singing their twilight songs.

In one swift motion, Cassie dipped and snagged his journal, opening it to the center, where she saw what looked like a poem.

"Hey now... those are private!" Ludo protested, but he made no move to retrieve his notebook from her, as Cassie had pulled it to the opposite side and was already starting to read aloud.

> *I do not trust the self-seeking advice that*
> *trolls across my social spaces.*
> *Falling prey to ill-informed intent might*
> *result in the reproduction of angry faces*
> *Smeared in hate-filled taunts that have no*
> *space in this life to which I intend.*
>
> *And how can it be that bias still exists in the*
> *second millennium of a progressive world?*
> *Yet if the change I wish to see doesn't start*
> *with me, I'm no less blind, nor less a cause*
> *of the things I hear and of which I've seen*
> *that cause me pause.*
>
> *Should I rather not be inspired by the daily*
> *toil of more mundane aspirations.*
> *Like the blinking ideals that mount an offen-*
> *sive despite the crushing uncertainty of*
> *future conditions.*

Can I not avoid the traps of my predestined
  glory
Or shall I just plunge to the dissipation of
  my own story?

Do I seem so much less if I cannot grasp that
  work is work and not play?
That what I do is for the future and not today?
Can I not find evidence to remain calm when
  faced with pointed questions
that are dangled before me like mere sug-
  gestions.
An over-ripened bowl of quips and tropes
succumbing to the underlying subterfuge of
  vapid hope.

Are they not more in need of what I can bring
  than they let on?
Their so-specific search can hardly overcome
  the thin-slicing
That intimates a choice well before their con-
  scious mind begins to voice.
And so perhaps it is less a matter of match-
  ing the impossible ideal that
Frames their solid state concept of meaning
  and is more
A matter of meeting their humanity with my
  own.

However frail mine may seem. However
drawn or weary my ideals
However simple-minded or short of sight I
feel. I know that I am not alone.
So long as I avoid the silly refrains that litter
the path along the way
Toward the inevitable but over-styled soli-
tude of the grave.

Must I truly be unique or must I be willing
to try?
Must I truly stand out or must I be willing
to stand by?
Is it trite to suggest that eighty percent is
showing up?
To be counted among the twenty percent that
are shouting stop?
Must I truly be prepared for a life I have not
yet lived,
Or am I already ahead by simply taking the
initiative?

"It's... It's not bad, Ludo. Makes me think there's something actually inside that head of yours." Cassie's voice had gentled toward him as she read, and after reading she closed the notebook and handed it back to him.

"Thought you'd find a poem about you in there, didn't you?" he retorted as he retrieved his notebook.

Cassie stopped walking and turned to him. "See... that's what I'm talking about. You don't have to try to be... whatever that is. Just be what's in those pages, Ludo, and people will like you." The young man stared back at her, having no reply for her directness, but Cassie could see him physically relaxing. "And no, the answer is no. You are not the only one who feels pressured to live an impossible ideal." Turning back up the path, Cassie continued toward the school, with a more subdued Ludo following alongside.

After a moment of silence, the younger man flipped to a page near the end of his notebook and began to read.

"Standing tall and slight.
Hair streaming, tossed and blown.
Like the eternal twilight.
Against the black cliff stone.

Observers are a-watching
Silent in the gloom
The prey they are stalking
Closer than the moon

Shadows, creeping, scouting
Danger to behoove
Silently I'm shouting
Wishing her to move

Standing on the stone
She is not alone."

"I've seen you, Cassie... on a stone cliff... drawing. I've had the same dream nearly every night, but it's not... It's not the same dream. It's a little different each time." Ludo's voice was earnest, almost imploring her to believe him.

"Are you serious? What kind of creepy thing have you been up to?" Cassie's mind was whirling. She began to pick up her pace, afraid to look back at him, needing space to think this through and all the while wishing she were just having some sort of nightmare.

Ludo had stopped in his tracks, hand clutching the notebook limply to his side as he called weakly after her. "It's true, Cassie... I'm not trying to be a creep... I just... I think you're in danger."

Cassie broke away in a run, the burn from practice forgotten. Not knowing what else to do, she merely ran without knowing where she was going. "This can't be real... it can't be real." There were too many coincidences, too many recent bits of evidence that were piling up to mean one thing.

The dreams might just be real.

As Cassie ran, a small group of faculty were gathering for an informal meeting in an upper conference room in Tripplett Hall.

"Now, Grimpen, why is it that you've called us all in such secrecy." Bale Adonis had agreed after much urging from Master Grimpen Galleon to meet, along with Cressida, Mistress Shileen Becket, the Dean of Writing, and Master Ignus Radcliff, Dean of Digital Arts. The only dean not invited was Cynthia Zeltrix, whose absence few paid any mind to, as she was new to the school and not privy to the history of student disappearances—which was the reason for the gathering.

"So, just to get my numbers straight. Bale, one of your students and one of Cressida's dancers disappeared last season. Two of my musicians, both vocalists, one lost last season, along with one from Shileen's society and one from Cynthia's. The most recent was another of yours, Bale, but also one of my vocalists. Is that correct? Have there been any others?" Master Grimpen had settled himself at the head of the small conference table and opened a notebook, in which he had jotted a number of notes.

"We all know these things, Gimpy darling. Pearl has assured me that she is looking into this personally. So why the sudden fuss? And the secrecy?" Even the way that Cressida sat in a chair was graceful as she slurred her words slightly in her alluring way.

Master Grimpen slid several thumb drives across the table, one for each attendee. "This is the song they were practicing when the students disappeared. I've tried to erase all copies of it, but you know how things are nowadays. Nothing is ever truly gone."

"Well, it certainly won't help to hand out another set of copies, Grimpen. And what are we to do with these? Study them until WE disappear?" Bale emphasized the word we but pocketed the thumb drive nonetheless.

Grimpen continued, nonplussed, "I think we need to take further precautions." He paused momentarily as if steadying himself for a suggestion that would not be welcome. "I think we should cancel our participation in this season's show..."

"What! Never! You must be mad, Grimpen!" Bale's response was immediate as he pounded the table with his fists. "Walgrove has won the Governor's cup for thirty-five years straight... Thirty-five years! And you want to just... not show up? Madness, pure madness."

"Come now, Bale, let us listen to Grimpy, I'm sure he has a reason for this insanity, don't you, darling?"

But Grimpen merely continued his sentence. "And I think that we should remove the senior painting from Quibbley Hall..."

This time Cressida interjected, "Cynthia will never permit that, as you well know, and there is no proof that the mural is connected with the disappearance."

"Now, dear, who is the one who should simmer down," noted Bale with a sigh before continuing. "You must see reason, Grimpen, We can't go shutting down the school. We simply can't. Certainly not without more information to go on." Bale had lounged back, once again completely in control of his demeanor.

Grimpen sat quietly until the other two had settled down. "Imortum is a fine musical, but it is at the very heart of these disappearances. The visual arts student WAS painting the mural on the backdrop when she disappeared. Both of my vocalists were practicing one of the songs. Your Dancer was performing choreography from a scene in the musical, and, Bale, your student was rehearsing a poem, which was translated by the writing student that disappeared!" Master Grimpen was red-faced with exasperation as he tried to drive his point home. "It's the play, I'm telling you, there's something about the play. Wherever did you even find the thing?"

"Heaven's, man, calm down. It's part of the Epic of Gilgamesh. You know, our *ancient Sumerian heritage* we are so fond of." Bale had accented the end of that phrase, making light of the oft repeated marketing line for the school. "The song and the scene as I understand it is nothing more than Gilgamesh's rejection of Ishtar. This stuff doesn't mean anything, and it even ends by admitting that the search for immortality is fruitless."

"It's connected, surely you can find something else to work on," Grimpen countered, but he was immediately interrupted by Cressida.

"The students work on these plays for two years. You can't just change it out. You know that as well as we do. It would destroy every senior season, it might cost some of these students the moment they need to get noticed for a bigger stage, and it would certainly destroy our chances at keeping the cup, which would cause a riot on the board and with our benefactors." Cressida pleaded with

Grimpen now, though her voice made it clear that she would not support his request.

"It might cost them a great deal more than a bigger stage. They might be lost forever."

Both Bale and Cressida laughed at this, taking it as simply melodramatic theater. The other two masters continued in their silence, until Grimpen sighed audibly and leaned back in his chair.

"Fine. You need more evidence, I'll find more, somehow. Just... just be careful with that musical piece, I'll make a new arrangement, and at least change the choreography, Cressida."

"Fine," Cressida responded as she slid smoothly from the chair to her feet, offering a hand to Bale. "Come along, Bale. We have some changes to discuss."

The meeting having drawn to a close, the remaining masters followed, leaving Master Galleon alone in the conference room.

Whittle was sitting on the edge of the fountain when Cassie arrived. The moon was just rising over the silhouette of the Lid as she took a seat next to Whittle, who had a duffle bag in one hand and a flashlight in the other.

"I guess a darker outfit would have been smart," muttered Cassie as she noted Whittle's thin figure wrapped head to toe in black versus her own gray athletic joggers and sweatshirt.

"You obviously don't have much to wear beyond your school clothes, so, here..." Whittle handed the duffle bag to Cassie, who unzipped it to find a pair of cleats along with the type of pads she had seen the other jammers wear and a practice uniform.

"You don't have to do that, Whittle..."

"Yes I do. If you're going to be on my team, you need to be equipped to win. Besides, I don't want to see my girlfriend all bruised up and limping around the campus." Whittle smirked in saying this but was already on her feet before Cassie could respond. "Hush now... we need to be quiet on this next part."

Cassie let the moment pass, closing the duffle bag back up and crouching as she followed Whittle quietly out of the maze-like garden. With a series of hand motions that Cassie could only guess at, Whittle took them swiftly across the lane to a medium sized building emblazoned with the name, "Quibbley Hall" across the front entry. But rather than approach the front, she nudged Cassie to follow her around the building to a small door in the rear that had been propped open. Deftly, the two slipped in and closed the door behind them, waiting a moment for their eyes to adjust to the dark interior.

Completely blind and confused at this point, Cassie caught Whittle's wrist gently. She could feel the other girl's steady pulse. "At least I'm not the only one out of breath..." Cassie whispered. She could feel Whittle smiling back at her as a light tug indicated they should move forward.

For a few minutes, the pair traveled the darkness hand in hand, until Cassie heard a metal door creak open and then the audible click of a flashlight, which was partially covered with cloth to mute its brightness.

"Why all the secrecy?" Cassie asked in a whisper.

"This is the senior project building. Seniors have been known to... treat those who are found here that do not belong very poorly."

Cassie nodded at this. "So, if we're here to see something, how did you know it was here in the first place?"

"So many questions, my little grasshopper. There... just follow my light." In response, the beam cut from the floor to the wall, and what appeared to be a large, painted mural or scene that Cassie couldn't quite make out. "One of your society students was working on this mural for the show this season when she disappeared."

A chill ran down Cassie's spine as she followed the light, which was tracing across the mural. "How can someone disappear by painting something?"

"Right? I thought you might know... but it isn't just the painting itself. Here, hold this while I go get the thing I wanted to show you." The flashlight was pressed into Cassie's hand as she heard Whittle walk slowly toward the mural, rippling the fabric as she pushed it aside at one corner.

Slowly, Cassie stepped back in the room and removed the layer of cloth from the beam, allowing the light to cast a wider glow over the mural.

Her breath caught. It was a scene of a stone cliff next to a long gorge and a waterfall. There were darkened crevices like caves cut along the cliff... but most extraordinary was the coloring. It was twilight... and it was exactly like her dream.

A sudden noise made her jump, but it was only Whittle returning with a can of paint that she had pried open. "Here, hold this." This time, the light was taken from her as Whittle handed the small can of paint to her and flipped off the light.

The room fell into complete darkness... but as her eyes began to adjust, Cassie could see a faint bluish glow emanating from the paint inside the bucket.

"It's phosphorescence... that's pretty neat..." Cassie was confused, her mind still dazzled by the mural she had just seen.

"No, actually, it's sonoluminescence... watch this." Softly, Whittle began to sing a simple vocal exercise, holding and changing notes like an ancient aria or arpeggio, and as she did, the paint began to glow more brightly. Cassie watched in fascination as the glow within the bucket pulsed with the notes. But as she lifted her eyes to say something, her breath caught as she took in the changes to the large mural. All along the edge of the huge fabric curtain, symbols began to emerge, all glowing in the same soft blue color, until the whole mural looked to be suspended in a frame of light.

A chill ran down Cassie's back as her stomach lurched into a knot. Something was wrong... something FELT wrong. The image on the huge mural was shifting... becoming almost three dimensional. Quickly, Cassie shifted the bucket to one hand and grabbed Whittle's wrist. "You need to stop that... Whittle... stop singing..." As Whittle did, the light began to fade, along with the tension in Cassie's stomach.

"There's more, I'm not even singing the most interesting piece. Some sort of ancient hymn, I think." Cassie could hear the excitement in Whittle's voice, matching her own rising fear.

"Whittle, you're going to think I'm crazy, but you have to promise me that you'll never sing that song again. Not here, at least... not around that mural."

In the faint hue from the open paint can, Cassie could see Whittle's eyebrows raise questioningly as she opened her mouth to respond, but just as she was about to say something, the lights in the room flickered on, blinding them both as a stern voice called out.

"Alright, stay right where you are. Alistair, I've got them... I'll keep them here until you arrive."

Eleven

Alone, the girl huddled in the rocky impression she had found after how much time she could not tell. In this strange place, there was no day or night, only an everlasting twilight that colored everything in amber and violet hues. Janice was not the outdoorsy type, but she was not frail either. She knew that water was the first thing she needed to fin, then shelter—she might have gotten that in the wrong order, but she'd found both in either case. There was a deep-flowing spring that broke the surface just inside the overhang of the massive stone cave she had found herself in when she'd first arrived. The landscape was sparse, mostly rock, with a few withered pines and some green plants that at least told her that this place must not be too different from her own world.

After a careful taste from the spring, which she found to be both cool and refreshingly clean, Janice had carefully searched along the cave mouth and then further across the rocky cliff to either side. Initially, she had yelled for help but quickly stopped after hearing what amounted to a low moan in response. Frightened, she had searched furiously until she came upon the small alcove she now used as a base camp of sorts.

Once or twice, she had tried to use the song as an escape, but after many fruitless efforts, she surmised that it was perhaps for one way use only—and the chances of stumbling upon the correct returning phrase was slim. With no other option at hand, she slept when she grew tired and investigated her surroundings otherwise. The only thing she had found so far that resembled any kind of human presence was a small, arched, stone bridge that led from one side of the stream to the other, located within relatively easy walking distance from her base camp.

It was there that she had first noticed the glowing light in the water. On two occasions as she had passed, she felt that she'd heard a voice calling to her. Both times, she'd scurried away in fear, but desperation was forcing her to take bolder steps, which was how she came to be squatting on the near shore next to the bridge, staring intently at the softly pulsing light beneath the rippling surface.

"Silimma hemeen."

The ghostly voice spoke with a lilting, otherworldly accent. Bracing herself for the worst, Janice took in a deep breath and responded, "Hello? Can you hear me?"

"Silimma hemeen," the eerie voice responded once again—the sound was muted, as if emitting from somewhere deep within the water, which made sense to her.

Shifting more closely to the water's edge, she stretched a hand out over the rippling surface. "Can you help me? Can you help me get back? I don't know where I am."

"Usha hehungun."

Janice nearly jumped in glee at the new phrase. Somehow, she was communicating with the creature. "Hello... I... I came here by singing I sang a phrase, it brought me here. Is there another phrase that you could share with me? One that can take me home?"

Maybe there's another phrase, something that could reverse the transition? Something that would let me travel back home and back again safely, she thought with rising excitement burning in her throat.

As she spoke, the glowing light below rose to the very top of the water but did not break its surface. Within its luminous shape, Janice could see what looked like a face—distorted yet beautiful in its own way. Plucking up her courage, Janice got down on both knees and held her hands out and over the water, then she began to sing the phrase that had brought her here. As she sang, the light pulsed, almost rhythmically to each note. When she completed the first refrain, the creature responded by mimicking her phrase, almost as though it were a digital recorder but with slight changes and deeply distorted... ethereal, with a darkness to it.

"U-sha-a heh-un-gu-un," the voice warbled from the depths.

Clapping her hands excitedly, Janice practiced this new phrase in her head before cupping her hands and dipping them into the water, softly repeating the musical phrase the creature had just given her.

As she sang, the water surrounding her hands bubbled and frothed, like a water jet in a jacuzzi. As Janice watched in fascination, a small mote of light broke away and floated softly over to settle within her open palm.

"You're... warm. Oh, I thought I would never feel warm again. So... you're friendly. Okay... let's try another phrase, then? This time, one that will take me home?" Even as she spoke, the glowing light in her hand grew suddenly heavy, pulling her hand more deeply into the stream. Surprised, she shrieked and cried out, "Stop! What... what are you doing? I don't want to go in there..." But the weight only grew heavier, threatening to pull her off balance as she struggled to free herself from its grasp.

"Help! Is anyone there? Please... Anyone?!"

But the weight in her hand was too great, and with a lurch and resounding shriek, Janice was yanked from the shore and pulled rapidly into the depths of the water below.

Cassie and Whittle sat side by side, facing the expansive mural as the man in fatigues they'd recently learned to be named Alistair paced back and forth. His compatriot stood at the door, burly arms crossed to indicate that any attempt to escape would be futile.

Whittle, for her part, had taken the lead in responding and was sticking to the basic story, she was now repeating for the third time. "As I said already... this is just a silly prank we were going to play on the seniors. We both understand now that it was a stupid idea, and we promise we'll never try anything this idiotic and childish again."

Garrot Black guffawed in response from his position by the door, earning him a cross look from Alistair.

"Miss Apple and Miss Cole. I was once a teenager myself... and I know a lie when I hear one. We'll just wait for Mistress Floquet to arrive, and she can sort this out on her own."

"So, the chief of security can't resolve a student prank without calling Mom?" Cassie was surprised at Whittle's cutting tone but then recalled that her new friend was seriously considering a switch from percussion to the performing arts. And if this were any indication, she would be exceptionally good at it.

Alistair frowned at that remark, looking back over to Black, who shrugged and added, "She may be a rich little brat, but she's got a point. It's not like we don't know who these kids are and won't be able to find them later."

"True. But I want to know what you were doing in here. The video feed showed this place lighting up like a Christmas party without the lights being on... same as last time."

"Last time?" This time it was Cassie's turn to speak up, but she was rapidly interrupted by Whittle.

"We could show you. It's just a little performance trick with some phosphorescent paint, but it doesn't work with the lights on."

"As if I'm going to turn the lights out with two young ladies in the room. I'm not that dumb. But I'll have you show me all the same."

"Okay... just step back against the curtain there..."

This time Cassie grabbed Whittle's arm, "You can't do this... it's too dangerous."

Another guffaw from Garrot as Alistair's smile broadened with his reply. "Look, kids, I've seen more scary stuff than you'll ever imagine... just go ahead and do your thing there."

With a stern look back at Cassie, Whittle began to sing the simple phrase she had used earlier in the evening. This time she sang it over and over with depth and feeling, allowing her voice to soar with emotion, until the mural behind Alistair began to ripple as a cool breeze filled the room. Before long, snowflakes began to swirl around the security chief.

With a look of wonderment on his face, Garrot Black began to walk toward his chief, "What the... blazes is this? I've never seen any stage tech that could do something like this... it's... it's actually cold."

Alistair nodded as he turned toward the mural, "Don't stop, girl... you keep singing... whatever you're doing, don't stop until I say."

Cassie was growing frantic now, as she sensed danger just beyond the mural... like a huge, lurking beast. "Chief Alistair... you don't know what you're doing... I don't think that's safe."

But just as Cassie began to shout her warning, she looked over at her friend, whose eyes had glazed over as she sang. Whittle continued mindlessly as if under some other control—in fact, it appeared to Cassie that Whittle was being played like a musical instrument.

A sudden concussive thud drew Cassie's eyes back to the mural. Chief Alistair had vanished.

"Did you... did you see that? He's gone... Just like that—he disappeared... Okay, kids, you need to stop that. You need to stop that now!" Cassie could see the security officer's right hand slowly reaching toward the pistol on his belt, unclipping the weapon, but as he did so, his elbow made contact with the mural screen, and with a second concussive thud and a clatter, the man was gone, his gun clattering to the floor along with his radio, phone, and flashlight.

The wind was whipping at them from the mural as Whittle continued to sing... her song a torrent of melody and tones that Cassie had never heard from a human before. In fear, she dabbed her fingers into the pail of paint she still held and lifted the strangely glowing substance to Whittle's face. Making strokes on either side, she painted with instinct, having no idea what she was doing other than madly dabbing and dashing and stroking until abruptly, Whittle's voice seized in her throat and she crashed to the floor.

Instantly, the wind died out and the howling subsided as a silent hush fell upon the room, broken only by Cassie's heaving breaths. The security officers were gone.

"Whittle... Whittle... Please... Come on... you have to wake up. We need to get out of here, now!" Cassie cradled her friend's head in her arms as she blinked back tears of fear and anger. She carefully set the strange pail of paint down and tried to wipe the remaining residue from her fingers as she inspected Whittle's head for injuries.

After what felt like an hour, but could only have been moments, Whittle's eyes blinked, her lashes fluttering and squinting under the overhead lights.

"What... What happened? Where am I?"

"You're safe. But, Whittle, we have to get out of here. The two guards... they're gone... they disappeared into the mural. I don't... I don't know what's going on, but we have to go." Cassie's voice was low and frantic as she helped Whittle back to her feet.

"Guards? I don't remember any guards... all I remember is... I remember singing that silly tune... and the edge of the mural lighting and then... here we are?" Even as she spoke, she allowed herself to be led from the room, down the dark corridor, and out into the cool night air.

Together, the girls made their way across campus, slipping from shadow to shadow until they reached the girl's dormitory and the propped open window of Cassie's basement-level dorm room. Quietly, the two of them slipped into the room, careful not to wake Sarah, who lay bundled under the covers after a late night studying in the lounge.

But just as Whittle reached the door to exit the room, Sarah rolled over, eyeing them both cooly in the darkness.

"The whole story... you're going to tell me the whole story. I don't know what the two of you are up to, but I want in... unless you want to be in a whole lot of trouble."

"Your roommate is tougher than she looks, Cassie. I'll let you two sort this one out. Whatever you put on my face is starting to burn, I need to get it off." Slipping the door open, Whittle disappeared down the hallway.

"It's better if you don't know, Sarah..."

"Everything."

Back in the security shed, the bank of video screens that moni-
tored the vast array of cameras set across the campus blinked once,
then twice, before all twenty tiny screens blinked out. The system,
sensing an issue with the power supply being cut, re-booted, but
as it was attempting to save the last four hours of footage, the
hardware encountered an error and logged the error to the server,
resulting in the last four hours of video content from every feed
across the campus being dumped from memory.

Twelve

"**W**hat do you mean there's nothing? We have how many cameras spread across this campus and we just happened to lose the data from every feed the night that my security chief and his senior officer went missing?"

"I don't know what to say, ma'am." The security officer who had reported the missing chief was standing just behind Mistress Floquet's shoulder as she looked across the array of security screens, her hand twisting the main dial that controlled the video feedback. As she hit play once again, the timing clock on the upper corner of each camera jumped forward by four hours. It was as the security officer told her when he'd brought the news of the Chief's disappearance from the night before.

Calmly standing back up and turning to face the security officer—a short but stout man in his late forties if she were to guess—Mistress Floquet leveled a stare at the man that made him wince. "I don't care if you have to personally tear this equipment apart yourself, I want answers. At the very least, I want more information than you've told me thus far."

"Yes, ma'am, we're doing everything that we can..."

"And what, exactly, is that? Looking for two men who have gone missing? Where are you looking? What exactly are you doing that is actually useful?" She knew that berating this man was no use, but at the moment, she felt like chewing steel.

"We've locked down Quibbley Hall and are dusting the room where the officer's equipment was found. We're also going through all door and window alerts. We'll find something if there is anything to find." A ring of sweat had formed under both of the officer's arms as he hesitated before saying anything further.

"What is it? I can see you're holding something back, what else."

"This would go faster, ma'am if we could get outside help, perhaps call the police in?"

If the man thought he had caught her withering gaze before, he was no longer disillusioned as the look he received now quite literally made him take two steps back and lift his hands over his face. Mistress Floquet's countenance warped in a snarl that was more beast-like than human as a cloak of darkness embraced her.

"You have more resources here than anyone but the NSA. Give me answers, or you may be the one we're searching for next."

The man whimpered as he curled down toward the floor, covering his head with both arms and mewling like a wounded calf as the headmistress pushed smoothly by and out the door. She had an idea of what had happened, and who she should speak to next.

"I'm in, too. Look, I get that you don't like me and all, but something big is going on, and you're at the center of it. I know you were out last night after curfew..."

Ludo got no further with his comment than that before Cassie grabbed him by the arm and clamped a hand over his mouth with the other, pulling him into a side hallway. She'd felt Ludo's eyes on her during the entire class and knew he was up to something. "Keep it down, you idiot."

"I'm right!" he shouted as she took her hand away, but her look was enough to silence him.

"You don't know anything, and nothing is going on."

"You're a terrible actor, Cassie. Besides, I saw you from my window. You and someone else. You were both heading toward the Quib. When I heard the two guards were missing, I just put two and two together."

"My word, Ludo, are you spying on me? Do you realize what a creep you are?"

"I can help. I know I can. In our writing courses, we've been poring over these weird, ancient texts, learning the history of poetic forms. I'm pretty good at translating them already."

"What?! Why on earth would I care about your translation abilities?" Cassie was both nervous and excited—she could feel her elevated pulse. If she were being truthful, she kind of liked Ludo, even if he were a complete idiot.

"Fine. What if you find a monster, or something worse?"

"Then I'll need something to feed it... good point." Cassie countered with a grin, cutting the young man off before he tried to say something stupidly macho.

"Monster bait, then. I'll take it." Ludo managed a bit of a smile and straightened his shirt as she finally let go of him. "You're deceptively strong..." The boy actually tried to feel her bicep before she swatted his hand away and glared at him.

"Jalaw, remember?"

"Noted."

"Okay. If you can keep your mouth shut, you can come along, but one word out of you..."

"Not a peep. Where and when do we meet?"

"We're meeting after dinner, on the bottom floor of the gallery."

"I'm in... you won't regret this." Ludo smiled as he pushed himself back into the flow of students, leaving Cassie alone in the side corridor.

Gathering her composure, she waited a moment longer for the crush of students to dissipate before heading to Diacus Hall for her next society block.

"Today, we see what you are made of." The looming figure of Mistress Zeltrix once again filled the space behind the small lectern. She had allowed the assistant professors to handle the last few society blocks, but Cassie felt that her appearance here today was not by mistake.

"How many of you are familiar with the Greek concept of the humors?" Mistress Zeltrix asked as she surveyed the class before her. No one made a move to respond. "Well then, Miss Dawson, why don't you enlighten us. I'm sure you've done your readings."

Sarah blanched at being called but responded without hesitation. Cassie was beginning to wonder if she was actually shy or trying to avoid looking like a-know-it-all, as she always seemed to, well, know it all. "The four humors originated in Greek medicine and likely earlier, generally referred to as phlegmatic, melancholic, choleric, and sanguine... they roughly correspond to the four seasons."

"Lovely. And can you name the colors associated with each and their temperament?" Mistress Zeltrix turned toward an easel that stood behind her, which held a large, blank canvas.

"Melancholic is black, winter, and associated with being tired or depressed. Phlegmatic is autumn, green, and can be fearful or stubborn. Choleric is summer, yellow, and aggressive or angry. Sanguine is spring, red, and impulsive or passionate." Sarah had grown more confident as she spoke, and now the whole class was looking at her.

"What do we call people who know the answer but do not volunteer to share it?" Mistress Zeltrix asked without turning around. While Sarah was talking, the mistress painted a smooth circle of each color in turn in the four corners of the canvas.

"I don't... I don't know, Mistress..." Sarah stammered.

Mistress Zeltrix held the red brush in her hand as she turned around to stare purposefully at Sarah. "Useless."

The class gasped as one, to which the mistress swiftly swung her gaze across the room while adding, "Equally useless are those who do not know because they are unwilling to put in the effort. Make no mistake, children, your talent and your money may have gotten you here, but it is only through hard work and fanatical dedication that you may remain."

Taking the red brush and turning the handle toward Sarah, the mistress indicated a second blank canvas that stood at the front of the class. "Miss Dawson. I want you to evoke passion in as many of us as you can. You may use only the red."

Carefully, Sarah took the brush and walked to the blank canvas, where she paused a moment before stroking out the smooth curve of parted lips before setting the brush aside and walking back to her seat.

"How many of you feel passion from this?" Mistress Zeltrix asked as Sarah took her seat. One or two of the students tentatively lifted their hands. "Adolescence can be aroused by almost anything, apparently. Perhaps this is not such a good test. Miss

O'Dine, would you please take the yellow and evoke a sense of anger in as many as you can?"

Molly had been keeping a close eye on Cassie ever since Mistress Maude had intervened in the dormitory hallway, and she rarely missed an opportunity to let Cassie know just how little she regarded her. In this case, she bumped Cassie's shoulder as she brushed past. Taking the yellow, the fourth year proctor dabbed heavily in the pail before dripping the brush sloppily and slashing the canvas with several strokes of yellow—sending paint flying against the floor and the far wall as she did.

A collective groan by the first years drew a smile to Molly's face as she walked back to her seat, adding, "Enjoy cleaning that up," her gaze was directed at Cassie, who blinked and shook her head.

"I'm certain that we could have done without the theatrics. I suppose a few more of you felt anger at Miss O'Dine's... performance?"

Several more hands went up at this point, including Cassie's, which drew Mistress Zeltrix's attention.

"Miss Cole, shall we try fear, then?"

The older woman smirked as Cassie stepped forward and took the green pail, but rather than painting in front of the others, she turned the easel around and flipped the canvas on its side. She knew what she wanted to paint, as it was something she had seen in her dream—something that made her fearful every time she looked at it. Quickly, she stroked with one hand, dipping her brush as necessary into the pail. She didn't worry about sharp lines but let the paint ooze as she moved rapidly, swirling in the blue and yellow until the strange and ghastly silhouette she had seen emerged on the canvas.

The class grew restless as Cassie painted, but Mistress Zeltrix watched with growing curiosity flashing in her eyes. When she finished, Cassie looked over the canvas at the class. As she started to slowly swing the painting around, the creak of wooden legs was the only sound that could be heard.

Simultaneously, a girl and a boy sitting together near the back of the classroom screamed, others looked anxiously at the pair, unsure what to do or think. Nervous chatter began to pick up in the classroom as three students abruptly left the semi-circle of chairs, half-running toward the exit. Cassie's hair prickled along her arms as she looked at Sarah's ashen face. Following her gaze, Cassie saw another student convulsing on the ground, as others around him began to whimper and cry.

In a few short strides, Mistress Zeltrix picked up the black pail of paint and splashed the canvas before turning abruptly back toward the class. "The lesson is over!" Rapidly, the classroom vacated, the students seeming only too happy to exit the space, which felt claustrophobic and stale.

"Miss Cole... you will follow me. Now." Her voice allowed for no alternative.

Mechanically, Cassie followed her professor, who led the way through a pair of doors that were situated behind the lectern. Cassie had never been in this section of the building and was surprised to find it both well-lit and exquisitely furnished. Mistress Zeltrix had taken the space over as her personal office and studio. An array of bizarre and striking paintings hung along both walls like some modern exhibit had been prepared, though Cassie had never seen anything like these paintings. Looking at them gave her the impression of movement, as though she were standing in the midst of an oozing wall conceived by Salvador Dali. Breaking her eyes away, she turned around to close the doors, and as she did so, the nausea receded.

"Oh, that won't be necessary Miss Cole. We'll only be together for a moment."

As Cassie turned back toward Mistress Zeltrix, the nausea began to rise again in her stomach as the images hanging to either side started to undulate in their grotesque display. "Those are... interesting paintings. Are they yours, Mistress?" The struggle to remain focused was all too real as Cassie sought some other point in the room upon which she could safely look.

"Yes... yes they are. Do you recall my first lecture, Cassie? Do you remember what I told you about art?" Her voice was like liquid metal.

"Art is magic? I think that's what you said."

"But you didn't believe me, did you, Cassie?"

"I don't... I don't think that's the right word for it, Mistress. I guess I didn't really understand what you meant by that." The buttons on the mistress' coat, those weren't moving. If Cassie could focus on those, the nausea and spinning in her head might recede enough to think.

"It wasn't a metaphor, dear. I meant what I said. Art is literally magic... for those who know how to wield it, and if I'm not mistaken... I believe you have the talent."

Cassie found the whole scenario to be beyond comprehension at the moment, so she simply remained silent, looking from one button to another as the mistress continued.

"While you may be only in your first year of enrollment, I believe you are both old enough and experienced enough to begin working toward your senior project. As of today, you will continue to attend this block but will also join the third and fourth year scholars in the senior society seminar and workshop."

"I don't know what to say, Mistress... thank you?"

Mistress Zeltrix chuckled lightly, "Oh, this is no free pass, Miss Cole. Tomorrow after dinner, you will join me at Quibbley Hall for your introductory seminar. That will be all."

"Tomorrow evening... Alright. I'll see you there, Mistress." Blinking at this turn of events, Cassie spun quickly toward the double doors, moving out into the main room, which was now vacant save for Molly O'Dine, who stood with a pail of soapy water and a mop.

"Not so fast, Judy. Seems you made all the other first years sick... it's only fair that you get to clean up the mess."

As Captain O'Dine roughly pushed the bucket and mop into her hands with a smirk, water and suds sloshed onto Cassie's smock, soaking through to her uniform beneath. "I'll be back to check on this, so be sure to do your best work." Another smirk, and the precept was heading toward the exit, leaving Cassie alone with a bucket and a mess of paint to clean before dinner.

THE DREAMS ARE REAL

Thirteen

Cassie couldn't remember the last time she had allowed herself to visit her special dream. Ever since the wild night in the Lid that resulted in the disappearance of the security officers, which followed Ludo's creepy revelation that he had been spying on her in her dreams and then was compounded by the increasing impact of her art on the world outside her canvas, Cassie had avoided the place at all cost. Yet, it was such a part of her experience that awakening once again within the cozy confines of her rocky nook felt reassuring.

Leaving the ever-present portfolio behind, Cassie crawled out of the cave and scampered briskly to the upper ridge, where she scanned the scene that spread before her as if seeing it for the first time. The cliff face appeared as it always had, with its numerous craggy outcrops that made for easy climbing, the simplest path leading to the large cavern opening that arced over the rushing stream that flowed off toward a forest of twisted roots and vines to what she assumed as south based on the verdant greens which provided a stark contrast to the cold, craggy, white mountains that stood shrouded in mist in the opposite direction. For some reason, she spent little time considering those majestic cliffs, her eyes scanning quickly past them at every errant glance.

As for the forest, Cassie had never ventured far enough to reach those verdant hills, trusting an inner instinct that told her nothing but nightmares awaited in that direction. Checking for any odd noises, Cassie proceeded to walk along the ridge until she reached the lip of the lofty cavern mouth. Here, she let herself down along a set of handholds that she used often enough that traversing them had become an afterthought. As her feet landed on the soft, sandy soil that covered the cavern floor, she was confronted by a prickling sense of being watched.

"Hello?" she called, tentatively at first and then with more authority, "Is anyone there? Ludo? If you can hear me, you better get out of my dream." Cassie didn't expect to hear a reply, but she also wasn't prepared for the sight of a single trail of footprints along the far side of the cavern spring. "Ludo? Did you manage to actually make it into the dream?"

Again, there was no reply as Cassie approached the rushing water and squinted in an attempt to bring the faint tracks on the far side into clearer focus. Whatever made the marks had been wearing some sort of flat-soled shoe, of that she was certain, for there were neither toe marks nor any marks indicative of heels or tread, but the shape was distinctly bipedal and shoed. Cassie estimated that the imprint was close in size to her own. "Could this be one of the missing students?" she mused aloud, her stomach fluttering nervously at the thought.

Judging by the direction of the impressions, the footprints appeared to have come from inside the cavern and were leading away and down, along the shoreline of the swiftly flowing stream. "Let's see... follow the prints back into the deep dark cave or out along the stream?" Cassie shook her head with a chuckle as she began to walk away from the cavern in the direction that the footprints were leading her.

After some time, she spied a small bridge ahead, straddling the water, but as she began to move more quickly toward it, she felt a jostling on her shoulder—and without warning she was back in her bed, with Sarah gripping her shoulder and shaking her awake.

"Oh no you don't. No going to sleep this early for you. You've been avoiding me for days, and tonight is the night we are supposed to be meeting."

Cassie let out a gasp of frustration. "But I'm so tired, Sarah... perhaps another night."

Sarah dropped a sweatshirt and joggers onto Cassie's bed in reply, which Cassie reluctantly pulled on before climbing down to the floor and stretching sleepily.

"We'll leave in a couple of hours, once the coast is clear and all of the evening activities are complete. Whittle couldn't join us until her audition, so this is the earliest we could all get together. The plan is to exit out the window and to the left. We'll keep going until we get across the lane and into the trees. Once clear of sight, we'll circle around the men's dorms to pick up Ludo and then head to the rear entrance of Diacus Gallery. I taped the latch open after cleaning up tonight so we won't have any problem getting inside."

Sarah smiled smugly at the thoroughness of her plan.

"Can't we just talk like normal people during the day? What's with all of this sneaking around?" Cassie was eyeing the covers on her warm bed, especially interested now in returning to her dream and investigating those footprints.

"Well, if you weren't Miss Perfect, being invited to the Quib with all the big kids, we probably could," Sarah responded with more than a hint of jealousy. "I never see you anymore, so this is how it has to be done. Now, I've got a couple more things to do, but I'll be back in about an hour. Don't you dare go anywhere... and no going back to sleep."

True to her word, Sarah left and returned within the hour, pointing quietly at the window after laying a finger to her lips to indicate silence. "Time to go. All is clear."

With that, the roommates climbed out the window, landing softly in the grass, a crescent moon shining brightly overhead. The planned escapade took little more than half an hour, before the four of them—Ludo, Sarah, Whittle, and Cassie—were huddled together outside the rear door of the gallery. Evenings had grown increasingly chill as the season turned toward winter, and Cassie was already feeling the cold seeping through her sweatshirt.

"Wait, what if Mistress Zeltrix is in her office?" Cassie was looking for any reason to avoid this inevitable meeting.

"She and the headmistress are both off campus tonight for a fundraiser in the city. You know that, Cassie, you're just stalling." Sarah pushed through the door and held it open for the others, slowly closing it as they all moved deeper into the room and away from the windows.

Once they were inside, Sarah pulled a few of the stools into one of the mud rooms down the back corridor and led the group in, watching like a hawk as each took a seat around a makeshift table. Atop the table sat a campus map with a number of markings and other notes. Sarah had been busy.

"Since our little princess here has been avoiding us..." opened Sarah after they were all settled.

"That's not fair," Cassie countered.

"I agree," responded Sarah with a look that indicated she was in charge of this meeting. "The rest of the team has been busy compiling notes and research, while you have been... napping? Cozying up to the masters, I assume?"

"Really?" Cassie was simultaneously reacting to both the statement and accusation, but the acknowledging gaze from each of the others suggested that she was the one out of the loop.

"Jealous, Cassie?" Whittle queried with a sly smile, though Cassie detected something of a somber note in her eyes.

Noting that she would have to ask Whittle about this later, Cassie turned her gaze to the map spread before them on the table. "So, what is all of this?"

"This," announced Ludo, who had remained quiet up to this point, "is our own string theory map. Each point highlights the disappearance of a student or staff member." Ludo caught Sarah's sharp gaze. "Uh... Sarah has been compiling it, I suppose it would be best if she explained."

Nodding, Sarah smoothed the map out slowly before responding, "Whit here was quite helpful in piecing together a lot of what happened last year..."

"Whit? We're going by pet names now?"

"Try to keep up, darling..." Whittle responded with that sly smile and hint of sadness once again.

"Are you alright, Whittle?" Cassie inquired.

"It's nothing. Auditions didn't go very well tonight..." Whittle didn't offer more, deferring to Sarah, who was waiting impatiently to get on with the purpose of their meeting.

"As I was saying," continued Sarah with a huff, "In addition to what Whit provided, I got my brother's help to dig up additional information about the other students and staff that have gone missing. If the timeline is correct, these disappearances started shortly after Headmistress Floquet's arrival."

"Wait... you brought your brother into this?" Cassie was envisioning word of their scheming spreading like wildfire across the campus.

"Geeze, Cassie, we'll be here all night at this rate!" Ludo interjected with feigned frustration.

"Trevor doesn't have a clue about what we're doing, and he wouldn't turn us in. I'm his 'adorable baby sister,' remember? Anyway, he's way too focused on completing his final season and getting into Remauld. Besides, we need to use the resources at our disposal, Cassie, or we'll never get anywhere. If you didn't notice, there's something big going on here, and the headmistress is at the center of it."

Cassie wanted to slap the whole lot of them but decided this wasn't the time or place, outnumbered as she was. "Fine. So, you have a plan?"

"Of sorts. We weren't expecting you to get access to the Quib, but that actually speeds our timeline up significantly."

"Well done, girl," Whittle noted with a nod. "Doing us Judies proud." This time her smile felt more natural.

"There's not really anything interesting in that building, aside from the room you took me to, Whittle," Cassie was not about to give way to Sarah's rather horrific shortening of what was a perfectly good name. "But I haven't gone down to the lower levels. It's just been a lot of boring lectures and weird one-off assignments," Cassie finished with a distinct lack of enthusiasm. Honestly, she had been hoping for something much more grand, but in reality it was just more work.

"Oh?" Sarah asked with renewed interest, "What kind of assignments?"

"They have me doing impressionist work. I'll watch one of the dillies or listen to a performance and just paint, usually with a limited color palette. Pretty boring, really. And no, I'm not using any of that odd paint we found, Whittle." Indeed, Cassie was definitely not going to start calling her Whit.

"Do they let you keep the art?" probed Ludo this time.

"No, but I usually sketch the likeness of them in my notebook."

As Cassie said this, Sarah dropped the very notebook in question on top of the paper map.

"Hey! That's mine! Why did you bring that? How did you get that... Without asking me!" Cassie was honestly upset at this, feeling even more betrayed than she had been when the meeting first began. Not only was she out of the loop, but now she felt like a tool.

"You leave this lying around all over the place Cassie. Do you have any idea how important your drawings have been to figuring all of this out?" Sarah's cavalier attitude was not in the least reassuring.

"What's going on here?! Are you all my friends or am I just some... tool for you to use? Going through my private things! Meeting without me? I... I think I've had enough for one evening."

"Cassie, listen." Whittle broke in, trying to calm Cassie's rising rage.

"No, I won't calm down. You can't... spy on me in my dreams... steal my artwork... tail me on campus... How does any of this feel right to any of you? You know what, I discovered something that's actually useful tonight, and I was going to share that with you, but now? You can have your little private club without me."

Cassie grabbed her notebook as she sprang to her feet and, ignoring their protests, ran toward the exit and out of the building, into the cold night air. Her cheeks were flushed with rage and embarrassment. How could they treat her like this? Why couldn't she just be a normal student without all of the insane positioning and intrigue.

"This was a mistake... just a huge mistake. I should never have come here," she whispered as she trotted across the quiet campus, clutching her notebook closely to her chest, eyes cresting with tears.

As Cassie ran, head down and careless of where she was going, she began to hear the bubbling sound of a swiftly flowing stream, which drew her up short, her breath coming in quick gasps from the exertion.

"How... how am I back here?" As she took in the familiar landscape of her nightly dreams, Cassie spun around in confusion, still clutching her notebook. The huge cavern and cliff face stood dark and ominous behind her, the rushing stream to her left and the bridge just ahead of her. It was as if the entire meeting with her friends was the dream, and this was the reality.

"Sarah? Whittle? Ludo?" Cassie called out. But as before, there was no reply, just the bubbling of the brook and the wisp of a light breeze.

"Confused yet? Well, I wouldn't be surprised if you were."

Cassie spun around with a start at the sound of the unexpected voice and nearly dropped her sketchbook as she saw what was talking to her, or at least what she thought was talking to her, for there on the ground, standing no more than a foot tall, was a slender, softly glowing creature that, if she was not mistaken, looked very much like the school's cartoonish dragon mascot.

"Brrrbipppitybrrrptum," the little creature bubbled contemplatively as it blinked big white eyes up at her, swishing its spiky, purple tail back and forth like a feral cat. "Looks like you'll be waking for real now. The next time you return, come find me. I'm not actually supposed to talk to you, but I think in this one instance, it's for the best."

Once again, Cassie began to feel a jostling in her shoulder, and then, without warning, she was back in her bed, with Sarah gripping her shoulder and shaking her awake.

"Oh no you don't. You've been avoiding me for days now, and tonight is the..." this time, Sarah's familiar declaration was cut off as Cassie shrieked and sat up in bed, nearly smacking the ceiling with her head as she did so.

Jumping back abruptly from the edge of the bunk where she had been standing in order to reach Cassie's shoulder, Sarah's fierce glare melted into a look of concern.

"Tell me... this is real this time, right?" Cassie sputtered as she untangled herself from the sheets and slipped down from the bed, noting the sweatshirt and pants that Sarah had gathered in her left fist. Before Sarah could say another word, Cassie interjected, "I told you what I'm doing at the Quib, right?"

"You haven't told me anything, that's why we're meeting tonight... Cassie, are you alright?"

"Right... we're meeting at the gallery, in mudroom C. You have a map set out, and you've invited Whittle and Ludo. Am I right?"

Sarah blinked at her in complete shock, lost for words.

"We need a change of plans. We need to meet somewhere else, and this can't wait... there's something I need to tell you all, but... I need to change the timeline just to know that I can."

"But Whittle is in auditions right now, she won't be free for at least an hour," Sarah protested, but Cassie was already dragging her out of the room and down the main corridor, Sarah still clutching her athletic clothes.

"That's perfect, we'll meet her there, and maybe we can stop her. I don't think her audition is going to go very well."

Fourteen

"Next! Who's next for Ishtar? I can't believe I have to recast this late in the season, what a disaster this is." Master Adonis stood poised at the front of the theater atop a riser that stretched over the first few rows of seats in the center of the auditorium, hands on hips. The disappearances were bad enough, but when they impacted his casting, well, he was fuming at this point.

"I believe Miss Apple? She is next, dear." Cressida stood on the floor next to the riser, clipboard in hand as the short list of eligible students dwindled ever further. Whittle was a stretch as a percussion major, but Cressida had heard her sing before and felt it was worth a try. "She is a third year... percussion."

"Percussion?! What in the devil's brooch..." Adonis trailed off as he stepped to the edge of the platform and held his hand out for the clipboard. "Let me see that. Are we truly down to percussion now?" Master Adonis snatched the clipboard and let out a long and dramatic sigh.

"We've been through all of the fourth years who don't already have parts and the third year vocalists. She has the right tone, and her physique is perfect. I've already tested her on the choreography, and she's flawless with that." Cressida was sounding just as exasperated as Adonis at this point.

"Oh, very well," Master Adonis conceded before raising his voice to be heard across the stage. "Miss Apple... Miss Apple, you're up. Just acapella... give me the first few lines of Gilded Cage."

Whittle had been waiting nervously in the wings. She had watched the last three girls get cut to ribbons by Master Adonis and felt that they were actually quite good. But at Walgrove, quite good was rarely good enough. With a calming breath, Whittle straightened her posture and walked onto the stage. She wore a loose fitting sweater, her hair was down, and she'd even put on some lipstick and mascara, which was exceedingly rare.

Quavering at first, Whittle began unaccompanied, her voice low and airy. She had gotten in only a few lines before Master Adonis cut her off with a wave of his clipboard bearing hand.

"No, no... come on, girl. You play percussion, you know how to hit something, don't you? I need to HEAR you out here, not just see you."

Nodding, Whittle cut a quick glance across the stage to where Willem and Trevor both stood—the two boys who were fighting for the lead role. Both, she felt, were exceptionally talented, and both looked determined as they watched her, knowing that she would be their duet replacement for Janice.

"Well, come on, we don't have all day!"

Whittle began again, slowly working through the lyrics until she reached the chorus, at which point she was again waved off with a furious fluttering of papers.

"Gracious, child! You're not a baritone! Take that up an octave and let me HEAR you!" The voice was cutting and sarcastic, making Whittle wince.

Seeing her recommendation flagging, Mistress McClaine walked to the edge of the stage and motioned for Whittle to come closer.

"You can do this, dear. Just put him out of your mind. You know the words, just sing..."

"No... obviously she needs someone to show her." The distraught voice of Master Adonis rang over loudly through the theater, causing many of the other young scholars to cringe, only too glad it wasn't them in Whittle's place. "Willem... sing her part, up an octave, and show her how it should be done."

Whittle let out a deep sigh of frustration as she knelt to the edge of the stage, planted a hand along the edge, and vaulted down to the floor next to Mistress McClaine.

"My dear, now isn't the time to give up..." The mistress' voice echoed hollowly in the back of Whittle's head as she stalked away toward the exit. Even if she stood a chance at gaining the part, nothing was worth this amount of humiliation. With her head down, she absently barreled straight into the chest of a young man, who managed to deflect the blow and catch her gracefully from tumbling headlong to the ground.

For a moment, the familiar arms of Willem encircled her. He was one of the two senior men vying for the lead, and his statuesque, almost too-perfect figure was only surmounted by the fact that he was also one of the nicest and brightest men in the school. "Sorry about this, Whittle. You're doing well, and Mistress McClaine is right, you shouldn't give up so easily."

Whittle softened a bit but extracted herself from his arms. "Too bad you aren't my type, Willem."

"So, there's hope then?" the senior responded with a grin that didn't reach his eyes.

"Well... your advice goes both ways."

"My what?" he responded quizzically as he turned toward the stairs leading to the stage.

"Don't give up hope," Whittle replied as she lifted a hand to gently cup his cheek, her dark eyes sparkling in the dimly lit theater. Everyone had noted how off he'd been since Janice's disappearance, but no one had yet been willing to broach the subject directly with him.

Taking her hand gently by the wrist, Willem blinked slowly and looked back into her eyes. "Let's hope so," he said before moving smoothly up the steps to the impatient call of Master Adonis.

"Let's go, Willem! Remember that everything you do between here and November goes into the decision. It's you or Trevor. Now, sing!" having shouted this, Adonis knelt on his stage and whispered knowingly to Mistress McClaine. "I suppose they do have chemistry..."

But that was all that Whittle heard as she pushed her way through the exit door, flooding the auditorium with light and a pillow of warm, humid air, to the collective groan of those inside.

Whittle hadn't made it more than a few steps before she caught sight of Cassie and Sarah jogging up to her, Ludo in tow.

"There you are!" Exclaimed Cassie, a little over-excitedly.

"Here I am," muttered Whittle in reply.

"Oh no... we're too late," continued Cassie as the trio came to a stop in front of Whittle.

"Too late for what?"

"To tell you not to try out... and I'm sorry it didn't go so well, Whittle."

Whittle stopped and turned her head slowly toward Cassie, "How could you know?" she wondered, color rising to her cheeks.

"Oh, goodness, I don't think you're a bad singer, Whittle. I just... somehow, the dreams are letting me see into the future now?" The words had tumbled out without any sense of caution at all, and Cassie found herself clamping a hand over her own mouth as Sarah grabbed her arm and tugged at her with a firm look on her face.

"To the gallery... all of you. I guess our talk can't wait now." This bought Sarah a look of annoyance from all three of the others, but she shrugged it off with a sniff and the knowledge that she was right and they would follow.

As the small group of friends slipped quickly across campus, Jimmy Franks peeked out from behind the tall column against which he had been leaning while waiting for Trevor Dawson to exit the auditions. He hadn't intended on spying on their conversation, but he had to admit that he had a certain knack for being in the right places at the right time. "I wonder what you four are up to..." he muttered as he stepped from behind the shadows and casually began to stroll toward the gallery, but just as he did, the auditorium doors opened once again, and this time it was Willem who stepped out and looked around until he spied Jimmy strolling by.

"Hey, Chopper... did you see that girl, Whittle? She just left through these doors a moment ago."

"Maybe, Marshall, what's it to you?" replied the slightly shorter Jimmy as he slid his hands into his pockets. If you were a man on this campus interested in catching the eye of one of the women... you would eventually come to hate Willem. At one point or another, you would either be compared to him by one of the professors or ignored in his presence by any of the girls who went doe eyed when he was around. Still, Jimmy tried to keep his frosty expression from creeping too far into his voice.

"Come on, Chopper, we're in the middle of auditions and Adonis wants her back inside."

"Well, I think I saw her heading back to the dorms," Jimmy lied with a smile growing on his face. "Say, I heard someone saw Janice the other day. Apparently she just left for home, probably couldn't take it any longer." Jimmy snickered as he watched the spark of hope light and then flicker out in Willem's face before he picked up his pace, now determined to trail the small group of students to the gallery.

Willem was left flat-footed, a sour grimace growing on his face as Jimmy loped away across campus. With no sign of Whittle, Willem turned back to the auditorium, belatedly realizing that the emergency exit door had no exterior handles. After a brief pause, Willem turned toward Jimmy's disappearing form and began to trail after him rather than return to the auditorium, where auditions were likely being halted for the day due to this latest disruption.

As the small group entered the lower hall, everything appeared as it had in her dream. The lower door of the gallery had been taped to prevent it from locking, the small mudroom had the same orientation of stools, and the map was spread in the center of the small, raised table.

This time, however, all eyes were on Cassie.

"The dreams I'm having are real."

"I knew it!" exclaimed Ludo and Sarah at the same time, as if they had just solved an amazing riddle.

"Apparently I need to be brought up to speed. You mentioned dreams... seeing the future? What's going on, Cassie?" Whittle's voice was tight and tinged with no small amount of worry, which surprised Cassie more than the consternation she heard in her voice.

"I've seen her there... that must mean... whoa..." concluded Ludo as if suddenly realizing that if her dreams were real, his must be as well.

"One at a time, Ludo," scolded Sarah as if she hadn't just blurted out her own exclamation a moment ago. Turning to Cassie, Sarah settled herself onto a stool and continued. "From the beginning... everything. And, Ludo," she added without looking at him, "take notes."

Thus, Cassie found herself facing her friends and recounting to them everything that she could remember about the mysterious dream world she had been visiting since she was a little girl.

"It all started a few months before my mother disappeared," Cassie began before being interrupted by Ludo.

"Wait, what? Your mother disappeared? You mean... like the students?"

"Hush, Ludo, let her speak," ordered Whittle with a sad smile directed toward Cassie, having talked with her at length about her mother during the climbing trips they had been taking on the weekends.

"I've always thought they were dreams, but I guess I should have known better. For a year or so, I would try things out—you know, see what I could do. I found out that I couldn't take electronics, but things like my clothes, thankfully, and my sketchpad, pencils, they would all go back and forth.

"As for the dream world itself, I haven't seen that much of it. I always wake up inside a small cave, and as long as I go back to that same cave, I can wake up in my bed. Otherwise, I just stay in the dream world. It's always cold... snowy... always cloudy and twilight. Time doesn't seem to change at all there."

For some time, Cassie shared what she could remember about the dream world. She described the great rocky cliff and the cavern and stream. She showed them some of her drawings of the place, including sketches of the strange glyphs that were etched into the cavern walls and in odd places on the ground all around the opening.

"Are there any people, anything else alive there?" This time it was Sarah asking the question as the others looked on, all of them absorbed completely in her tale.

"I see prints in the snow... I hear animal calls and other sounds? But I've never seen anything else... until tonight."

Jimmy had followed the small group to the back side of the gallery and found the door handily propped open. For some time, he had simply waited outside for them to exit, assuming that they eventually would need to and that would allow him to catch them by surprise in the midst of breaking a school regulation—which would give him leverage to learn more about what they were up to without exposing himself.

But as the evening crept on, he began to edge closer to the door and had just grasped the handle and tugged gently on it when the sound of footsteps behind him caused him to lurch around, letting the door close with a soft thud.

"What are you up to, Chopper? Planning on mischief with the first years again?"

Whipping around, Jimmy found himself staring up into the too familiar face of Willem. "And what's it to you, Dudley?" Jimmy sneered. "I just saw the door propped open and was checking on it. No harm in that, is there? Besides, big boy, what brings you to the back of the gallery? Fancy trying the finger paints?"

"Out for a jog... saw someone snooping around and thought I'd have a look. Seems like I was just in time."

"Careful, Dudley. With so many students disappearing these days, you might want to keep your insufferable nose in your own business. But word has it that parents are getting a nice payout, so perhaps daddy would get a better return on his investment if you did disappear." Jimmy sneered as he shoved his way past the larger scholar. He was getting hungry as it was, and the little information he'd gained would be rewarded in any case.

Waiting until Jimmy had cleared the corner of the building, Willem slipped quietly into the rear of the gallery. He wanted to see what had been of such great interest to Jimmy for himself.

"No, no... this isn't coincidence. There has to be a connection between the disappearances and these dreams. Are you sure you've not heard any other voices? Seen any other people there?" Sarah was staring intently at the small map with its markings as she spoke.

"Like I said," Cassie responded thoughtfully, "Unless you think our mascot could come to life... that was the first living thing that I've seen. But I did hear singing... maybe a voice."

"Singing? What kind of singing?" queried Ludo, who had been studiously jotting notes into his digital tablet.

"Singing singing... you know... singing." Cassie responded with frustration.

"He means—female voice, male voice, was it a song that you have heard before?" Sarah translated.

"Female? I'm pretty sure it was female. I feel like I've heard it before, but it was, I don't know, just notes... like... da da da da da daaaa." Cassie wasn't a musician and had never pretended to be, so she wasn't sure that she was even singing the song she had heard correctly. But as she sang those few notes, she saw Whittle stiffen immediately. "It sounded a lot like the song you were singing, Whittle, the night the guards disappeared. I guess I didn't really connect it until now."

"That's exactly what I was singing... it's part of the Infinitum. It's... it's the tune that was playing on Janice's digital player the day she disappeared..." Whittle leaned in toward Cassie, her voice dropping as she spoke in a hush with the realization that was dawning on her. "You might have heard Janice! If these dreams are real, maybe... maybe Janice is still alive."

"What do you mean Janice is still alive?!"

All four of them nearly leaped out of their skin at the unexpected fifth voice that confronted them from just outside the mudroom doorway.

"Willem? Look, Willem... I swear we had nothing to do with it." Whittle's normally strong voice sounded hollow, frightened. Cassie had never heard her like this.

"I've been here long enough... if any of you have information about Janice, you'd better tell me now." The voice indeed belonged to Willem, whose athletic body filled the frame of the door, his normally cheerful countenance replaced by something much darker, something almost dangerous.

"It's not what you think, Willem. I swear to you..." encouraged Whittle once more.

Cassie noted absently in the midst of her shock that Whittle had stepped between Willem and herself and was pleading with the senior scholar, who looked to be on the breaking point.

"Then somebody better start talking. Now."

Fifteen

"Listen, Trevor. You know how much I like you and your sister. I don't want anything to happen to either of you, but whatever she's gotten herself into with this new girl... it isn't a game." After retreating from the gallery, Jimmy had made his way back to the Lid, arriving just in time to catch Trevor Dawson as he was walking out of the towering glass entryway. Trevor paused as Jimmy strolled up quickly, sensing the concern in his suitemate's voice.

"Sarah's bright, she's not going to get in too deep with anything, Chopper. You just need to relax," Trevor coaxed as he adjusted the backpack on his shoulder. "Besides, Willem is actually giving me a run for my money this year. I need to be focused, or the lead will slip to him."

"Nah, no way that happens. He's pretty and all, but his dad has hollowed him out so badly he'll crumble when it really matters... he always does."

Trevor chuckled at that, he liked Willem well enough, but auditions were... well, it was no different than facing a friendly foe on the field. Besides, talented competition raised everyone's skills, and getting the lead was no guarantee of moving to the next level.

As the pair were talking, Mistress McClaine and Master Adonis exited the building arm in arm. While there were many rumors, no one was really sure how to describe their relationship. Neither wore a wedding ring, nor bore the same name, but given how inseparable they were, most assumed they were in some form of long-term commitment, and one that clearly worked better than many more traditional arrangements.

"Oh, Trevor, you're dancing has really improved this year. If I'm not mistaken, you must have spent half the summer in rehearsals." Mistress McClaine smiled demurely at Trevor as Adonis looked on appraisingly. Anyone meeting Cressida for the first time would have no idea how ferociously protective she was of her dancers. From the first day that Trevor stepped on the stage, she had been recruiting him to invest more and more time in studying dance over vocals.

For his part, Trevor enjoyed dancing, all the more so as his skill increased. "Not half, Mistress. I spent the full summer break at La'Fette's... ballet, mostly." Trevor was proud of his progress, and rightly so given the amount of work he'd put in. "I intend on earning the lead this year... and the solo."

"Well, well, you've a better shot than you think. With Janice disappearing like that, I wonder if Willem will ever be right. He just can't seem to focus any longer. Tell me, Trevor, of the remaining female leads, do you have a preference?" Cressida slowly tilted her head toward him, her eyes flashing mischievously.

"Why not make Willem the female lead?" interrupted Jimmy with a sly sneer, receiving a thump in the arm for his trouble.

"Jimmy," responded Trevor, but he in turn was cut off by Adonis' thoughtful response.

"Actually, Mister Franks, that... that is a very interesting proposition. Willem has the range... it would be a blow to the women's houses to lose a lead role entirely, but what am I to do?" Adonis made a dramatic gesture of surrender before stepping away, pulling Cressida along with him, his attention now seemingly on to some other matter of greater importance.

"It's not a bad idea... not entirely unheard of either," the boys could hear the mistress respond as the pair of masters strolled away through the garden.

After they were out of earshot, Jimmy thumped Trevor on the arm in return... adding with another smile, "Hah, that would solve it. Can you imagine, Willem as your leading lady?! Too bad your sister isn't old enough to take the part. She'd be magnificent."

"She hates singing. And I've already put a good word in for you, Jimmy, no need to keep blowing that horn. She has a mind of her own, you know. I can't force her to take you to the winter formal." Trevor shook his head slowly but chuckled lightly. He could at least appreciate Jimmy's undaunted pursuit.

"What? I would never take advantage of our friendship!" Jimmy feigned looking hurt as he continued, "I care about you both, your whole family. We've been friends for years, and I'm telling you that all this snooping around and looking into the disappearances is only going to end one way—badly. And that roommate of hers is a bad influence. She should never have been paired with a Judy! Seriously, it's an embarrassment to the family name."

Trevor sighed and shook his head in mute acknowledgement. "I'll talk to her. I can't promise anything, but I'll talk to her. Just... keep an eye out for her, Jimmy. I've got to be able to focus on winning this part. If I do, Remauld's is a shoe-in."

"You can count on me, Trevor. I've got your back, even if she doesn't say yes to the formal." Jimmy smiled slyly once more and clapped Trevor on the shoulder one last time before slinking off, leaving Trevor alone near the fountain as an owl's hooting call ushered in the darkening night.

As Trevor was turning to leave, the jingle of a heavy set of keys alerted him to a familiar presence making his way into the garden.

"Mister Dawson! I say, you couldn't possibly have a head full of worries on a night like this, could you?" Bentley's voice preceded the appearance of the rotund bus driver and handyman. He was one of the few people on campus that everyone liked and in whom many confided. His sure and easy presence was as much a part of Walgrove as the ancient trees that dotted the campus.

"Oh, hey, Bentley. Nothing serious going on. Well, actually, since you're here, perhaps you can give me some advice." Trevor settled himself on the wall that ringed the fountain and waited for the older man to plod over, setting a small pail and a pair of hedge shears down on the fountain's edge.

"Not about girls, I hope. No, you've always been too busy and focused for that," Bently mused, lifting thick fingers to stroke his rounded chin. "Can't be the audition... for the same reason. Must be..."

"The disappearances."

"Ah... I thought as much. You know, Trevor, that I can't really talk about any of that." The older man looked about as he said this as if expecting to see a school official striding up to them at the very mention of the topic. Oddly enough, nothing more than a single bird could be seen fluffing its feathers as it settled atop a shrub about halfway across the garden.

"I'm worried about Sarah, that's all. Anything you could tell me, anything at all would be helpful." Trevor paused, looking up at the older man until Bentley sighed and settled himself down on the fountain's edge as well. Taking out a neatly folded rag, Bentley dabbed unnecessarily at his forehead for a moment before replying.

"The night the guards disappeared... somehow. All of the security footage was erased." Bentley folded the simple cloth and placed it back into his pocket without looking at Trevor. Across the garden, the small bird fluffed its feathers noisily as a light breeze pushed a few scattered leaves along the stone walkway, their sound the unmistakable scraping of winter to come.

Keeping his voice calm, Trevor nodded and stood slowly. "There are only a few people on campus who could pull something like that off. And as it happens, I know one of them very well." Lifting his backpack to his shoulder, Trevor smiled down at Bentley, who had remained seated. "Thank you, sir. Just one last thing..."

Bentley took his time standing, even as he lifted a hand to stop Trevor from finishing his question. "I know what you're going to ask. The new girl, Cassie. Seems like everyone is interested in her... especially the headmistress." This time Bentley looked at Trevor, pausing just a moment before adding, "She's a good girl. Talented. I think you'd like her if you gave her a chance. I think she's in trouble, Trevor. I don't know whether to recommend that you help her or stay away."

Nodding at this response, Trevor spoke softly in reply, "I think I know what to do. Family has to come first, after all." Saying this, the young man slipped out of the garden and down the path, but rather than heading toward the dorms, he took the lane that led toward Quibbley Hall, determination cutting across his angular features.

Janice scrabbled at self-awareness—like grasping at a soap bubble in the air. Breathing didn't seem to be an issue for her, but other basic mental functions like thought, reason, and even that tentative sense of self were like fireflies flickering in the shadows.

She knew that her eyes were observing, but it was as though the images were never processed into recollection as she floated within a void of sights unseen and sounds unheard.

"Let me go... I promise... I promise I'll never come back... Please... please let me go." Janice thought the words as much as speaking them, the sound of her voice echoing oddly in her own mind. Somehow she knew she was not alone. There were others here as well. Some seemed familiar, though she didn't know how she knew this. And then there was the darkness. She shivered as she thought of it. "You don't scare me... you're just an imagination. Just wait... someone will come looking for me, and when they find me..." Janice's voice drifted off. What was it she was talking about? The thought floated away in a swirl.

The creature watched her... watched them. Its growing collection. Their odd and gangly bodies floated in a kind of temporal stasis like so many corporal dolls. This was not enough, or perhaps the ones it had collected were simply wrong. Either way, the creature needed to collect more, to study them and discern why they were of so much greater interest than the other creatures that walked the surface above. Surely one of them held the secret to the creature's release from captivity.

Gliding over to the most recent in its collection, the Ningalix stroked fingers softly across its face. "Jaaaannnnissss," it purred. Immediately the captive's countenance changed into a rictus of pain or longing. The Ningalix knew this somehow but could not yet distinguish between the two. It knew that its touch on this one was different than the others, and so the Ningalix sang to it soothingly until the captive creature settled into silence once again. The sounds this one made were different each time, giving the Ningalix the opportunity to practice its voicings.

"I need... I need to tell Willem. Willem..." Janice mumbled, her voice muted as though spoken through a mouthful of honey.

"Willll... Emmmmm," the Ningalix murmured, repeating the word once again. It was not an unpleasant utterance, thought the creature, as it glided back toward the surface, where it could sense the opening of the gateway once again, and with it the presence of more of these creatures... more to add to its collection. "Willll... Emmmmm, come... my Will... emmm." The Ningalix could feel anger flowing from these, mixed with fear. This sensation it knew well, licking its teeth in anticipation of the feast to come.

As the Ningalix caressed her cheek, self-awareness returned in a jolt to Janice. With it, the cold and the terror of her situation, but this time she saw something more... something familiar. It was Willem... along with another boy, whose face she could not make out, and perhaps two additional scholars behind them. They were walking toward her, walking toward the creature... toward the trap. In that moment, Janice screamed the only thing that she could think to scream... Willem's name.

"Willlllleeeeemmmm! Willlllleeeeeeemmmmmm!"

"I'm not going back down there. Besides, they've locked that room up tight." Cassie and the others had arrived at the Quib and snuck quietly to one of the labs that she had been using over the past few weeks. It was Willem who suggested—no, demanded— that they go to the large room in the lower floor where the security officers had disappeared.

"If what you are saying is true about how the guards disappeared, then this is the only thing that makes sense. Trace your steps back to the beginning, to the only thing we know."

"Listen to Willem, Cassie. He's right, you know it. I can see it in your eyes." Whittle's voice had been uncharacteristically soft ever since Willem had arrived, an observation that was irritating Cassie to no end.

"Didn't you say that you were the one to open the... portal... thing... whatever it is, Whit? If Cassie doesn't want to go, no one is forcing her. But time is running short. I say we at least try to confirm that this... dream world... exists." Willem's gaze had brushed across Cassie but only briefly as he turned a shoulder toward her while replying to Whittle, his body separating the two.

"That's like, the worst bad-movie idea ever..." Ludo interjected before being hushed by a harsh stare from all three of the women simultaneously. "What?! Don't any of you watch movies? You know I'm right!" he defended weakly.

"What dreamworld? What are you talking about?"

As one, the group turned to the now-open door to see Trevor Dawson, silhouetted against the darkness of the hallway with his hand grasping the doorknob and a critical look spread across his brow.

Sarah and Ludo both shrieked briefly before covering their mouths, Ludo's face going crimson as Whittle lofted an appraising eyebrow at him.

"You're making enough racket for the whole academy to hear you..." Trevor said as he looked the group over, his gaze lingering on the first year students, who were not permitted to be in this building let alone to be out after curfew. "Sarah, whatever you're getting yourself mixed up in, this needs to end now."

"You can't tell me what to do, Trevor!" Sarah shot back with feigned indignation. "I know exactly what I'm doing..."

"Clearly, you don't." Trevor's voice had softened as he took a step into the room and closed the door softly. "None of you know what you're doing. Look," He held a hand up to ward off something that Willem was about to say. "Let me speak."

Trevor paused a moment until the others had all nodded sullenly, and turned toward Willem as he responded. "I get it, Willem, you want to find Janice. If it were Molly, I'd feel the same... probably be doing even more to try to bring her back."

"You and Molly?" Cassie blurted incredulously before yelping as Sarah stomped on her foot and gave her a fierce look.

Ignoring Cassie's outburst, Trevor turned toward Sarah. "This isn't a prank, Sarah. It's not a play, and it certainly isn't a game. People we care about are disappearing. They aren't coming back, and no one knows how it's happening or what to do to make it stop."

"But that's the point, Trev, the school isn't doing anything. Worse, they're covering it up," Willem interjected as he looked back to Whittle, who had laid a gentle hand on his shoulder. Cassie's stomach knotted as she watched the pair of them, bewildered at her own reaction. Whittle was just being kind. "You all know that I'm right," Willem continued. "You've thought about this, Trevor, I know you have. How many more people need to disappear before we do something about it? And now... with Cassandra here, who somehow has access to her strange 'dreamworld' where she has heard Janice's voice? It's the first lead we've had, the first bit of information that anyone has that they might still be alive. You said it yourself—you would do anything."

As Willem spoke, Cassie watched Trevor, trying to gauge his response, noticing subconsciously that he too was quite handsome, though different than Willem, not as chiseled, but very...

"Ouch! What was that for?!" Cassie yelped as she pulled her foot up. Sarah had apparently stomped on her foot again and was now giving her a look of stark disapproval.

Ignoring the back and forth between the roommates, Trevor replied to Willem, "If we want to help, we need to take what everyone knows to Headmistress Floquet. That's what reasonable people would do. Willem, if we have a chance to save Janice and the others, we will need help. We can't and shouldn't try to do this on our own."

Crossing her arms over her chest, Sarah strode up to her brother, her diminutive height in comparison to him not dimming the force of her will. "We're doing this, Trevor. You can help, or you can get out of the way. Your choice. But make it quickly, because I have a feeling that we don't have much time left."

Sixteen

"Thank you, Mister Franks, Miss O'Dine. I appreciate you bringing this to my attention." Mistress Audrey Maude sat primly behind the simple wooden desk that was the sole piece of furniture in an otherwise starkly appointed dormitory office. Molly O'Dine and Jimmy Franks were two of her newest prefects, and as such had tended to bring more to her attention than the others. But this bit of news concerned the dorm mistress.

"If I may add, Dorm Mistress, I don't think that Sarah Dawson has anything to do with this." Jimmy's mouth curled slightly as he recognized Molly's desire to protect Sarah given her interest in her older brother. Ignoring his smirk, Molly continued in her serious manner, "I believe Miss Cole..."

"You do seem to have taken an inordinate amount of interest in Miss Cole..." Mistress Maude cut in smoothly.

"Truly, Dorm Mistress, I am not trying to show disfavor toward her, but she has shown no interest in adopting to life at Walgrove. Rather the opposite... she seems intent on upending all of our traditions."

"All of them, oh my. That's very ambitious of her." Mistress Maude cut in again, watching carefully as Molly blushed at this second rebuke.

"What Molly and I are trying to say, Mistress, is that with the recent disappearances, we're worried. Having scholars ignoring the curfew and meeting secretly across campus..." This time it was Jimmy's turn to be interrupted by Mistress Maude's curt but not unkind reply.

"Clearly their meetings are not so secret if you are so quickly aware of them, now are they, Mister Franks?" It was Jimmy's turn to blush this time, but Mistress Maude relented with a small wave of her hand. "I understand you are both worried, you are both observing that our reasonable rules are being broken, and that the problem is spreading rather than remaining with just a roommate or two."

"Yes, Mistress," Jimmy replied with a simple shake of his head.

"As it happens, I have a meeting with the headmistress tomorrow evening. I will bring this matter to her then. In the meantime, you are both prefects. You are aware of your responsibilities and the limits to your authority. I encourage you to think for yourselves, act within your roles, and offer some amount of leniency, remembering that you too were once first-years yourselves. And as I recall, neither of you perfectly adhered to every rule and guideline."

After a long sigh, Molly nodded and stood with Jimmy before expressing her thanks to the dorm mistress and departing the small office.

After they had moved beyond earshot of the dorm mistress' office, Molly stomped a foot to the ground as she spun toward Jimmy, staring up at him with fire in her eyes matching that of her hair.

"I swear, she takes that girl's side constantly."

"We did it the right way, Molly... you'll see. We've covered our tracks, and we've essentially received the mistress' permission to take action. If we're a little harsh, we'll feign ignorance." Inside, Jimmy smiled as he saw the rising ire of his fellow prefect. He could see why Trevor liked her, even though the couple had not yet had the "DTR" talk. Still, the girl could be scary tough... which he was finding more endearing all the time.

"Whatever. So, where are they? At the Quib, you say?" Molly had already begun striding toward the exit, her hands closing in fists as determination set about her shoulders like a cloak.

Chuckling lightly, Jimmy dug into his pocket for the ever-present digital recorder. This was absolutely going to be worth capturing, he only wished he had his camera on hand as well.

Mistress Audrey Maude remained seated, scribbling idly on a writing pad, until the sound of the exit door opening and closing reverberated in her office. With a click, the mistress turned off the small electric lamp on her desk, and in a blink, the tall woman disappeared. In her place fluttered a small starling, it's oily black feathers blending perfectly with the shadows of the room.

The small bird chittered once as it hopped about before springing with a flutter into the air and out a window that had been propped open on the far side of the room.

The air of the large prop room rolled out in a stagnant sigh as the small group of scholars clung to the wall of the darkened corridor. Whittle turned back toward the group and winked as she slowly pulled the previously locked door open. "You can learn useful things growing up in the flats..." she whispered as the others walked cautiously together into the dark room.

"This is the part of the movie where half the party is eaten by the monster..." Ludo quipped hesitantly, receiving a firm kick to the shin for his efforts, from whom he couldn't tell in the darkness.

"Last time I'll say this... this is a really, really terrible idea. I mean, all they did was lock the door but left that... thing." Cassie paused and threw an arm over her eyes as a bright beam of light swung toward her.

"Sorry..." Sarah's voice called as the light slipped away from Cassie, sweeping across the floor and up toward the huge tapestry that covered the majority of the far wall. "It sure is creepy... even for a set backdrop. What's it supposed to be?"

"Sumer. It's a scene looking out from the city across the landscape. Those are date trees, probably, and the two rivers are the Tigris and Euphrates... the cradle of civilization..." Ludo's voice trailed off as Cassie and Sarah both chastised him.

"Show-off."

"Know it all."

"Shhhhh," cautioned Whittle, who had joined them after having inspected the room. "None of you are very good at this clandestine stuff are you?"

"Okay... so, now what?" Willem's voice was tinged with anxiety as the dim hue from Sarah's flashlight revealed his face, transfixed by the mural that hung before them all, its frame edged in strange designs.

"Whit knows the song... I think she just needs to sing it," Sarah answered, her voice just as flat as Willem's.

"Neither of you were here last time," Cassie cut in with urgency. "Last time, two... two grown men... disappeared! No one has ever come out... they always go in."

"Someone find a rope and tie it to my waist," Willem commanded, ignoring Cassie as he strode toward the hanging screen.

"Think about it, Will..." Whittle cut in.

"I have been thinking of nothing else. Janice returns... if there's even the smallest shred of hope, we have to try. None of you have to get close to the thing. I can handle this."

"Cassie has a point, Will. We should get help and not try to be heroes." Cassie was a bit shocked to hear Trevor come to her side, but he too was quickly rebuffed, this time by Sarah.

"For the love of... Whit, we need you to sing the phrase, or teach it to me. We're here, we have a chance. Let's get this done instead of sitting around like we're in some ethics class discussion!" Sarah threw her hands in the air, casting withering looks toward anyone who dared to look in her direction.

"We need to do this. We need to try. The rest of you can leave if you want, but I'm staying until we at least try. This might be our only chance to figure out what's going on." Willem paused, looking toward Trevor, who was frowning and looking at his feet, slowly shaking his head.

"Oh, for the love of... Look, everyone stay away from the... the thing... the backdrop." Whittle shook her head as she took a slow step forward and steadied her breathing. After a quick backward glance toward Cassie, Whittle began to sing the phrase she had sung the last time the pair had been in this room.

In a moment, Will's ethereal voice joined hers, then Trevor as well, until at last the entire rim of the screen began to glow... faintly at first, but as the notes continued, the strange symbols shimmered, cascading between blue and deep violet hues.

Then, just like before, a chill breeze swept into the room, and with it... cascading snowflakes.

"It's open," Sarah breathed, excitement evident in her voice. "Whittle, Trevor, keep singing. Will, call to her, maybe she'll hear your voice."

Cassie, Ludo, and Sarah had unconsciously huddled together, nearly standing on one another as the air continued to chill and the image on the large, hanging screen grew translucent, revealing what appeared to be the dark inner walls of a vast cavern.

"I shouldn't be here, I shouldn't be here... Please stop... please... all of you stop." Cassie's voice was tight with concern, fear creeping up her spine as a deep sense of foreboding washed over her. She wanted to run but somehow felt rooted to the floor.

"Janice...?" Willem's voice echoed hollowly, not just within the room but deep within the cavern that stretched before them like some monstrous, gaping jaw. "Janice? Are you there, Janice?" Willem took one hesitant step forward, followed by another.

As if in reply, the wind began to whistle, its undulations within the tunnel sounding all too much like Willem's name.

"Willllleeeeemmmm... Willllleeeeemmmm..." the wind seemed to call.

This was the nudge that Willem needed as he picked up his pace, heading toward the sound blowing from within the shimmering veil.

"The rope!" Sarah yelped as she sprinted to the side of the room, grabbed a coil of thick hemp cord, and dragged it back awkwardly toward Willem, whose eyes remained transfixed on the shimmering veil before them.

"I can help..." chimed Ludo as he aided Sarah in pulling the rope further forward before wrapping and cinching one end around Willem's waist. "Okay, Will... umm... one tug if you want us to pull you out? I think that's how this is supposed to work."

Ludo's voice cut off abruptly as the sound of a scream rent the silence.

It was Cassie, her face pale, a look of horror gripping her normally beautiful countenance. As one, Whittle and Trevor stopped singing, turning toward Cassie and then following her gaze back to the shimmering portal that began to fade along with the last echoing ring of the song and the sound of Willem's name twisting within the wind.

"No! Keep singing! Janice!! I'm here, It's Will... it's..."

As the window to the other world began to fade, a last breath of snow shimmered through the portal, swirling about the legs of a young woman who stepped once then twice into the room before collapsing into the arms of Willem, who had lunged forward as he saw the figure appear out of the gloom.

"Janice... Janice, it's you ... it's you, Janice... it's you..."

In sheer panic, Cassie threw herself through the door and bolted down the dark corridor, careening into an exposed pipe that threw her to the floor. Quickly, she rose, scrambling frantically before exploding through the back exit door and out into the cool autumn air. For a time, she ran... she ran as fast as she could run, not fully knowing why. She had seen nothing, only... felt... something... felt as though something were being torn from her.

After some time, Cassie collapsed, her legs burning. And there she lay, curled on the ground at the foot of a large oak with the towering shadow of the sleeping turtle looking down at her. Her breaths came in quick, short gasps as she fought back sobs that wanted to bubble to the surface. There she stayed for a time, allowing the quiet of the night to soak in, until she heard the low rumble of an engine and the crunch of gravel beneath slow-rolling tires. A door opened... followed by the crunch of booted feet, slowly making their way toward her before stopping just shy of where she lay.

"Well now... are the beds really as hard as that?" The familiar and kindly voice of Bentley seemed suited to the night. As Cassie made no move to reply, Bentley knelt and lay a warm, calloused hand gently on her head. "There, there, little one... you're much too big for these old bones to lift you on my own, but I can't just let you stay out here at night. You'll catch a cold, or worse."

With a groan, Cassie rolled over and then up onto her knees, accepting the offered hand that lifted her easily up and tugged her gently toward the waiting truck that sat idling on the path. "I'm... I'm okay, Bentley. I don't know what came over me..."

"Well, I certainly do. Seems you and those friends of yours have been getting into more trouble, but I suppose, if you really did find the girl, then... well, that's certainly something."

"How did you...?" Cassie began just as Bentley opened the passenger side door to reveal Ludo sitting in the middle of the truck's lone bench seat.

"Your frenemy here... young fellow what gave you all that trouble—peas from a pod it seems—came by in a crazy panic, woke me out of bed to come help find you." Bentley shook his head as he pulled himself into the driver's door and closed it with a rusty thud.

"I had to find you, Cassie... the others... I think I... I," Ludo stammered as if he was trying to find the right words.

Cassie settled into the seat beside him and pulled the door closed as he finished his thought.

"I think I felt it too..."

BOYS ARE TROUBLE

Seventeen

The dreams were gone.

Weeks had passed, and Cassie remained unable to return to her beloved craggy cliff—she even missed the muted hues of that forever twilight landscape. And worse were the headaches. Rather than awakening refreshed with a head full of creative ideas, she felt as though she were living in a perpetual fog. Her work was suffering because of it, and both scholars and faculty were beginning to take notice. Perhaps more precisely, Cassie was becoming invisible. Her celebrity star had not only fallen, it had cooled and faded to muted stone. And as far as anyone else was concerned, she was just another forgettable Judy.

Sarah, on the other hand, Cassie noted with a sour smirk from her perch atop the bunked beds, had become something of a celebrity. With her central role in the events leading to the return of Janice Tremaine, Sarah no longer wanted for attention of any sort, garnering more than a little adulation from scholars and faculty alike. Rumor had it that she had even been exempted from taking several recent exams as a kind of recompense for her 'heroic' actions. Indeed, Cassie now learned more about her own roommate from whispers in the hallway than from their ever-limited interaction. The fallout of their friendship had increased to the point that Sarah rarely slept in the room, bunking with a variety of upper grade girls on various nights of the week.

"Even Mistress Zeltrix likes her now," Cassie breathed with no small amount of disdain as she dropped to the cool tile floor. Sarah's vacant bed was so perfectly made you could bounce a coin on it. "You are quite the miss perfect, aren't you?" Cassie mumbled sourly as she threw on her uniform and trudged out the door, only to run into the waiting figure of Captain O'Dine.

"Well, if it isn't our star pupil," Molly began before cocking her head as a quizzical look overtook her normally dour demeanor. "You look perfectly dreadful. Why the long face?"

Cassie blinked at Molly, disconcerted by what sounded suspiciously like genuine concern.

"Oh, don't look at me like that. I don't actually care, I've been instructed to keep an eye on you, is all. If you disappeared tomorrow, I'm fairly certain that no one would miss you." Molly drew a mock smile on her face, but once again, Cassie sensed an almost maternal note of concern emanating from the fiery society captain.

"What can a poor Judy like me do for you this lovely morning, Captain O'Dine?" Cassie felt a twinge of regret over the brimming sarcasm in her voice, slumping her shoulders as she finished the statement and looking toward the stairwell leading up and out of the lower floor.

"Oh, it's not for me. I want nothing to do with you. On the contrary, you are wanted by Mistress Zeltrix for questioning regarding your role in the... in Janice's return. I told the mistress that you participated in the trespass but were seen running away wailing like a frightened child... so you couldn't possibly have been the one aiding Janice and likely would have no useful information to share."

Cassie gritted her teeth and looked at the floor. Here was the old Captain O'Dine she had come to loathe.

"You need to look at me when I speak to you, Judy!" Captain O'Dine stomped her foot as she drew closer. She was smaller than Cassie, but her stance was anything but weak, and her chin was only inches away from Cassie's own.

Cassie swallowed and slowly looked back at Molly, locking her eyes with a determined look of her own. "Is there anything else that the captain requires of me?"

"Actually, there is." The smaller girl stepped back and folded her arms across her chest before continuing. "As it happens, you are not entirely incompetent at Jalaw... and with the upcoming match against Saint Eustace, we could use a deeper bench." Molly stared Cassie down for a moment as if regretting having to make the request, but eventually her face softened as she continued, "You've got a little... urban... in you. Pretty much the only thing about you that's worth anything."

Cassie actually chuckled at this as she responded, "You never cease to amaze me, Captain..." but she was cut off by the familiar and dismissive sneer she had come to expect from the upperclassman.

"We'll see you on the pitch. Be early, you need to help prep the field." Molly was already spinning away as she said this, leaving Cassie standing flat-footed in the corridor.

"Wonderful," Cassie muttered as she turned toward the stairwell and made her way slowly up the winding stone steps and out into the adjoining lounge, where she was immediately beset upon by a familiar voice.

"Cassie!" The voice was followed by the somewhat gangly loping of the slim young writer as he nearly leapt up from the table at which he had been sitting, spilling a pile of books to the floor in the process but leaving them as he approached.

"Ludo," Cassie replied, her voice not entirely flat. While she sincerely appreciated all that Ludo had done for her, she was finding the attention he was now paying her to be a bit... overwhelming.

For his part, Ludo let her tone slide past as he hefted a neatly folded piece of paper in one hand. "I've figured something out... or, well... I think I've found something that might be useful."

Cassie sighed as she continued walking. She was already late for her block as it was and just couldn't muster up the energy to care. "Maybe after lunch?" she mumbled as she continued to walk through the lounge. "I'm behind in history... math... everything... I just... I need to focus on my classes, Ludo."

Nonplussed, Ludo slipped up beside her, leaning in conspiratorially as he unfolded the paper to reveal a series of shapes and symbols, not unlike the many symbols Cassie had seen and painted from her dream world. "It took some digging, but I found this, and I think I've figured out what each symbol means. It's definitely a form of writing, similar to cuneiform but different in subtle ways and way more complex."

Cassie was about to silence him with a curt response when a scholar appeared around the corner at a run, and with a yell barreled toward them at full speed, arms flailing to either side. It was only her quick instinct that saved them all from a collision as she tugged and spun Ludo aside. Without looking at them, the scholar, a first year, she was quite certain, shrieked wildly before crashing into the large wooden doors that led outside, knocking several scholars down who had been unlucky enough to be entering at that moment.

"Geeze... what was that?!" Ludo exclaimed but hushed himself quickly as Cassie silenced him with a finger pressed to his lips.

Streaming behind the boy, she could make out what seemed to be a trail of... something she couldn't describe. It was like the pulsing waves of heat you could see rising from the asphalt outside her building on a hot summer day, but this seemed to be marking the path of the scholar like the contrails of a jet.

"You see something, don't you... I know you do, Cassie," Ludo exclaimed excitedly. And then she was the one being spun around as Ludo took hold of both of her arms and drew her around to face him. She found herself dizzily looking up at him, noticing how much... stronger... he appeared to be this close up. "Cassie, look at me."

Trying to shake the fog away, Cassie blinked up at him but was having trouble converting thoughts to words as her eyes traced the line of his jaw and she felt a distinct urge to kiss him.

"Cassie... something bad is happening... something really bad. Ever since Janice returned, things are... things are getting weird." Ludo paused, his eyes furrowing as he looked down on her. "Not you too!" he exclaimed, as he released her and took a step back, scrambling into his pocket for a pen, but Cassie snagged him by the arm and tugged him in toward her, lips pursing for a kiss.

With their faces mere inches apart, Cassie could feel the breath coming in quick gasps from Ludo even as his face flushed in embarrassment, but consciousness of her circumstance slammed back into Cassie like a crashing wave just in time to push him back and away. "Ludo! What are you doing?!" she exclaimed as she gulped for air, her own heart thumping in her ears as she searched for an explanation.

"Me?!" he yelped in reply. "I didn't have anything to do with that! You... you..."

"Well, that is... unexpected..." The familiar voice of Sarah shocked both Cassie and Ludo to silence as they turned toward

Cassie's roommate, faces reddening in embarrassment. But Cassie's feelings changed abruptly as she took her roommate in, standing as she was and holding the hand of none other than Jimmy Franks, whose face contorted in a wicked grin.

"I hear you've been recruited to the team, Cassie. You'll probably just sit it out on the bench, but glad to have you all the same." Jimmy's smile was joined by a slight arching of one brow as he lifted Sarah's hand, held firmly by his own. "Well, we should leave you two lovebirds be... and, Ludo... well played, I must say. Well played."

Ludo sputtered, his face turning yet another shade of crimson as he hastily refolded the parchment he had been carrying and shoved it into his pocket.

"Jimmy!? Seriously, Sarah?!" Cassie blurted before realizing she was talking.

"And why not?" Sarah shot back, her face growing dark before Jimmy cut in smoothly.

"Our families have been friends for ages. Actually, we have quite a lot in common, but I wouldn't expect a Judy like you to understand these sorts of things." Jimmy chuckled lightly as he drew Sarah toward the exit. "See you on the bench, Miss Cole," The upperclassman added without looking back.

Sarah, however, did look back, shooting a look of pure menace toward Cassie, as if daring her to say more, but Cassie quickly turned away, still shaking from the emotions that had overtaken her and now awash in confusion and uncertainty.

"Cassie... I'm sorry..." Ludo tried, but his voice was a mere buzz in her ears as she turned up the hallway toward the adjoining building where her next class was already in session, leaving Ludo standing awkwardly in the hallway as scholars trundled past.

"It is getting out of hand, Headmistress."

A small knife flashed quickly into Floquet's hand, catching the morning sun as she expertly snipped away a long stem from one of the many rose bushes that grew in the garden surrounding her quarters.

Mistress Zeltrix watched the headmistress moved about her work with a practiced grace.

"Do you know why I trimmed this stem?" Floquet asked as she stood and offered the stem to her Dean of Visual Arts.

"No, Headmistress, I cannot say that I have spent much time with... gardening."

"Well, then, perhaps a bit of instruction. You see, autumn pruning begins after the first killing frost and before the winter storms arrive. Long stems like these have a habit of damaging other branches or causing the entire plant to be uprooted if they are not properly maintained." Floquet lifted the leafless stem and looked at it in an almost spiteful manner. "It would have been better to have harvested this stem while the blossom was still young and beautiful... such a waste." Floquet dropped the stem into a wicker basket that stood next to her along the path.

"I'm not sure the child can handle much more pressure... her work has already suffered significantly since the crossing."

Floquet snipped another stem, lifting it for inspection before replying with a sigh, "I'll have to clean this knife now. I believe this is rosette diseased, I wouldn't want to pass it to the healthy plants." In saying this, the headmistress dropped both the knife and the stem into the basket before turning back to Mistress Zeltrix.

"If you are not up to the task..."

"I assure you, Headmistress, I can do this."

"But..."

"But I fear that the timing could have been better."

"The timing could always be better. And that is the point, after all." The headmistress began to walk slowly back toward the manor. "Have you forgotten what we are doing here, Cynthia?"

Mistress Zeltrix allowed the other woman to pass before following, the chill autumn wind whipping up suddenly, scattering dried leaves across the stone path in a light staccato rhythm. "She is losing faith in herself... and therefore losing control."

Floquet turned smoothly but swiftly to face the slightly smaller woman, her white hair pristine in the morning light and framed like a majestic cloud against the bright blue sky above. "Faith is most readily birthed in the very heart of adversity, is it not? Perhaps you have been... too gentle?" her voice lifting at the end was punctuated by a swirling mass of migrating birds that began to dance in swooping patterns overhead. "Or do you think there is someone else more suited to our needs. You think perhaps that I have chosen poorly." The ice in the headmistress' voice was sharp.

"No, never, Headmistress... Cassie is the one... I will... she will do what we need her to do."

"Excellent. Would you like to join me for breakfast?"

"Thank you, Headmistress, but I have work to do. Perhaps another time." Mistress Zeltrix bowed as she spoke and waited a beat for permission to depart.

"That you do," replied Floquet simply before turning back toward her manor as the Dean left the garden at a brisk walk, her heels clicking on the stones as she went.

Eighteen

"You're up, Judy." Captain O'Dine jogged to the sideline, soaked in sweat but with a determined look in her eyes. "You're replacing Kelly as a scamper. Grab her vest and get out there."

Cassie blinked and hesitated, not entirely sure that she was the Judy Captain O'Dine was referring to.

"Yes, CASSIE, I'm talking to you, do you need a personal invitation?!" O'Dine shouted with disgust and no small amount of frustration. "And one more thing… don't screw this up." With that, the small but powerful jammer turned back toward the fray, stepping up quickly to send a much larger player from the other team tumbling to the turf.

The match had been fierce, and far more violent than Cassie had been led to believe. Both teams had served a considerable amount of penalty time, which had increased the scoring substantially with just two banners remaining on both sides.

Scrambling to her feet, Cassie ran quickly down the sideline to the entry point on her own team's free zone, taking the sweat-soaked vest from an exhausted looking Kelly Striver. The girl looked positively beaten as she exited the field and offered a perfunctory nod before collapsing onto the grass.

"Well, there's my girl. 'Bout time you joined the fun." The familiar and welcome voice of Whittle met her before Cassie's eyes caught sight of her athletic friend. Even soaked in sweat and sporting a new scrape across the jaw, Whittle cut an alluring figure against the blue sky and green pitch. "Like it?" Whittle laughed as she tilted her chin to show the large scrape that was bleeding slightly. "That's gonna hurt real bad tomorrow. Stay away from the tall lanky one with the tied back hair... girl must have filed her nails down for the match."

"She did that on purpose?" Cassie queried before huffing as Whittle slapped a Velcro banner to the front of her vest.

"Just retrieved this one. We have two more of these to go and we win. So, just follow me, and we should be able to put an end to this quickly."

"Ah... okay... I just need to run to the other side without getting this tag pulled off..."

"Easy as pie, except for the half dozen murderers out there who would just as soon rip an arm or leg off. These rival games are the best, aren't they?"

Cassie had no idea if Whittle was joking or not, but her enthusiasm was infectious, drawing a smile to Cassie's face, as she was only too glad to be talking to her friend again after several weeks of botched schedules and missed meetups.

"Alright, you've got what it takes, and fresh legs to boot, let's start behind that wedge being set on the left side and see if we can't win this thing." With that, Whittle was off in a loping run, her long legs quickly covering the distance.

With adrenaline coursing through her limbs and her heartbeat thundering in her ears, Cassie followed, nearly tripping herself on a tuft of grass at the start but picking up pace quickly until she was shadowing the other girl. The pair zigged and zagged across the pitch, dodging and spinning as they sought shelter behind their jammers. A bellowing yell close to her ear was followed by a tearing grab at the side of her vest that nearly sent her to the pitch, but at the last moment, the lithe form of Whittle was beside her with a steadying hand.

"Halfway there... now it's going to get tricky, just stay close."

It was all Cassie could do to nod and duck after Whittle as a muddy arm nearly took her head off. "This game is insane!" she yelled as she ran.

"Don't get too cocky there, Judy!" the familiar but heaving voice of Bobby lifted from her right as he plowed into a player on the oncoming team, sending the other hard to the ground, where the player remained motionless.

A sharp whistle cut across the field indicating a penalty.

"What! That was legal! I barely touched her!" screamed Bobby in a rage as the referee ran up and indicated he was to move off the pitch to the penalty area.

"Five minutes for flagrant fouling!" intoned the official. "Restart in the Walgrove quarter!"

Cassie jogged to a stop just behind Whittle. Only one defender stood between them and victory.

"Bobby! That was completely unnecessary! We had the field!" O'Dine barked in angry frustration. This was the angriest Cassie had ever seen the diminutive Captain.

"That was garbage! A clean hit!" yelled Bobby from the sideline as he pounded the ground with a fist in frustration.

Whittle placed a hand on Cassie's back as she leaned down to her ear. "You did well. A restart all the way back here is going to be really rough. If I go down, I need you to just leave me and run as fast as you can."

"But..."

"It's just a game, Cassie... I'll be fine. I won't let them get my tag, but I may need to go to the ground to open a hole for you to get through. Got it?"

"Got it... follow you until you go to the ground... find the hole and run for my life."

Whittle clapped Cassie on the back, wincing as she smiled from the swollen cut on her jawline. "Ouch... that really is going to hurt tomorrow."

Once the teams were in position well within the Walgrove half of the field, Whittle coaxed Cassie to follow her in a weaving trot along the back line. Feinting twice to test the defensive line, Whittle offered a quick, "Here goes nothing," as she darted forward.

The other team converged on them quickly, one grabbing hold of Whittle's vest and yanking her to the ground, but true to her prediction, this movement drew the attention of the other opposing Jammers, leaving Cassie free.

Her hesitation gone, Cassie leaped forward, literally hurdling one of the diving jammers as she broke free up the field in a full on sprint. The home crowd went wild, but Cassie didn't relent, feeling the thump of feet just behind her and possibly gaining, she noticed one last defender angling toward her from the far side of the field, but just as the other dove, Cassie leaped and twirled before bounding into the safe zone and planting her banner on the scoring pole.

The crowd erupted in wild cheers and applause that just as quickly turned to boos and howls.

Turning, Cassie found herself alone on the far side of the field, her pursuers having given up the chase and returned to support their team in taking down Whittle. What Cassie saw was shocking.

Whistles were blowing fiercely as the referees tried to bring the scrum in the center of the field under control. Cassie could see punches being thrown, and then from the side of the field a darting figure like a charging bull sprinted across the field and directly into one of the opposing team players who had remained outside the milieu, hands to their side in as much shock as Cassie at the brawl that had erupted.

With a sickening crunch, Bobby smashed the other player into the turf, followed by a flurry of punches that landed with dull thuds.

"Bobby!! Don't, what are you doing!" Cassie shrieked as she sprinted toward him, grabbing his arms as she arrived in a failed attempt to stop the larger boy from pummeling the hapless student he had targeted.

"Leave me alone, Judy!" Bobby shrieked back... his eyes glossy and mouth frothing as the back of his fist slammed against her temple.

And everything went dark.

A blue-hued sliver of light split in a vertical line before Ludo, expanding slowly to form a translucent window that gazed out upon a stark and stony landscape. A frosty breath of air puffed out toward him, and with it, a sprinkling of crystalline snowflakes.

"I've done it!" Ludo yipped excitedly, and then, "I've done it..." he repeated softly with a hint of awe at the fact that he had just opened what appeared to be a portal to the other world, the world he had visited only in shallow dreams, aside from the most recent portal opening in the basement of the Quib that resulted in Janice's return. "Well, here goes nothing..." Ludo murmured as he checked the contents of his backpack once again. After the weirdness that morning with Cassie, Ludo had decided that he might be the only one left capable of finding out what was going on and then figuring out a way to stop... whatever it was. He had packed all of the essentials, a flashlight with extra batteries, some climbing rope that he didn't really know how to use, a recording device to capture any evidence that might present itself, his trusty notebook and several pens, and of course, a smattering of snack bars he had grabbed from the lunch hall.

He stood along the base of the Sleeping Turtle, the large taprock mountain that framed the northwestern end of the campus. Ever since he had found the tome of glyphs buried in the "Sleeze," which was the name the scholars had lovingly given the H.C. Leezicus Library, Ludo had been hard at work building interpretation models on the brand new battery of computers in the Rezek Digital Arts Center. While many of the scholars dismissed Ludwig as an odd boy, the faculty knew well how intelligent he was, especially his photographic memory. One look was all he needed of the symbols ringing the mural in that lower room in the Quib and he could recall their exact shape and location. Plugging them into the models he had been constructing made short work of the remainder of the task, which was to convert the sequence into an audio signal.

"First to test the switch on the other side," Ludo mused as he withdrew a small battery-powered speaker he had affixed to a digital player. With the built in wake up function, the sound would play on the other side to ensure that he could return from this little venture. "Your mother would definitely not approve of this, Ludo..." he murmured to himself as he tossed the device in and powered down the device he had used to open the portal in the first place.

"Could this possibly take any longer?" Ludo had taken to his feet after several minutes had passed, pulsing with nervous energy and unable to wait any longer. Just as he was about to look at his watch for the umpteenth time, he heard the telltale lyrical pulsing of his manufactured sound as the portal blinked and slid open once again. "Genius! Pure Genius!" Ludo remarked enthusiastically, only a little disappointed that his triumph had gone completely unnoticed. "Well, she'll notice me now, won't she." Saying this, Ludo grabbed his sack, set the first device down with a thirty minute timer just in case, and with a deep breath stepped through the shimmering curtain into a whole new world.

To his amazement, the air was crisp and clean, and while the sky above was dimmed in twilight crimsons and golden hues, he could easily make out the landscape that stretched before him.

"This place needs a name..."

"Well, if you must have a name, you can call it Eridul."

Ludo shrieked like a child and jumped in the air as he looked about for the source of the strange little voice. "Who... what?"

"No. It's pronounced Ehhrrrr-ihhhh-Duuuullll." The voice responded rather crossly. "I must say that you outworlders are not very bright at all." Ludo's eyes finally caught sight of the strange little creature that was speaking to him and then shrieked once again as he turned to make a dive back through the portal but to his dismay stepped on the device that had opened the gateway. As his foot crunched down on the speaker and the attached digital audio device, the portal winked closed, a stone wall taking its place.

"That's just as well... there's a number of things on this side that you wouldn't want over there." The creature moved swiftly and smoothly across the ground until it came to rest atop a small stone a few yards from where Ludo was now crouching.

"You look... You look like... like Wallie..."

"Whatever is a Wallie?" replied the creature, which Ludo could clearly see to be something like a miniature dragon with tails and scales and all. Its eyes, however, were comically large and round.

"It's the school mascot... Wallie the Wyrm."

"I see. I've taken the shape of the creature I saw on the patch all of the other young soft skins wore on their uniforms... a Wallie, is it?" Standing on its hind legs, the small dragon looked down upon itself as it swished its tail about, "Perhaps something less frightening, then, if this seemingly innocent shape is so fearsome." With a snap of its tiny, clawed fingers, the strange creature transformed into the monstrous shape of a bear, easily tripling in size and letting out a bellowing roar that shook the ground beneath Ludo's feet.

Ludo shrieked again and began fumbling with the broken device, hoping he could somehow fix it and escape as he leapt back against the stone wall.

"Well, clearly this is worse, but would a little help be too much to ask for? I've never actually spoken to one of you before, and this is a bit confusing, you must admit." With another snap, the creature shifted back into its prior form, flicking its tongue thoughtfully for a moment.

"No, no... this is good... this is just fine... do... do you have a name?" Ludo stammered as he tried to collect himself. Oddly enough, he was suddenly appreciative of the fact that he was alone after all.

"Well, I do wish you would make up your mind, but yes, why don't you call me Lananna." The small dragon-like creature's mouth widened in what Ludo could only assume was a smile but which in fact looked quite threatening with its glistening rows of sharp teeth.

"Maybe do less of that."

"Show my teeth?"

"Right... less teeth."

"You don't like my teeth?"

"I like them just fine... but... less."

Lananna hissed out a puff of air as it settled to the ground and blinked back at Ludo. "So, then, why have you come to Eridul?"

His pulse having returned to a more normal rate, Ludo sought his memory for where he had heard such a familiar sounding name. "Eridul... like the ancient Mesopotamian city of Eridu?"

"Eridul as in the place you are right now. I've never heard of any such... mess of potamia." Lananna tilted its head to one side and blinked once while continuing to look at Ludo. After several moments of silence, the small dragon continued. "You aren't very good at this communication thing, are you..."

"No... not my strong suit."

"I see. So, perhaps you could tell me where you are from and we can take it from there."

"Walgroves... well, I mean Earth, probably."

"You do not know the name of the place you are from?"

"I mean... of course I do... it's a planet called Earth, in a solar system in the Milky Way galaxy," Ludo cut himself off of his own accord.

"Milky Way..." the creature repeated dubiously.

"Uh... yeah, it's a bunch of stars, you know, a galaxy... and we live on a planet in it."

"I see..."

Just as the creature spoke, the stone wall upon which Ludo was resting split open as the device on the other side turned on, sending Ludo sprawling backward into his own world at the foot of the Sleeping Turtle.

With a hop, Lananna followed him, its feet crunching against a layer of fallen leaves that covered the ground beneath the towering trees.

"Wait, you can't..."

"I can't what?" Lananna queried with a hint of menace in its voice. "This is how treaties are made... you inspect my world, and I inspect yours... or are you soft skins so lacking in common decency that you would deny me this right of passage?" Lananna blinked back at Ludo, its tail swishing from side to side.

"Uhh... but... people will... I don't know... no one has seen anything like you here, they might do all kinds of things."

"Ah... I see, you wish to protect me. That is honorable. I would have protected you had we remained, though I dare say that there are far more things in Eridu that would simply eat you on sight. From what I have seen of the creatures of your world, it would seem I have little to fear." With a final swish of its tail, the creature began to saunter away from the rocky cliff face along the trail. "And besides... one of us is already here... and that one... that one is not very nice at all."

Nineteen

"Will you just listen to me!" Janice screeched as she tossed the papers she was holding in a spray across the stage, where they fell like autumn leaves, shimmering as they were highlighted by the blinding sheen from the spotlights above the stage. "It's not Mortis Isle... it's Azilem! And there is no Gilgamesh and Ishtar!" she roared with disgust as she paced toward the edge of the stage, eyes blazing furiously.

Master Bale Adonis stood slack-jawed at her sudden onslaught, looking down toward the script before offering a reply. "But of course it's Gilgamesh and Ishtar... it's right there in the script," the professor countered at last with no small amount of incredulity.

"Then change it, you idiot!" Janice raged, looking at her empty fist as though she wished she had something more to throw. "It's bad enough that I have to suffer through this... farce..." she seethed as she walked along the stage edge like a prowling cat. "But at the very least you can get the facts straight..."

"Perhaps you are right, Cressida my dear, and it is too soon for her to come back..." This comment Adonis addressed in lower tones to the ever-present Director of Choreography, whose own brow was furrowed in puzzlement.

"I can hear you... you froppy worm!" yelled Janice as she paced back toward the center of the stage. "Azilix, Ningalix, Lananna, Parci..."

"But that doesn't make any sense, darling," Cressida interjected at last, easing a few steps closer to the raving scholar. Janice, however wonderful it was that she had returned, was clearly unwell. But Cressida's usually calming demeanor seemed to have no effect.

"Write it down, fool!" Janice demanded before letting out a yell that echoed across the auditorium. "I don't have TIME for this! I have work to do!" The young girl stalked over to Willem, who had been practicing the scene with her. "You... At least you seem interested in doing as I say. Pick those papers up, I've made corrections where I can, give them to the lackwit down there, and then come fetch me when you have completed your task." With this, Janice spun on her heel and leaped from the stage, landing with astounding grace at the far end of the orchestra pit before heading out the side door to the auditorium with a crash.

Scholars and Masters alike stood or sat in stunned silence until Willem broke the palpable tension as he knelt to pick up the strewn papers, his eyes red, his mouth pursed in a thin line.

Minutes more passed before Trevor called softly from the right wing of the stage, "Willem..."

"Not now, Trevor..." Willem cautioned without looking up from his task. His hands were visibly shaking as he tried to pick the papers up from the floor.

"Well, then... I think we should all take a break for... for the rest of the day," Adonis suggested, his voice lacking its normal pomp and authority.

Picking up on Bale's tone, Mistress Cressida reached the edge of the line of light that rimmed the stage and lifted her steady voice in support of the master's declaration. "You heard Master Adonis. Take the rest of the day to work on your lines and movements... there is plenty that all of you have to work on. Be back here sharply tomorrow after your blocks are over."

Cressida's voice seemed to cut the lingering tension in the room, and conversations began to spring up in low tones amid the scuffling of feet and zipping of backpacks as scholars and staff made their way reluctantly out of the auditorium.

Trevor paced softly to the center of the stage and began to retrieve papers along with Willem until they both held a neat stack and stood facing each other in awkward silence, which Trevor broke in careful tones. "She'll be alright, Willem... you just need to give her time." But Trevor was cut off immediately by Willem.

"She isn't alright! Whatever this is... it isn't all right. She's... she's angry... she has weird memories... Azilix? Parci? What kind of nonsense is that?"

Willem sighed heavily, his hand clutching the stack of papers in his fist, the first sheet clearly visible as he lifted it for Trevor's inspection. "Does this look alright to you? These aren't notes... this isn't even a... a language!" Trevor could see clearly the myriad of scribbled symbols that covered the page—it was the work of madness.

"Willem, you have to breathe. Just... just give those to me... let me take care of them for you." Trevor gently took hold of the edge of the bundle of papers and tugged them away from Willem before adding them to his own stack.

"That isn't Janice. I'm telling you, Trevor... she's still in that place... and whatever that thing is that came out... that isn't her."

Willem said this with a quaver in his voice, as though he were trying to convince himself of the truth.

"She's been through..."

"What?! What has she been through?" Willem cut in once again, exasperation on his face as he looked into Trevor's eyes for the first time.

The two rivals stared at one another for a few moments before Trevor replied, "I don't know..."

"That's right, Trevor. You... don't... know. No one does, because all she does is skulk around the Quib and demand that everyone run idiotic errands for her. It's like she thinks she's on some amazing mission, but..." Willem trailed off.

"I know, Willem, I've heard. Her room is full of scrawlings. Her roommate has told everyone about her screams in the middle of the night... it's awful. Here." Trevor placed a hand on Willem's shoulder, the firm weight of it seeming to quell Willem's shaking. Trevor had never seen Willem like this. He had never seen anyone like this, for that matter.

"I have to go back... I have to find her... the real her," Willem muttered to himself.

"Willem, are you nuts?! We can't go back. What does that even mean? You can't just open another portal... or whatever that was. If it isn't her and it really is something else, you could just let more of them in."

"I know what I have to do," was all that Willem offered in reply as he turned away, shoulders slumped in resignation, and made his way out of the auditorium, his exit emphasized by the clang of the exit door slamming shut.

"Man, that guy is whack." The voice of Jimmy Franks drifted hollowly from the far side of the auditorium, soon followed by slowly approaching footsteps.

"Geeze, Chopper, give the guy a break. His girlfriend is..."

"Even more whack than he is," Jimmy chuckled with a grin as he jogged up the stairs at the edge of the stage. "Ah, come on, lighten up. You did good there, bringing him down like that. Pretty masterful acting, I gotta say." Jimmy thumped Trevor's shoulder in a good-natured gesture as he arrived, peering down at the pages that Trevor was still holding. "That's disturbing."

"It actually is... she can't be well. Surely the school has someone helping her. Can't imagine what sort of nightmare she was in, but whatever it was, it was bad."

"Yeah, well... no chance he gets the lead now."

Trevor sighed and eyed Jimmy with a look of reprobation.

"Hey, I'm just looking out for you, Trev. You get this lead and you're a shoe-in for that guaranteed slot to Remauld. But, uh... I have an idea about what to do with these, if I may?" Jimmy gripped the stack of papers as he said this last, but noting the concerned look growing in Trevor's eyes, he added, "I'm a hacker, remember? I can have the crew image these and put them through a couple of models... maybe see if there really is a pattern here."

Realizing the sense of this approach, Trevor relented and allowed Jimmy to take the stack of pages upon which Janice had furiously scratched the numerous odd shapes in what appeared to be no pattern at all. "Makes sense... I guess. I'll go check in on Sarah... see how she's getting along with her roommate these days."

"Oh, Sarah is fine... very fine indeed," Jimmy responded with a wink and a chuckle before slipping back down the stairs and out into the blustery afternoon.

"Hey, buddy, what're you working on there?

Ludo stretched his fingers over the keyboard in an attempt to blank out the screen of the computer he was working on but reconsidered, as the voice was coming from directly behind his shoulder and such an action would only look suspicious. "Uh... nothing much, just a little personal project," Ludo replied lamely as he spun his swivel chair around to discover none other than Jimmy Franks peering at him suspiciously while hefting a messy stack of papers under his arm. The computer lab was otherwise empty, leaving the two to a private conversation.

"Ohhhh... personal projects are always the best," noted Jimmy as he slid onto his own wheeled chair and pushed himself over to Ludo's desk with a bump.

As Jimmy's chair hit the table, Ludo's book bag seemed to jump of its own accord, drawing Jimmy's attention. As he looked toward the bookbag, Jimmy could have sworn that the thing hissed at him. "Say, what's in the bag? You got a cat in there?"

"What?! No, I don't have a cat," Ludo said defensively as he pushed the book bag further out of reach. "In fact, I was just finishing up, so if you want to use this terminal, you can have it." Ludo made to stand up but was held in place by a firm hand on his shoulder.

"Don't be silly, buddy." It wasn't lost on Ludo that Jimmy likely didn't know his name, which in fact Jimmy could not recall at the moment. "There's a hundred empty terminals in here, I don't need to take yours. But goodness, you are more jumpy than normal. Almost makes me think you might be up to something." Jimmy laughed as he watched Ludo's face redden and then slapped Ludo's shoulder heavily as he rolled back a foot or two before setting the papers he was holding on the desk in front of Ludo with a dull thump. "Actually, I was hoping to find you here because... I could use your help."

Jimmy had paid no attention to Ludo since his arrival, and thus Ludo could not have been more surprised by this request. What assistance could he possibly provide as a first year? "You need my help?" Ludo queried with a slight hint of suspicion tingeing his voice.

"Why, yes I do. Have you ever seen anything like this before?" Jimmy tapped the pile of scribbled-over papers with a thick finger.

"Obviously you're not talking about the typed lines... these ... scribbles?" Ludo was about to say more when the shape of them caught his eye and triggered a feeling of familiarity. They had a slant and order to them that was unmistakable... but these had been hurriedly scrawled by someone who knew much more about the shapes that he had used to enter the other world... or Eridul as his new little friend called it.

Jimmy caught the subtle shift in Ludo's focus and smiled. His guess had been correct—the first year had indeed been working on something with the new Judy girl, and whatever it was, it was tied to Janice and these symbols. "Any idea where these came from?" Jimmy asked idly.

"Uhhh... no idea... I don't think I've ever seen anything like this before... looks kinda crazy, actually." Ludo was struggling to find the right words and tone to hide his growing interest. His mind was already racing ahead, piecing the shapes together with what he had already discerned about the odd language. Idly, Ludo moved the first page to the side to look at the next, before picking up the stack and rifling through it with a critical eye, now fully absorbed.

Waiting for Ludo's focus to drift into the pages, Jimmy offered another question, his voice sibilant and soft. "Would it surprise you to know that Janice drew those?"

"Not in the least..." replied Ludo unconsciously. "These patterns... they're starting to make sense... it's obviously some kind of code or language... maybe something she picked up when she was on the other side?" The book bag jumped once again, startling Ludo, who blinked as if coming out of a trance. As he turned his head back, he found Jimmy staring at him with a quizzical expression.

"Tell you what, buddy... everyone says you're a whiz with weird languages and poems and what not... why don't you scan these in, work a little magic on them. In fact, I might be able to get you time on the Dauntless at the Quib."

"Yemp!!" Ludo blurted, forgetting everything as he spat out the nonsensical word before recovering enough to add, "I mean... I can use the supercomputer?"

"What are friends for, buddy?" Jimmy smiled as he rose to his feet, leaving the stack of papers with the kid. "Just bring that stack with you to the Lid later tonight... meet me by the lower entrance, and I'll let you in and give you access to my account." Jimmy took another long look at the bookbag before adding, "Sound like a deal?"

"Deal," Ludo responded, watching Jimmy closely but wanting nothing more than to look back at the stack of papers.

"Excellent. I'll see you later." With this, Jimmy stood before walking slowly out of the computer lab, leaving Ludo alone once again.

As Ludo swiveled back around to the pile of papers, he gasped in shock at the sudden appearance of his small dragon-like friend. "What are you doing?! He nearly saw you! And you can't be walking around out here where other people will see you!"

"Posh..." remarked Lananna as it swished is tail. "You should let me eat that one."

"What?! You can't eat people!" Ludo remarked with fervor and a small amount of fear, recalling the monstrous shapes that Lananna could take.

"Certainly I could... it is not that large."

"No, I mean... you are not allowed to eat people."

"You have strange rules here."

"You have to promise me that you won't eat anyone."

"Fair enough, but one promise requires another... that is the way of things."

"Uhhh..." Ludo stalled, his mind wondering what kind of promises this creature could try to extract from him. "I guess that is only fair."

"It is the way of things, fairness has nothing to do with it," replied Lananna, who had not moved from its perch on top of the stack of papers.

"Okay, well... let me take those... scribbles."

"No, you cannot look at these, your mind is too open."

Ludo slouched back in his seat, thoroughly confused. "What is that supposed to mean?"

"These 'scribbles' as you call them? They are not what you think they are. They are mind tangles. Only the Ningalix uses these still. They are very dangerous but also very easy to avoid—you simply don't look at them."

"Okay... mind tangles? Ninja..."

"Ning-gah-lix" interrupted Lananna. "You really must learn to listen better than you do. I will not waste my vow exchange on this... I will only suggest that if you desire to continue to live, you should not look directly at these... scribbles."

"I see... so, can I feed them into the machine? Or will they damage a machine as well?"

"Why would anyone want to eat a written mind tangle?" The creature cocked its head to the side and blinked back at Ludo.

A bell rang suddenly, announcing the beginning of a new block and drawing the conversation to a quick close. Feeling like a fool,

Ludo closed his eyes while shoving the papers into his backpack before ordering Lananna to slide in as well, then, hefting the backpack, he trudged off to his next block, wishing it were already evening.

Jimmy watched the scene unfold from behind the one-way glass observation screen that flanked the far end of the room. While it appeared from the inside of the computer lab to be nothing more than a tall stretch of opaque glass, the electrified material provided a clear view of the room while obscuring everything on the other side. The interior suite provided a number of additional features to the observer, including audio and video controls, temperature settings, and feeds from every screen. The observation room was used primarily for research projects and the like, and few first years had been made aware of its existence, as it was a tightly held secret. For Jimmy, the situation could not be better. The first year scribbler was indeed hiding something—and what a secret it was.

Twenty

The week of the winter festival had arrived with a light shower of snow that covered the rolling acreage of the school's expansive grounds in pristine white. While the rest of the school had already partnered up for the coming dance and festivities, Cassie had neither been approached nor asked anyone and had finally concluded that she needed to put all of the worry behind her and focus on just being a normal student—which meant finding someone to accompany her to the dance. It was also one of the last days remaining for climbing, which was how Cassie found herself nervously crossing the campus toward the field house, where she knew she would find Whittle. A loop of climbing rope slung over her shoulder, Cassie made her way across campus in the hope of sharing some personal time on the craggy climbing surfaces of the Sleeping Turtle.

As she pushed the doors open to the field house, however, her stomach clenched at the sound of raised voices, but she entered anyway, finding herself facing two seated and familiar faces. A cold breeze followed Cassie into the common room, and with it a scattering of dried leaves that momentarily drew the attention of the pair of faces that turned toward her, one grim, one sad and shocked. After taking note of Cassie's arrival, however, they turned back to their conversation as if Cassie's appearance were of no concern.

"Willem, I won't do it, not again. I admit that she's not doing well, but the school has resources to help her. It's not your responsibility, it's not your fault." Whittle sat astride a low bench opposite the athletic form of Willem, whose face was a mask of misery and emotion.

"It's not your place to tell me what my responsibilities are or are not. I thought... I thought after all of this time... I thought that I could count on you, Whittle..."

Cassie's gut clenched involuntarily as Whittle grasped Willem's forearm tenderly, her countenance imploring the other to listen to reason. "Willem, don't say that. You know that I'm only trying to help you, that I would do anything for you..."

"Uh... is everything okay?" Cassie interjected.

Willem turned toward Cassie and leveled a blank stare at her but did not reply. Instead, he rose to his feet and picked up his sports bag, looking intent upon leaving.

"Cassie, could you give us a minute?" Whittle asked as she too rose to her feet and cupped Willem's chin with a hand. "Willem, don't do this... Please..."

Cassie dropped the rope she had slung over her shoulder, her cheeks coloring with shame and indignation and a rainbow of feelings that washed over her ranging from anger and fear to a deep malice that she had never felt before. "Oh, I see what's going on here... you...two... Go ahead and deal with... whatever..." Cassie growled before turning quickly and running from the small building, but not quickly enough to miss a sharp response from Willem that rang in her ears as she ran.

"What do you see in that kid? She's not loyal, she's not helpful, she's just in it to make a name for herself, Whittle... and look... she's running... but I'm here, and I need you..."

Cassie ran from the words as they trailed her like buzzing hornets. She couldn't run fast enough, as it seemed the words just followed her, until she had broken into a free sprint across the fields at the Swamp, through the parking lot behind the Lid, and down the lane.

Her feet carried her aimlessly until she found herself gasping for air along the lane near the small maintenance garage where the old bus driver Bentley happened to be washing down the little white bus with the school's name blazoned across the side.

"Gaaaahhhhh!" Cassie yelled, her voice echoing through the trees and rattling within the open garage. The old bus driver dropped the hose with a start and then struggled to bend to grab it in order to shut off the flow of water. "I hate this place! I hate it here!" Cassie screamed. Again, her voice echoed against the facility. Having just retrieved the hose and shut it off, Bentley dropped it to the ground once again and strode as swiftly toward her as he could, hands rifling through his many pockets as though trying to find something he had stowed in one of them.

"My dear... my dear, please, please... there is no need to shout. Breath ... please, just breathe... you are not alone."

Cassie felt as though her lungs were going to explode, as though the world were falling in on her, to crush her. She felt ill, doubling over in a dry coughing fit before feeling a warm hand thump her back softly. She began to sob then, wracked with grief and rage that tore at her like a tumbling and unrelenting series of waves.

"Shhhh... there, there... has it gotten so bad so quickly?" Bentley murmured softly. He seemed to have at last found what he was searching for in his coveralls and withdrew a small, smooth stone, upon which was carved a single symbol. This, he pressed to her temple briefly. "Perhaps this will help."

As the cool stone touched her skin, the world spun around her, causing her to drop to a knee and place a hand on the ground to catch herself. The ground was cool and moist from the water that had flowed away from the hose. A light breeze tickled her cheek, and in that breeze she smelled... "Am I dreaming again? ...I know that smell..."

"Well, I think that will be enough for now..." Bentley's voice sounded just like Bentley always had, but in this moment, it seemed to dull as he lifted the stone away from her head.

As the world came back into focus, Cassie's head throbbed, but the rising emotion had abated. In fact, everything seemed muted in comparison to the waves of feelings she had just experienced. Slowly, she opened her eyes again and looked around, half expecting to see the familiar hues of her dream world. But it was just she and Bentley, the bus, and the little maintenance garage.

"It's like a drug withdrawal," Bentley explained in soft tones. "Worse probably, from the look of you," the old bus driver added in matter of fact tones.

"Withdrawal? Do you think I was drugged?" Cassie asked as she gathered herself back to her feet and brushed her hands against her trousers, leaving a pair of muddy streaks.

"Not in the sense that you are thinking," Bentley replied. Instead of answering her question, he asked one of his own. "This dream world you..."

"Ahh... I don't know what you're talking about," Cassie hedged quickly, cutting Bentley off mid question.

"Come, my dear, I am an old man with a good bit more experience reading people than you give me credit for. I suspect that your dreams stopped the very day that young Janice returned."

Cassie didn't know what to say and for a moment remained silent, until a thought struck her, "Wait... did you know about... all of this? Are you connected to all of these disappearances? And what was that thing you did to me? Where did you get that stone?" The questions were rising quickly now as Cassie struggled to piece things together.

"Now, now... before you go working yourself back up again, let me answer one thing at a time. First, I have been here quite a bit longer than you and have indeed learned as much as I can about the disappearances. They trouble me more than you can know, for many of the young scholars come from families that I know well and admire. Second, I don't think it would help either of us to trade lectures about who should be doing what or who should have told the other something..." The old man crinkled an eye at her until she relented with a sigh.

"I just... I don't know who to trust anymore."

"And that is exactly what they want us to believe. They want us to feel alone, isolated, and before you go asking me about who THEY are, I don't actually know, all I can do is speculate... but I suppose that you might be the only one capable of discovering the truth." Bentley paused to ensure that Cassie intended no comeback. Seeing her relent once again, he continued, "If you don't destroy us all in the process, of course."

"Well, that's worse than anything else you've said!" exclaimed Cassie with no small amount of exasperation.

Bentley chuckled lightly before turning toward the little white bus. "Come, why don't you let me take you for a short ride, I think there is something that you should see." Bentley paused before turning toward the bus and lifted the small stone. "Here, I believe this little pebble actually came from this... dream world of yours.

Perhaps it will come in useful." Saying this, Bentley tossed the little stone to Cassie, who caught it easily.

The stone was heavier than she expected given how small it was. It was smooth and oblong, and to her artist's eye, very pretty. It had a depth to it and colors that shimmered in the light, with a thin, speckled layer that seemed to glow as she held it in her palm. Once again, her vision began to swim, and the sky seemed to dim, until she swiftly slipped the stone into her pocket. "I guess I should be careful with this..." Cassie murmured as her head began to clear.

After waiting for the odd sensation to dissipate, Cassie followed Bentley up into the bus, sitting once again in the same seat she had taken on the day she arrived at the school. As the engine groaned to life, Cassie settled back into the seat and peered out the window, remembering the day that seemed so far away. "It feels like forever ago..."

"What's that?" asked Bentley as he shifted the bus into gear and pulled out onto the narrow lane, turning the little bus toward the hulking silhouette of the Sleeping Turtle.

"Oh, nothing... things are just changing so fast."

"Indeed they are, indeed they are..." replied Bentley as he and Cassie trundled down the road toward the darkening forest line and the towering stone crown that peaked above its jagged edge.

"Thank you for reporting this directly to me, Mister Franks. While this... creature... is certainly interesting, I'm much more concerned about your observations of Miss Tremaine." Mistress Audrey Maude eyed the young man who sat perched on the chair before her desk like a pleased tiger cub who had just discovered its first sign of prey.

"I really think I should bring this lizard to you, Mistress Maude...
for your inspection, of course." Jimmy's left leg tapped idly against
the ground as he tried to keep his hands still. He hated having to
report back like this and yearned for the day that he would rise
high enough in the Order to make his own calls. Or at the least; to
earn a more accomplished magister.

As if reading Jimmy's very thoughts, Mistress Maude dismissed
him with a wave, "You have your orders already. If you ever hope
to make Practicum, I would advise you to execute on the orders
you are given rather than continually pursuing your own ends."
Mistress Maude looked up in time to see Jimmy's crestfallen
expression, adding in softer tones, "You are a brilliant and skilled
young man. Follow the path you are given, and you will rise as
quickly as you desire. As for the creature... pet... whatever it is...
leave that to me." The mistress looked back down to the desk and
the letter she was writing. With a flourish of her pen she signed
the dossier, folded it neatly, and sealed it with a lump of warm
wax pressed with a stamp that rested on the top of her desk. This
she handed toward Jimmy with a smile. "Take this to Miss O'Dine,
if you would..."

With a nod, Jimmy accepted the note as he stood and without a
word exited the study, allowing the door to close softly behind him.
When he was safely away from the mistress' office, he paused and
cracked the still-warm seal on the letter, scanning it briefly before
tearing it in half and tossing it into a nearby trashcan. "Bureau-
cratic rubbish. It's time someone did something about all of this
nonsense." In so saying, Jimmy pushed his way through a nearby
exit and out into the last remaining rays of light, which were painting the sky in deep crimson shades.

A bird called from its perch in a tree high above as Jimmy
passed quickly below—it's deep yellow eyes watching the young

scholar leave a trail of footsteps in the new fallen snow, before lifting into the air with a flutter of feathers and circling off toward the great tower at the center of the campus.

It had taken only a few minutes for the little white bus to make its way to the trailhead, where Cassie and Bentley exited the bus. Claiming that he was much too old to be walking the trails in the gloom of the waning daylight, Bentley had walked with Cassie to the large map that sat framed just outside the tall strand of evergreens that circled the mountain. Having pointed out the lower trail she should take and the spot to which she should go, Bentley handed Cassie a large flashlight and bid her to stick to the low path, and under no circumstance should she go on any of the climbing surfaces. With one last mutter to himself about how this might not be such a great idea after all, he watched for only a moment as she slipped down the trail and into the trees toward the adventure that awaited.

Having jogged down the winding path, Cassie found herself standing at the foot of the Sleeping Turtle, its dark rock surface slick and clear before her as it rose quickly above her. But she knew instinctively that she had found the spot, for there... shimmering on the stone before her, were a series of familiar symbols, glowing with a faint, bluish hue.

"I can't believe it..." she breathed as she approached the stone surface and examined the glowing script. "It's... it's like a mirror image... I know these symbols... but there's something missing..."

It was then that Cassie felt the weight of the small stone that Bentley had given her. Fishing into her pocket, Cassie produced the stone, which now she understood to be not merely a smooth stone but a key. "And if there is a key, there is... a lock!" She said this last with growing excitement in her voice. Her eyes had traced the odd runes until they found one small, oblong indentation that looked to be the exact shape of the stone she now held—the stone that had grown warm in her hand.

"Well... Bentley wouldn't send me here for no reason... perhaps I am the one to bring the rest of the scholars back home."

As Cassie had surmised, the stone was an exact fit, sliding into the hole so perfectly that she could barely make out the edges as she pushed it flush. And as she did, the stone wall shimmered and then dissolved, leaving an opening that led into a dark cavern... with the sound of rushing water filling the silence almost immediately.

"It really is real, then..." Cassie noted in a hushed whisper as she stepped from the world she knew into the world of her dreams.

The Ningalix cackled as it drove the little white bus back toward the small maintenance building... eyeing itself in the rearview mirror and admiring the old man's face that stared back at it. "These soft skins are so easily fooled... so desperate to be needed." It chuckled once again as the last light of the dying day slipped beyond the tall trees, ushering in the night.

NOTHING IS AS IT SEEMS

Twenty-One

"There are too many complaints, Pearl... far too many." Willem Marshall III rested his hands atop the heavy wooden table that filled the ornately appointed private meeting room that formed the center of the main floor of the headmistress' manor. He wore both a dark suit and a scowl as he clasped his hands together and eyed the headmistress, his lips drawn downward in a frown.

"Oh? I hadn't heard anything, Willem. Please, expand." Headmistress Floquet sat primly at the head of the square table, wearing the dark robes and hood of her office and academic station, as this was a formal meeting of the Board of Directors for the Governor's School for the Arts. Floquet sat passively, fully aware of the many sets of eyes that shifted from her back to the director, whose son was now in his final season at the school. The Marshall family were multi-generational backers of the school and therefore felt they were entitled to more than their actual say in matters of governance, especially those that might impact the reputation of the school, as the issue of the missing students indeed was.

Willem Senior opened a folder containing a number of letters and newspaper clippings from local publishers. "Fifteen letters in the last week and rising interest by not just local reporters but news outlets from the city as well." Marshall pushed the pile of papers toward the center of the table for emphasis. "You told us that the issue would be handled. This doesn't feel handled."

"I see... and I suppose that others of you feel the same?"

"For the money my family has donated to this institution, it shouldn't matter what anyone else thinks," interjected Marshall with a sour tone.

A deep laugh interrupted Marshall's growing petulance, drawing the dozen or so pairs of eyes to the oversized director who sat at the far end of the table opposite Floquet, his large and muscled frame shrouded in shadow cast by the uneven placement of light fixtures across the room.

"Something amuses you, Harvey? Perhaps you wish to share with the rest of us." Marshall's tone was anything but welcoming.

"So predictable, Marshall. Always parading your Daddy's investments like you had anything to do with the wealth you hold." The solid figure leaned into the light, his grim face appearing more ragged than usual. "What Marshall is trying to say, Pearl, is that we want results. Haven't we been patient enough? Perhaps a little... something... to let us know that this isn't getting out of your... control."

Floquet bristled at the tone but showed nothing as she replied. "As it happens, Mister Kettle... I did come prepared this evening with a... demonstration." Floquet paused as she rose smoothly to a standing position, leaning forward with both hands placed against the smooth, dark wood of the conference table. "But let me remind you that all of this was discussed at great length and agreed upon by every member in this room. And I have maintained my part of the bargain, have I not? For none of your own family have been... selected."

"More of your parlor tricks, Pearl?" quipped Marshall with a light chuckle that earned him a stern look from several who sat at the table.

"Perhaps you would do me the honor, Mister Marshall, and uncover the portrait behind you," countered Floquet, who waited stolidly as the Director stood slowly from his chair and moved to the wall behind where he had been seated to a frame that had been covered by a black cloth.

With a slight tug, Marshall pulled the cloth covering down, letting it fall to the floor, revealing a beautifully detailed portrait that looked unmistakably like, "Is that Master Galleon?" Marshall turned back toward Floquet, anger blooming on his face. "Is this some kind of joke?"

Mister Kettle began to chuckle then, his mirth leading to a full-bellied laugh as he clapped slowly in response. "Wonderful... wonderful, Floquet. Is that..."

"Master Galleon, you ask? Why, yes... yes it is." Floquet's face remained impassive as she watched the director turn from her gaze to address his fellow board members.

"Now, why would I care about a faculty portrait?" Marshall asked, his frustration palpable as he indicated the portrait behind him with a wave of his hand.

"Didn't you mention that Master Galleon was unfairly treating your child, young Willem the fourth?" Floquet's voice sounded like that of a cat toying with a mouse.

"Yes... but..." Marshall's assured tones were muted now.

"Well, then... now you may tell him yourself..."

"You think I'm a fool!? I'm not going to talk to a... to a painting!" Marshall looked to the other directors as if hoping for support from them but noticed that none of them were looking at him, instead they appeared to be staring at the portrait that hung on the wall behind him. Slowly, Marshall turned back toward the portrait, leaning toward it for a closer inspection. "It's lifelike, I'll give you that... but... I fail to see the..."

"You always do, Will... fail to see the point, that is," intoned Floquet as she completed the thought.

"Wait... Is that...?" Very slowly, the older man extended a finger to touch the face on the painting, pulling his hand back to observe. "Is the portrait sweating? What kind of strange trick is this?"

"That's no trick, you clown..." added the mirthful voice of Mister Kettle. "That's your dear old Master Galleon." Kettle turned his attention back to the headmistress. "Did the girl do this?"

"More or less. This was a practice exercise that Mistress Zeltrix had her perform as a test... a captionem. She is completely unaware of what she has done. And I had her create a blank for each of you." The headmistress let her words hang in the air for a moment as several of the Directors responded with slight gasps. "For you to use as you see fit, of course... I would never think to turn our work against a director..."

Marshall's face went pale as he turned back toward the table, his hands trembling slightly.

"If this... demonstration is satisfactory enough for you, Mister Marshall, perhaps you will take a seat so that we can move on to more pressing matters." Floquet's eyes flashed dangerously as she waited for the senior Marshall to slump back into his seat. As he did so, the rest of the room turned their full attention to the headmistress, who smiled demurely at each of them in turn—though her eyes were lit like crystalline fire.

"Wonderful. I will arrange for your frames to be delivered to your residences. We would not want an accident to take place should one of you... mishandle your gift." headmistress Floquet then turned to a pair of large doors that had remained closed behind her.

Nodding to an unassuming woman who had been sitting quietly upon a chair by the doors, the headmistress stepped to the side as the assistant opened the double set of carved oak doors to reveal the slim figure of what looked to be one of the scholars.

"Allow me to introduce an emissary who is here to open... negotiations with us now that a bridge has been established..."

The Ningalix's smile stretched wickedly across the face of the young scholar known as Janice as it glided into the room to stand next to the headmistress at the head of the table. "I'm afraid that you have neither held to the timeline, nor the quantity of our agreement, but we have decided that it is acceptable to re-negotiate the original offer... though I'm afraid that you may not like the terms."

The cavern was darker than she remembered from her dreams, but this was certainly the same place. She had never ventured this far into the cavern, but as she walked, the faint vermillion hues of the perpetual twilight cast the walls with a sinister look. She had never really thought of it in those terms, but recent events were now reshaping what she understood of the little world she had visited so often in her dreams.

For some time, Cassie walked along the water's edge, until she reached the mouth of the cave, taking note of the large glyphs that were carved into the walls on either side. "Yep... this is definitely the same place. I wonder if..." Cassie dipped her hand into the backpack she had been wearing only to confirm her suspicion that the flashlight was indeed gone. "I guess technology can't pass through the real world portal either."

Scanning ahead, she noted several sets of undisturbed footprints that led away from the mouth of the cavern, along the edge of the rushing stream. This, she decided to follow, until she arrived at a strange stone bridge that crossed in a heavy arc over the widening flow of water.

Suddenly, rough hands grabbed her and lifted her from the ground. Cassie let out a scream that was closed off by a thick hand covering her mouth.

"Now, little missy, let's not wake the monsters, shall we?"

Cassie bit the fleshy part of the hand... hard... and was instantly released to the ground, where she sprawled to the dirt and spit out a chunk of flesh.

"Tarnation!!" yelped the voice of her previous captor as he hissed through his teeth.

Another voice to Cassie's right chuckled. "Gotta admit, she's got a lot of fight in her, Garrot."

Recalling the name, Cassie slid herself to the edge of the wide stream, placing her back to the bubbling water as she turned to see the pair of security guards who had disappeared through the portal nearly a month ago in the lower rooms of the Quib. "You two!" Cassie breathed as she edged still closer to the water, thinking of diving in to escape should they make any sudden movement toward her.

"I wouldn't go in there were I you, kid," Alistair advised. Both men positioned themselves to block any attempt to flee but didn't come any closer.

"Bah, let the little maggot jump in and disappear... would serve her right, Alistair. I can't believe you bit me, you little brat!" The one called Garrot ripped a strip of cloth from the edge of his filthy shirt and began wrapping it tightly over the palm of his injured hand.

"What... what do you want with me?" Cassie stammered as she looked back to the water that bubbled invitingly at her fingertips.

"If you got in, that means we can get out, so you need to lead us out, because we've had all we ever want of this nightmare." Garrot's reply carried an edge of threat in his voice, but he backed off a step at a wave of Alistair's hand.

"Look... you're... the Cole girl, right?" Alistair inquired as he lowered himself into a squat near the ground. "You're the one the headmistress always talked about... had some kinda power over this place."

"I don't have any idea what you're talking about," Cassie stammered.

Alistair sighed and hung his head. "Look, kid, here's the deal. You and your little friend tricked us into this place to begin with. We've only barely been able to survive. Now you're here, which means you had to have opened a new door... or whatever it is... and we're ready to go home."

"You had to have seen me, all I did was walk out of the cave back there, I'm sure the door is at the far end." Cassie was about to add more but jumped at a sharp reply from the other man.

"There's no door! There's no darn door! You don't think we've checked... over and over and over again! There's no way to get back out once you've been in... this is a waste of time, Alistair. Just shove her in the water with the rest of the kids, and let's go back and wait for someone to come looking for her." Garrot's frustration was clear. He was filthy, and his eyes had a wild glint to them.

"What... what do you mean... other kids?" Cassie asked, her concern rising enough that she scooted slowly away from the water's edge.

Alistair replied next, "They're all in there..." Alistair pointed toward the bubbling water of the swiftly flowing stream. "As far as we can tell. The thing nearly got both of us, but I don't think it was prepared for two grown and experienced men."

Garrot spat on the ground and patted a large bowie knife that was sheathed along one thick thigh. "They didn't expect us to be able to fight back, either... but we've shown 'em we're not to be trifled with."

"We can't hold out forever, Garrot." Alistair sighed once again and rose smoothly to his feet. "Look, kid, you won't survive here on your own. You're the best chance we've had of getting out of here. If we could rescue the other kids, we would, but we're going to need help... a lot of help. So why don't you work with us to find a way out, and we'll figure out how to bring the kids back... all of them." Alistair's gaze shifted quickly to the sky above as an odd, screeching cry echoed overhead.

"We gotta get to cover..." Garrot breathed as he crouched back to the ground.

Cassie had never encountered any living creatures in her dreams, just the odd footprints that she would find from time to time, so this was something new. But from their reactions, it was also something very real—these two would never fake this kind of fear. "I know a place... I can take you there. We should be safe long enough to come up with a plan."

"That's a good girl... lead on," Alistair replied. The three of them slipped quietly down the path that ran along the side of the stream toward the cliffs that Cassie knew so well.

High above their heads, a creature soared. It could see them clearly, but its interest was not on the larger of the three. Those, it had been watching for some time and saw as neither threat nor opportunity. This third soft skin, however, this one presented a rare opportunity. The creature had felt this one in the past... but this time... the diminutive soft skin was here in the flesh. *Oh, how foolish*, the creature thought to itself as it swooped in ever widening circles before heading further north toward the cold reaches of the snow-capped peaks of Azilem.

Twenty-Two

"**Y**ou ready, kiddo?"

"It's Ludo..."

"Yeah, whatever... just follow me, and I'll have you logged in and rolling in no time." Jimmy had been waiting for Ludo's arrival after being alerted that the first year was heading his way. He had been spending some quality time with Sarah and hated to break away from her for this, but the presence of the backpack gave him hope that Ludo's secret had traveled with him. If not, he had one of the boys rifling through Ludo's room while he was out—so either way, he was prepared.

After punching a security code into the door on the back of the building, Jimmy led a tentative Ludo inside and down a series of hallways until the unmistakable hum of the cooling units permeated the very walls around them.

"Big day for you, kiddo. Your first chance to use ol' Dauntless here. Nothing like getting your hands on this kind of raw power for the first time." The electric lock beeped to indicate that the lock was about to open, which it did after a brief moment with a click and release of air pressure. Jimmy spun around toward Ludo, barring his entry to the room. "Now, you're cool, right? You aren't supposed to be in here yet, but I can count on you not to tell anyone about this..."

"Yes... yes, I'm cool, Jimmy." Ludo was actively trying to peer inside the room, completely absorbed by what might lie within.

"Great, why don't you go to station thirteen, and I'll get you set up from the control room above." Jimmy made to move before pausing one more time and sticking a hand out, palm held upward. "Yeah, one other rule, can't have other electronic devices or static causing materials in here... I'll need to hold on to that bookbag while you're in here."

"Uh..." Ludo hedged, now torn between handing over his backpack and the prospect of getting to log in to the machine within. "There's nothing that would cause static in here... also no electronics..." He sounded less than convincing, even to his own ears.

"Hey, it's not like I'm gonna go through your stuff. I mean, My 'rents are loaded, there isn't anything that you have that I couldn't buy ten times over." Jimmy left his hand open and watched Ludo's face, knowing that he was nearly at the tipping point. "Tell you what, I'll set it in the control room window, you'll have a perfect view of it from where you are... no funny business, I promise."

Ludo could think of no further valid argument and so slid the backpack off his shoulder and laid the strap into Jimmy's open hand.

Swinging the backpack over his own shoulder in a single smooth movement, Jimmy stepped aside and waved Ludo into the room. "You'll take console thirteen like I said. All security access is handled from the control room. I'll set you up in just a moment, and I had the boys scan in all the documents earlier today, so everything is ready for you to get going with model testing... or whatever it is you do." Jimmy smiled broadly and clapped Ludo on the shoulder, pushing him fully into the room before pulling the door closed and chuckling to himself as he skipped up the short flight of stairs to the control room.

"I need your backpack, Molly," Jimmy stated as he entered the control room with a beep, click, and woosh of air.

"What for?" As always, Molly's reply was succinct. The only one she let her guard down for was Trevor, and Jimmy was definitely not Trevor Dawson.

"Don't ask, just toss it on the ledge over the window, it looks just like this one," Jimmy replied as he lifted Ludo's backpack with a smile.

Following his order, Molly set her own bag on the ledge, where it was clearly visible to Ludo in the laboratory below. For effect, Jimmy stuck his head into the window and waved before offering a thumbs up and looking back to Captain O'Dine. "Is everything set up?"

"We're good to go," she replied with a stern nod.

Pressing the intercom button, Jimmy relayed this information to Ludo, who was seated at console thirteen, staring aptly at the set of four screens before him. "Okay, buddy, I can give you four hours of time. If you need anything, just hit the intercom button to your right... and happy hunting."

Ludo nodded below but quickly turned his attention to the screen as his fingers began to work quickly on the keyboard. Before long, a string of code and symbols was streaming before his eyes.

Jimmy continued to watch for several more minutes before turning back to the awaiting Captain O'Dine. "Alright. He'll be busy for several hours now. That bag comes with us, but don't open it just yet. Is everything else in motion?"

Lifting the strap to her shoulder, the fiery-haired upperclass-men wrinkled her brow at the weight of the bag, "What... does he have rocks in here or something?"

"Something much more interesting... much more interesting, I hope," Ludo repeated as he walked to the door and set the light timer for four hours.

"And yes, everything is ready. I sure hope you know what you're doing. If either Sarah or Trevor get hurt from this..."

"Relax, they're the reason we're doing what we're doing."

Captain O'Dine nodded at this and followed Jimmy out the door and off to their next destination, Ludo's backpack in tow.

Ludo was awed by the sheer cost of what surrounded him. "This place redefines state-of-the-art..." he murmured as he twirled around before seeking out console thirteen. Finding it, he took a seat, and as he did so the console in front of him whirred to life. A keyboard slid out from the desk, along with a second shelf that featured a long touch screen and a range of knobs and toggles that he could only guess at. The quad screen hanging like a wall of liquid glass before him shimmered and began to glow like the great eye of some living thing. "I could stay here forever..." he said as he felt around idly for his near-always present backpack.

"Man, I hope that wasn't a mistake," he noted to himself as he looked behind him and up to the control room window where his bag now rested next to the smiling face of Jimmy. "He's too self-absorbed to look in there... surely," Ludo added before turning eagerly back to the screens, which were now flipping to an array of icons and widgets that fed him information on the available processing power, temperature, and a number of other readings that were unfamiliar to him.

As he lifted his hand toward the keyboard, he accidentally lifted it over the shelf to his right and noted that a pointer on the screen moved. "No way!" he yelped as he swiped his hand over the shelf one more time. Sure enough, the cursor moved again. Ludo was transfixed. Like a starving man entering a master chef's kitchen, Ludo threw himself into the experience of orchestrating this technological marvel. He felt alive in a way he had rarely felt before and barely noticed Jimmy's crackling voice over the intercom.

In moments, he had found the files that he needed, set up a virtual environment, and tapped out some exploratory code. The interface even began to make recommendations for him and started to run an initial model over the data as he worked. It was like magic. "This is better than magic," Ludo chimed with the enthusiasm of a kid on Christmas day.

"When did you become so clingy?" Willem asked sourly as he crunched his way through the crusty layer of ice that was forming over the snow which had been falling throughout the day and now covered the campus in a thick blanket.

"Willem, please, you have to listen to reason. We can't go back to that place, you just need to give Janice more time. She'll be fine, you'll see. And besides, you're likely to catch a cold out here, you didn't even wear a coat!" Somewhere in the recesses of her mind, Whittle knew that this was not like her at all, yet at the same time, she didn't care. Willem was everything now. In fact, she was amazed that she hadn't seen it clearly before. He was intelligent, athletic, wealthy, and caring—well at least until recently. "Why won't you come back to the lounge with me. We can talk through your feelings."

"My feelings?! What…" Willem censured himself with a shake of his head. They had arrived at the front door to Quibbley Hall, and so he pulled it open, half-tempted to close Whittle outside. "If I didn't need your help, I'd leave you here. Now, if you're going to come with me, you need to keep quiet and just do as you're told."

Whittle gazed meekly back at him, a crestfallen look enveloping her face.

"Oh jeeze…" Willem swore as he entered the building, a warm rush of air biting at his ears. "Alright, we go downstairs, back to the tapestry…"

"But won't it be locked, Willem?" Whittle pleaded. Again, a tiny voice in the back of her head railed at her for this simpering, but her waking mind brushed it aside as she stared back at Willem's handsome face.

The pair of them walked quickly through the empty hallways and down several flights of stairs. Yet as they entered the lower floor, Willem noticed the "occupied" light above the room to Dauntless was lit, and so he paused by the door. "Now, who would be here this late at night?" As he turned back toward Whittle, he noticed that she had skipped back up the stairs they had just descended and was entering the control room… which oddly enough was unlocked.

"Hey, there's no one in here, but I think Ludo is down in the lab." Whittle had poked her head out of the room as she said this and motioned for Willem to join her in the command suite. Following her lead, he strode up the steps and attempted to enter the room, only to find his way blocked by Whittle, who's eyes smoldered as she draped an arm along the doorframe to block his entry. "Hey, my boy… gotta pay the toll to enter." Her eyes flashed as she smiled thickly at him, her lips pursing in an expectant kiss that was not returned.

"Quit fooling around, Whittle. Maybe Ludo can help us out since you've clearly lost your mind."

Pushing past Whittle, who crossed her arms and huffed at him, Willem entered the command suite and noted the backpack that was sitting on the shelf by the observation window. Walking up to it, he lifted it down and unzipped it to peer inside. After fishing around, he found a notepad with the owner's name written in clear block lettering: Molly O'Dine. "What could Molly have been doing here?" he wondered aloud as he set the bag on the floor and peered through the window.

"I knew it, I knew you liked her." Whittle's voice was uncharacteristically petulant, and as Willem looked back at her, he saw her slump to the floor, her back resting against the wall as she hid her face in her hands... and started to sob.

"Oh, come on! I don't care about Molly! I don't care about anybody but Janice! I'm here to bring her back... you need to pull yourself together, Apple!" Something deep inside warned him that he was sounding very much like his father, but there was a buzzing sound rising in his head that was so irritating... if he could just get it to stop.

"You hate me! I know you do! I won't help you unless you tell me that you love me!" Whittle slapped her hand painfully against the hard floor and sobbed loudly once more.

A sound like hissing came from just outside the door and down the hall, followed by a dull thud and then footsteps. Suddenly, Ludo's face popped into the doorframe that had been held open by Whittle's slouching body.

"Guys, am I glad to see you! You'll never guess what..." Ludo stopped cold as he took in the sight of Whittle in tears on the floor with Willem standing over her... and then his eyes caught sight of the open backpack sitting on the ground. "Hey! What have you done! That's mine! You had no right to get into that!" Ludo stepped furiously into the room.

"This belongs to Molly, you idiot!" countered Willem as he kicked the backpack toward Ludo. "Here, have a look for yourself if you're so interested, and who let you in here anyway?"

Ludo snatched the bag up and rifled inside, tossing the contents around the room in a frenzy. "They took him... they took Lananna... this is... this is terrible!" Ludo turned swiftly and was about to run out of the room, when a strong grip fastened itself on his shoulder.

"Oh no you don't, you're not going anywhere. First, you need to help me get back to that place..."

"What?! Let me go, Willem! I need to find Lananna!"

"Banaaaaannnna" Whittle slurred on the floor as she slipped from tears to laughter. "Laaaa banana," she chuckled as she played with the phrase and giggled where she sat on the floor.

"What is wrong with you two!" Ludo yelped as Willem pulled him back into the room. The sudden yanking on his shoulder threw Ludo off balance, causing him to stumble backward into Willem and sending both of them crashing into the console.

"Oh no..." Ludo whispered as the laboratory below them suddenly dimmed as a whirring sound filled the room. A bank of warning lights flashed on a panel to the side as Ludo broke free of Willem's grip and rushed to the wall, stabbing buttons and swiping at objects on the touch screen interface. "You've run the program..." Ludo said softly. "I didn't intend to actually run the program..." Ludo turned toward Willem, his eyes wide, and this time he was the one grabbing the other's shirt in a fist. "You ran the program, Willem!!" Ludo shouted as the sound of the great computer rose in a whine and a roar.

Whittle laughed as the lights in the command center went dark, the sound of her laughter an echo of the chaos that was ensuing.

Willem stood dumbly in the center of the room as Ludo released him and fled back to the command console, furiously stabbing at more buttons in a vain attempt at stopping the program.

"I can't make it stop!! Someone help me! Someone make it stop!!"

But Willem was transfixed as he gazed down into the laboratory through the observational glass screen. There, in the midst of the rows of consoles with their arrays of screens, swirled a vortex of bluish light, churning slowly and somehow beginning to smash and then displace the consoles as it increased in size.

"Is it..." Willem began in hushed awe.

"Yes," Ludo replied before Willem could finish his thought. "We've reopened the portal to Eridul..."

"Perfect..." Willem replied as he watched the swirling light spring wider and wider until it snapped into a large circular portal, the outer edge bristling with power that sawed through the lights above and the floor beneath.

"No, this is a nightmare..." Ludo breathed as he watched his creation spring into reality. "I figured out the sequence... this... this wasn't supposed to happen and... I don't know if I can turn it off."

"Why would you ever want to turn it off?"

Willem, Ludo, and Whittle all turned to the door, their jaws falling slackly open as they recognized the source of the voice and the figure who stood in the middle of the doorframe..

It was Janice... and her smile was not kind.

Twenty-Three

"You know, for an art kid, you seem to know your way around a climbing surface." Cassie paused in her assault of the cliff face to look back toward Alistair, who she could see was breathing hard as he tried to keep pace. *Big tough military types my foot,* she thought to herself as she resumed her climb, at long last pulling herself to the top of the final ledge, where she rolled to the side and into a seated position to check her fingers for knicks. Knowing that she was here for real had made the climb much more challenging than the numerous times she had visited in the past.

"Try to keep up, gentlemen. We're almost there, but if this doesn't work, I'm all out of ideas." After several minutes, the two large men pulled themselves up to the ledge and rolled out on their backs, breathing heavily. "Special forces... really special..." Cassie commented with a little more than a hint of humor in her voice. "Let's go, boys, you can rest when we're safely away from here." Saying this, Cassie wiped her hands on her trousers and rose smoothly to her feet, hesitating briefly, as she felt she had caught a note of movement in her peripheral vision. A cold chill swept over her as she turned back toward the men, who were still lying about on the ground. "We really need to be moving, I don't think we're alone anymore."

The tone of her voice must have been sufficient motivation, for both men slipped quickly to their feet, eyes searching the sky warily. "Alright, kid, lead on." It was Alistair again, who took position just behind her and flashed a silent hand signal toward the other, who responded with a solemn nod. The trio set off along the top of the ridge, the twilight-tinted world spreading out and away from them in undulating tree and rock-covered hills. In the far distance, Cassie could make out the sinuous shape of a wide, winding river, and still further in the midst, the towering white-topped peaks of a jagged range of foreboding mountains.

A scream from behind her was the first notice Cassie had of the attack. She spun with a squeal of her own to watch helplessly as the final member of their party was lifted away in the taloned grip of some monstrous, mythical creature, whose shimmering feathers shifted in and out of visibility.

"Run, child! Run! They've found us!" Alistair's voice rang out as he slipped a smooth stone into the middle of a makeshift pouch that he had attached in the middle of two long pieces of paracord. He was already swinging the makeshift sling around his head as he watched his friend struggle against his captor high in the air above. It took a solid several seconds for Cassie to react as she watched Alistair let the rock fly with a snap, followed by a zinging sound as the rock found purchase against the nearly invisible creature that had snatched the other security officer.

"Get out of here, Alistair! Don't waste your shot! I've got an angle on it now!" Garret yelled back, his voice growing fainter as the creature winged away, emitting an ear piercing cry as the stone from Alistair's sling struck it solidly.

Cassie could look on no more as she saw what she believed to be the flash of a knife in the captive man's hand, followed by his bellowing howl as he dove the blade up into the creature.

"Blaaaaaack!" Alistair yelled into the sky, his tone heart-wrenching as his face blanched in a mask of horror.

Cassie ran full tilt toward her familiar little burrow, diving inside as she reached it. "Here! Here! I'm over here!" she called frantically as she scooted further back into the shallow space, the smooth red rock lending some small amount of comfort as her hands began to shake.

Another piercing cry from just outside the opening was followed by the snap and zing of the sling and then a series of heavy footsteps. And then silence. Cassie could feel her pulse pounding in her ears as tense moments ticked by, and then sounds of cloth against dirt and stone were followed by heavy breaths as the security guard slid into the opening and collapsed, a long gash ripped open along his pantleg.

"There's no... there's no way out... I'm... I'm sorry," Cassie cried, her voice broken as her mind fought to come to terms with the nightmare that was unfolding in her beloved little world of dreams.

"Stay in here, kid. Whatever you do, don't go back out there. They know where we are now... those things. They won't stop..." The man's words were cut short as a shadow blocked the dim light from the entry to the small alcove. "Oh no you don't!" Alistair cried as he was whisked from the cave as though he weighed nothing at all. His yells were silenced quickly with a sickening crunch.

Cassie shivered as her panic-stricken thoughts drew the grisly scene in her mind's eye. "I just want to go home... please take me home... please take me home..." Huddling against the far wall of the low alcove that had once held so many fond memories, Cassie repeated the phrase as she rocked back and forth.

Outside, the wind whistled against the stony cliff faces and hummed as it cut across the opening of the small alcove. There had to be something she could do, somewhere else she could go.

A light fluttering sound broke the silence that had descended, followed then by the nearly imperceptible clicking of tiny taloned feet. Peering over her arm, Cassie held her legs to her body, waiting for death to take her, but instead of some gargantuan creature, she saw the glossy black feathers and sharp beak of a starling. The smallish bird hopped a few steps closer toward her, its movement erratic, as birds can be.

"Cassie?" chirped the bird.

Cassie screamed in reply, shutting her eyes tightly and sending the small bird scurrying outside in a burst of feathers.

A deep rolling note of laughter sounded then, its resounding tones reverberating in her little hideaway and reaching deep within the rocky cliff. The light outside dissipated as shadows swarmed over the face of the cliff.

Once again, the little bird landed at the edge of the cavern and hopped tentatively inside, tilting its glossy black head back and forth.

"Goodness, child, this is not the time to lose your wits. Have you a pencil, a piece of chalk? Anything on you at all with which to draw?"

The words were definitely coming from the strange little bird, but Cassie was struggling to hold down her rising terror.

"Child... you do not have long... please... I'm not the one you need to fear... but it is coming... and it is coming swiftly. Now, can you draw something for me?" The bird chirped at the end of its phrase and hopped several paces closer still.

Pushing aside her panic, Cassie fumbled numbly through her pockets until her fingers closed on a simple pastel stick. It was cobalt blue, she noted idly. "Yes... I can draw," she replied softly as she held the small implement like a talisman before her.

"Quickly then, on the ground in front of you. The symbol for opening... you must have guessed it by now." The bird's voice sounded agitated and hurried, as if it fully believed that there was very little time to waste.

Miraculously, one of the symbols she had been practicing came to mind, and she drew it swiftly on the dirt floor in front of her, having to brush aside a few small pebbles to fix the lines. "There..." she whispered as she finished the drawing.

"Gracious, child... you didn't have to draw THAT one." The bird chirped as it hopped over to her. "But I suppose it will do, just... just place your hand in the center of it and hum that little tune your friends are always spitting out like nitwits."

"But I can't sing!" Cassie whined. Nevertheless, she placed the palm of her hand over the oddly shaped symbol she had drawn on the floor.

"Always making this harder than it needs to be... fine..." chirped the bird in frustration. "Well, this is going to sting... but you only have yourself to blame." In saying this, the bird hopped into the circle and with a quick motion struck Cassie's hand on the edge of her thumb, drawing a small bead of blood and an annoyed yelp from Cassie, who had not been expecting this sort of barbarous requirement.

Another booming laugh shook the cliff, and with it the wind whining more loudly, its blowing becoming fierce, as though a storm were brewing outside.

"Hold steady, child..." the bird chirped as the vision in Cassie's head began to swirl, causing a sick feeling in her stomach as nausea speckled her brow with small drops of perspiration.

The world dropped from beneath her then, first expanding vertically into bottomless depths and then wide... so wide that she felt her mind would split. Then, with a pop and a hiss, Cassie's vision went dark, the air went still, and she collapsed in a heap, her head striking the ground with a hollow, wooden ring.

Then light and warmth filled the void, and as the vertigo subsided, Cassie slowly opened her eyes to find her head resting on her arm across a desk in a cozy little room.

As the swimming images stilled, Cassie found herself seated in a firm wooden chair, and as she pushed herself up and pulled her rumpled hair away from her eyes, she discovered herself to be seated before the desk of none other than Mistress Audrey Maude, in the Dean's cozy office in the women's dormitory.

"Well now... It seems we have much to discuss, Miss Cole. For indeed, there is far more to you than anyone knew."

Cassie felt exactly the same sentiment for the even more enigmatic Mistress Audrey Maude.

"What is it? Where on earth did you find such a thing?" The questions were springing freely into Sarah's head as she gazed down at the amazing little creature that had coiled itself up on the far side of the cage that Jimmy had found who knows where. "It's some sort of Lizard, right? But those eyes. That's just... creepy. Or darling, I can't decide."

Sarah circled around the cage and jumped with a light screech when Jimmy thumped the cage playfully. "Don't hurt it!" she commanded, but her crossed look faded from her countenance as she looked over at Jimmy. He'd been a family friend for so many years that she found it hard to believe that she had never really

noticed him before. He had always been like a second brother, but...
he was gorgeous, and smart and sweet and absolutely everything
she had ever dreamed of. And best of all, he was completely hers.

"Come on, guy, I know you can do more than sit there in that
cage. Let's give the lovely lady a little show." Jimmy shoved the
eraser end of a pencil through the wires of the cage, poking the
creature in an attempt to elicit a response. But the strange animal
refused to move or even make a noise. It only looked up at them
with those large, unblinking eyes.

"It's definitely from the other side. There's nothing natural about
that thing." Molly had just walked back into the room, holding a
heavy reference book about animal anatomy with one hand while
she paged studiously through it with the other. Molly aspired to
enter medical school someday and, as Sarah had noted, tended to
act like she had already graduated from one. She liked Molly well
enough but sometimes wondered what her brother saw in the girl.
Molly was pretty and petite, she was smart as well, but she had
the personality of a snapping turtle... you didn't notice her until
it was too late.

"So, tell me where you found that thing again?" Sarah asked
as she knelt down by the side of the cage, peering intently at the
purplish hue of the iridescent scales. "I mean... this thing looks
uncannily like the school logo... how is that even possible? It's a
cartoon."

"Uh..." noted Jimmy as he flashed a look at Molly. He didn't
think it a good idea to mention how he had nabbed the creature
from Ludo's backpack, but he hadn't settled on a decent story
either, so the only option left was to deflect. "I wonder if it's hungry
or thirsty? I don't have any idea what something from that other
place would eat."

"People, if they can."

All three nearly jumped out of their skins at the sudden reply that came from the doorframe. Mistress Zeltrix was standing, hands on hips, and staring at all three of them as if she had just caught them breaking every possible school code.

"Ah, Mistress Zeltrix," Molly began, but the mistress dismissed whatever she was about to say with a wave of her hand.

"I'm glad that I found all three of you here. I'm less glad that I've discovered that you have been harboring a creature like this without having reported your discovery immediately."

"So it IS from the other side..." Jimmy murmured excitedly. But the baleful look Mistress Zeltrix gave him was enough to quell any further comment.

"They only just found it, Mistress. We were all about to report this immediately as you arrived. If we intended to hide it, we would certainly not be in an open classroom." Sarah was mildly amazed at how calm she sounded and how well thought her excuse was. And she noted with satisfaction the appreciative look that Jimmy flashed at her, which made her face flush slightly.

This was evidently not missed by the new dean, as her eyes drifted to Jimmy for a moment before returning to Sarah. "That may be, but now that I am here, I should take this with me."

Jimmy was about to object, when the mistress held her hand up once more. "I'm not finished, Mister Franks. Sarah, perhaps you would accompany me in taking this cage to the headmistress. I'm sure that she will be very interested in your full and accurate report on how this thing came into your possession."

Sarah blinked at the invitation but could think of nothing other to do than nod, which she did. "And what I said earlier is the truth. While I have only recently been made aware of the research the school has been doing, I can assure you that this very special creature is to be viewed as being extremely dangerous. It was wise of you to cage it immediately."

Up until this point, the odd little creature had not moved, but as the mistress mentioned this last, the creature swiveled its head around and let out a low hiss... it was as if the thing could understand exactly what she was saying.

Given that an appointment with the headmistress was not something that could easily be ignored, Cassie tossed a black drape over the cage before lifting it easily in both hands. "Will I be finished in time to prepare for the dance, Mistress Zeltrix? I haven't completed my costume yet for the winter formal this weekend."

"Oh... like you did for the masquerade?" Zeltrix's reply cut deeply, but the mistress softened as she led the way out the door. "Yes, Miss Dawson, there will be plenty of time to prepare for the ball. I wouldn't want you to miss that for the world."

Sarah smiled as she hefted the cage and followed the mistress out the door, only pausing briefly to toss one last smoldering look at Jimmy before laughing lightly as she turned the corner.

Twenty-Four

"Where to begin," the mistress sighed as she settled back into her high-backed wooden chair. The mistress' office was situated at the far end of Wolfmeck House along its own corridor that provided private access to the rest of the women's dormitory directly from the office and its own external exit to permit visits from the male captains on campus to help reduce the likelihood that they would find themselves unchaperoned in the women's halls. Aside from a pair of windows that were set at the top of the room, the office was sparsely appointed and featured only the desk, a small filing cabinet, and a standing wardrobe.

Having recovered as much as possible from the horrific ordeal she had just experienced, Cassie lightly fingered the thumb on her left hand, the one that had been so unceremoniously pierced by the bird-form of Mistress Maude. "So, you are one of them?" Cassie queried, having begun to connect a number of dots on her own.

"Well... 'them' is a rather broad and disagreeable term, wouldn't you say?" At this point, the middle-aged woman, if she were even a woman at all, slid open a drawer on the side of her desk, pulled out a false bottom, and withdrew a neatly folded parchment that she immediately began to unfold to reveal a map. "This... is Eridul."

Cassie gazed at the beautifully stenciled image of continents, oceans, rivers, mountains, cities... it was immense. "It's like a fairytale kingdom... bigger, even," she remarked as she studied the central landmass and read through the names. "Erdu, Bhursag, Am 'Rimu... They sure sound like made up names."

"I suppose it depends on your perspective. These names are very close in meaning to your ancient Mesopotamian languages for... well, I guess there is no better way to say it... we have a shared history... Eridul and Maridil." Cassie noted how the mistress carefully smoothed the lines from the map, almost lovingly caressing the paper. She could see the longing in her eyes.

"You miss it, don't you... your home."

"Oh yes, of course." Mistress Maude replied quickly, smoothing her facial features.

"Well, if you can go back there as easily as you did, why don't you stay?" This was not the first question that came to her mind, but it seemed to Cassie to be the most pertinent.

"That wasn't really me that came to retrieve you, Cassie... it was a... oh, what would you call that here... it was the genius loci of my people... a kind of spirit that I can reach from this side."

"Oh... so you are not really a bird?" Cassie was actually a little disappointed at this news.

"Well... bird is not our name for it, but yes, that is most certainly my natural form. I am a wing commander in the Flight of the Forest. I'm sure you've never heard of that, but my people are known as Woodlings... protectors of all the forests that stretch across Eridul. Since we most resemble the lifeforms here, it was decided quite some time ago that we should be the ambassadors between worlds." Mistress Maude was looking solemnly at the map once again, lost in memory.

"So, why Walgrove? Seems like a truce between worlds..." Cassie couldn't believe the conversation she was having but had decided to just go with it for now. "Seems like something that important would be handled at... I don't know... anywhere other than a private boarding school for kids."

"If you think about it, this is the perfect place. A private and secluded campus, access to enormous sums of money that no one questions. Greedy parents who are connected at the highest levels of society. And this isn't the only location... this is the exchange... a place where both worlds work to understand each other better, though, admittedly, that has been rather one sided in recent decades on account of the war and the trouble with transitioning from one side to the next. Good intentions are so often and so easily displaced by the baser instincts." Mistress Maude sighed heavily, giving Cassie the impression that she had agreed to this responsibility with a much rosier view of how it would transpire.

"Goodness... we really have no idea what is real and what isn't... do we?" Cassie made the remark off hand, not intending a response, but the mistress replied anyway.

"No, my dear. You humans are not only hard-headed but quite limited in your ability to conceive anything that is beyond your own immediate interests. Frankly, the closest creatures we have in Eridul are the jackfoles, and that is not a compliment. Still, it is not your fault alone. As you discovered... there is powerful evil at work in Eridul as well." The mistress smiled rather ruefully at that but lifted her eyes to the door behind Cassie before noting, "We seem to have a visitor on his way. I'm sorry, Cassie, but the tales will have to wait for another day. This feels... urgent."

True to her word, the outer door opened with a bang, followed by the clump of heavy feet and a heavy knock on the mistress' office door.

"Come in, child!" the mistress called through the closed door, "it is not locked."

At her command, the latch clicked and the door swung open to reveal the wide-eyed and panting frame of Sarah's older brother Trevor. Instinctively Cassie recoiled from him, for she could sense a strange and cloying darkness that clung to him like heavy sludge.

"Ah… you see it now too, Cassie. That is good. Let me show you another trick." In a few quick motions, the mistress had leapt to her feet, grabbed an old-fashioned ink pot and quill that Cassie had thought to be purely decorative, and with a firm grip snagged Trevor's arm and drew a mildly familiar rune across the back of his hand.

With a snap, like the tail of a whip, the air around Trevor trembled, and the thick phantasmal ooze dissipated like frost in the morning sun. Trevor sagged to the ground immediately.

"Well, don't just sit there, child, get up and help me lug him to the other chair… I don't have enough room for all manner of scholars to be stumbling about this tiny little office."

Leaping to her aid, Cassie took Trevor's other arm, helping to steer him to the only other chair in the room, where he collapsed with a thud and a groan.

"Okay, first… what happened to him? Second… what exactly did you do there…"

"Third," Mistress Maude cut in. "I will answer all of your questions, but I need you to fetch Mister Bentley for me. I fear that things have escalated much more quickly than either of us had hoped."

"I knew it! So you're BOTH from…. From Eridul… how many

more of you are there? Wait... don't tell me... Master Grimpen too... and..."

"Don't be a Ninamus about it... I need you to fetch Bentley now... and Master Grimpen is most certainly not one of us... he's his own kind of strange old bird." Mistress Maude shook her head from side to side as she tilted Trevor's head back to inspect each of his eyes as the young man moaned softly in the chair.

Realizing that no more answers would be forthcoming from Mistress Maude, Cassie slipped quickly from the room and out into the brisk breeze of a blustery winter day. Her feet knew the path well, and without checking her surroundings, Cassie began to jog quickly toward the maintenance shack, which was why she did not see the pair of eyes watching her from halfway across the campus quad.

"Welcome, my dear, come in, and let's see what you have brought us, shall we?" The headmistress had been waiting for Sarah and Mistress Zeltrix in an inner room of her manor, one that featured a beautifully stained mahogany conference table framed by tall-backed leather chairs and a ring of portraits that hung along the walls to either side.

Carefully, Sarah settled the cage on the near end of the table and lifted the black covering, folding it neatly before setting it on the table next to the cage. She watched the headmistress' eyes open in evident interest as the white-haired and statuesque woman gazed on the creature within.

"My, my, Cynthia... where did the child say she found this?"

Sarah bristled at being ignored and spoke up in confident tones. "Actually, Jimmy and Molly found it inside Quibbley Hall, perhaps the room with the tapestry has activated itself. I've actually been thinking a lot about it, and I have a theory."

Mistress Zeltrix scowled at Sarah and was about to reply, when the headmistress lifted a hand to hold her off as she turned a grim smile toward the young scholar. "Please... I would love to hear your... theory. You Dawsons have such bright young minds."

Sarah was pretty sure that an insult lay in there somewhere but pressed on, nonplussed. "The night that Janice returned, I was there, if you didn't know..." Sarah paused to ensure that this point of her argument was well understood.

"I am aware... please go on," the headmistress replied smoothly.

"Well, that wasn't the first time that the tapestry was activated. The other students told me about that, and I've heard about other experiments in the past." Sarah smiled smugly as she noted the slight lofting of the headmistress' brow. *So, she wasn't aware of that*, Sarah thought to herself. "Having done a bit of research, I found out that it normally takes several minutes of singing for the tapestry... the portal to activate. That night didn't take long at all. I decided to follow this lead and talked to a number of other students about their experiences, and I'm convinced now that the... veil?" Sarah stumbled for a word to use here. "Well, whatever separates their world from ours is growing thinner... it's weakening... so it makes sense that some of their creatures might be able to make the crossing."

She could see from the looks on both of their faces that they were impressed with the logic of her argument.

"Brrrip di pid idip! Wisdom from the mouths of children. Seems your little scheme is not so sneaky as you'd hoped." The creature in the cage pipped, the humor in its voice clear as a bell.

Sarah gasped as the thing spoke, and stepped away from the cage involuntarily.

"That will be enough from you, little imp," Mistress Zeltrix snapped, though Sarah couldn't tell if she were addressing her or the creature in the cage.

"Well, this puts us in a precarious predicament, doesn't it, Lananna..." Headmistress Floquet had turned smoothly toward the caged creature, seeming to have forgotten Sarah. "Had you kept your mouth shut, I'm sure we could have made this little incident go away, but... alas." With a wave of her hand, the heavy doors in the room crashed closed as the lights dimmed in the room.

Sarah felt a heavy and oppressive weight drop down on her shoulders as fear struck her. It felt as though her limbs had turned to stone as her heart leaped to her throat, its rapid beat pounding in her ears.

But the little caged creature just burbled in an infinitely cute way and laughed lightly as it lounged in the cage. "Dibidib ipity... So scary... I'm so afraid," the creature laughed, and its laughter lightened the room, instantly relieving the growing tension building in across Sarah's forehead. "They said that one of you would be here when I arrived... I had no idea it would be the infamous Kispa of Shihar." The little creature chuckled once again as it rolled to its feet within the cage and leveled a stare right back at Floquet.

"You have no right to be here, imp," Floquet clarified in dignified tones. "Be thankful that I am feeling generous tonight..."

"You don't know who I am, do you," replied the creature as it sat back and licked its paw, not unlike a cat.

"I know well enough... and I know that you can do nothing as long as the agreement stands."

"And does it still?" the creature asked cryptically.

Sarah was completely lost at this point, but having been completely forgotten, she had managed to maneuver herself to the wall by the door and close enough to the door latch to give it a careful tug and discover that while it was closed, it was not locked.

"We are fulfilling our end of the bargain... there have been some regrettable gaps in fulfillment, but nothing outside of the terms of the agreement."

"And yet... I managed to cross over..." The creature emitted a sound halfway between a laugh and a burp as it tapped a thin bar of the cage with an outstretched claw.

In the blink of an eye, the once small creature tripled in size. In fact, it transformed into a monstrous, furry shape that towered on the table and snapped the cage like it was made of twigs. Zeltrix screamed. Sarah slammed her hand down on the latch, opening the door, and didn't wait another moment as she leaped free of the room.

She had not made it far when a concussive blast ripped the door from its hinges, tearing a large chunk of the wall with it and hurtling both past Sarah to slam into the wall to her left, missing her by fractions of an inch. She was in full sprint now, hurtling a chair and ducking debris as she lifted her forearm to shield herself as she crashed through the front door and out into the brisk air of the fading afternoon.

Another boom and another crash, this time followed by a billowing ball of fire that leaped from the door and burst through the glass windows all along the front of the manor. Sarah screamed this time as she fled toward the buildings, wondering where she could possibly go.

But this was not the only scene of chaos. Before her, groups of students were running through the campus, some screaming, some laughing... but all in a maniacal hysteria. A group of scholars to her right were running barefoot over the snowy grounds as they carried a large effigy made of cloth and wood... of something she couldn't make out. A voice shouted at her to her right, giving her just enough time to dodge as a balloon filled with water flew over her head.

Sarah continued to run, her feet taking her toward her dormitory, but as she ran, a realization dawned on her that slowed her pace. "It's just the festivities before the dance... that's it... that's all it is... well not... not what happened back there, but..." Sarah's breathing began to slow as she dropped her pace to a light jog and then to a walk. As she looked around campus, it became clear that the students were not breaking into full hysteria but that this was just the normal celebrations that preceded the Winter Formal. By the time Sarah was turning the bend toward the rear entry to Wolfmeck House, she was chuckling slightly... still scared out of her wits but immensely relieved that all was not total madness.

Until the door at the side of Adicus Lounge burst open to reveal Jimmy and Molly hand in hand, laughing as Jimmy planted a large... long kiss square on Molly's mouth. Sarah blinked, as Molly not only did not resist, but pulled the much taller boy down toward herself, breaking free only after what seemed like a good sixty seconds to Sarah, who by that point had stomped up to the pair of them, her face like a thundercloud.

"Oh, hey, Sarah!" laughed Jimmy as he swung Molly into an arm. "Isn't it a wonderful night!"

That was all he got out as Sarah leveled him with a single shot to his chin before turning toward Molly, whose face had taken on its own dark shade. "Your turn, you witch... You were never good enough for my brother anyway."

"Why, you filthy little snot... I think you'll find my jaw is not nearly as soft as Jimmy's," Molly replied as her lip curled and her hands balled into fists.

And the fight was on.

THE ART OF THE DEAL

Twenty-Five

The sound of machines thrummed and echoed inside Whittle's head as she fought to make sense of what was going on around her. Slowly, her mind tried to pick out the things she knew. A girl stood in the doorway... her name... "Janice... That's Janice," she slurred. Her voice sounded funny to her ears, eliciting a light giggling laugh as her eyes moved to the next person in the room. "Luuuuuudoooo." That one she remembered because it was easy and fun to say. The person who belonged to the name didn't even turn around, as he kept staring intently at a computer screen with lines and lines of code streaming down its glossy face.

Another familiar face was approaching, the one she had named Janice. This one looked angry and sad at the same time. "So sorry... so lonely... so sad..." she muttered as she watched him lift his arms to the girl in the door. He looked angry once again and shouted something unintelligible. The girl he was shouting at... her face grew... "strange... gross... are you a monster? You can't be real. Why is my head spinning?" Whittle rocked her neck from side to side as she looked about the room. There was a deep humming noise filled with crackling sounds that were coming from the other room.

Whittle couldn't see through the glass from where she sat on the floor, and so she braced her back on the wall and pushed herself slowly to her feet. No one paid her any notice at all. "No one likes me anymore," she muttered sadly.

But now she could see through the window, "So bright! How pretty! Luuuudoooo... look, how pretty!" Whittle lifted her arm to point to the shining circular thing that was definitely expanding in the room below. Ludo, however, was ignoring her, which made her sad. The other boy said something mean and shoved his way past the girl in the door. Her smile as she watched him head down the stairs was grotesque. "That's it! It's a grotesque! See, I did pay attention in class, you... silly little girl." Whittle giggled again and then hiccupped as the girl walked over to her and looked at her with malicious intent.

"You are all so weak and fragile... your minds... so easily led astray." The Ningalix smiled, her face twisting in an incongruous manner. "Now, what shall we do with the two of you. An untimely end is in store for certain. But it will need to look accidental... wouldn't want to draw undue attention to this most perfect disguise of mine."

"THAT... is no disguise... you look hideous." She laughed then as the creature's face soured in front of her. But the strange looking girl ignored her, turning instead to the young man at the computer.

Deep within her mind, Whittle knew that none of this was right, and so she sought to quiet herself. Digging deep, she found a memory, one of the few bright memories she had of her childhood. It was her coach, Coach Janet Washington. Her coach had been tough, very tough, but fair, and most importantly, she had always been present in the most difficult of times. Something she'd said had always stuck with Whittle. "When you are your worst... Get out of your head. Get back to your heart." Whittle had always dismissed the phrase as nothing more than a trite saying, but something about it rang true. And so, Whittle began the long, slow fight to win back her own mind.

Preparations for the Winter Festival were in full swing. Groups of scholars were prancing across campus, some pulling large, decorated floats, others playing or banging handmade instruments, and still others generally looking as though they were up to no good. And Cassie wanted nothing more than to be able to forget all of her troubles and be swallowed up in the school atmosphere that had eluded her all year.

"Why can't you just be normal, Cassie... fit in for once in your life. But no. You have to have weird dreams, have weird friends that send you on strange quests to save imaginary worlds. Sometimes I wonder if I'm just losing it." She had picked up her pace and reached the lane that would lead her around the campus toward the maintenance shack where Bentley was most likely to be. The path swung her past campus and down the main lane. To her right was a large commotion with students shouting and yelling as they gathered in a circle around what looked like two combatants. "Who knows what that's all about..." she muttered as her eyes fell upon the headmistress' manor.

"What the..." Cassie quipped as she came to a halt in the middle of the paved lane. The manor literally looked as though a bomb had gone off inside. The front door had been blown out into the garden, the windows all along the front had also been destroyed as black smoke billowed out into the cold night air. A quick check over her shoulder told her that none of the other students had either noticed or cared about this at all. "Am I seeing things?" With a shrug and a tinge of fear, Cassie jogged over to the door of the building, peering through the windows to see if anyone was still inside. While a few draperies were engulfed in flames, the fire appeared to be confined to the front and not spreading. Edging a few paces closer, Cassie thought she could hear a muffled moan coming from within.

"You have to be nuts, Cassie," she said to herself. "You have absolutely no training that will be useful in this situation..." But while her own advice was sound, she knew that she would ignore it, which was exactly what she did as she approached the house quickly and entered through the gaping hole in the front of the once beautiful building.

"Hello? Is anyone here?" Another muffled sound came from deeper in the interior of the building. Carefully stepping over debris, Cassie made her way through the wreckage of the once pristine entryway that led through a sitting room and back to an interior conference space that she had not yet been in before. But here, she could clearly see through another gaping hole in the wall where a door once used to be. And that is when she saw the crumpled figure of Mistress Zeltrix lying face down on the ground.

"Mistress Zeltrix!" she yelped as she hopped over a broken chair, downed end table, and shattered lamp. As she entered the room, the smell of smoke shifted to something more metallic and visceral—its acrid stench burned her nostrils. "Mistress... can you hear me? Mistress?" She felt along the woman's neck as she had seen in the movies and found a thin rhythmic thrum she assumed to be a pulse.

"Oh, she'll live."

Cassie froze at the sound of the voice, too scared to look around like some foolish child in a horror movie who thought they could escape by not seeing the thing that chased them.

"Just a bit of a bump on the head... brrriptidipit" The voice added with a funny sounding note at the end.

This time, Cassie looked up into the bulbous eyes of a creature that was most certainly not from earth, recognition dawning slowly.

"Annnnnnd there it is... you remember me!" chirped the voice of the small dragon-like creature as it swished its tail back and forth.

"You're from..."

"Yep."

"How did you..."

"One of your friends let me in..."

"And you're..."

"Real? But of course."

"Are you..."

"Reading your mind? No... softskins like you are highly predictable. You really should consider mixing it up every once in awhile. Go against your instincts, you know?" The little creature moved back and forth as it spoke, oblivious to the burnt surroundings and the still form of Mistress Zeltrix lying on the floor between them.

"Where is the headmistress?" This time Cassie got her entire question out before the annoying little creature managed to finish her sentence. She watched as the creature sat back and smiled at her without responding. "Wait... Did she do this to Mistress Zeltrix?" Cassie said with a quickly inhaled breath.

"Sort of, I guess... she tried to cinder me, but... I am a Lananna... rookie mistake that I'm surprised she would make." Cassie had no idea what the dragon was talking about.

"Do you mean singe? Like she tried to burn you and that's why everything is scorched?"

"You don't listen very well, do you."

"Apparently not."

"Well, she got away. But we have more pressing matters at the moment." The creature hopped lightly to the top of the table, where it was now eye level with Cassie. "If you check that one's pocket, you'll find something useful." The little dragon tilted its head down toward the still form of Mistress Zeltrix, who emitted a low moan.

"I can't steal from a mistress!" Cassie exclaimed, her face the very image of shock and indignation at the idea.

"You won't last long where we're heading if you don't... go on now, I think your friends would appreciate it if you did not dawdle."

Shaking her head, Cassie knelt to the floor and checked both pockets of Mistress Zeltrix' slacks before at last seeing the neatly concealed pouch that was sewn down the side of one leg. "This is interesting..." she noted as she withdrew a slender paintbrush from the pocket and lifted it for closer inspection. "It's beautiful... looks like a series seven kolinsky sable..." she mused as she tested the brush edge with her fingertip.

"It's the proper tool of your trade... and quite surprising to find it on one with such little talent," the dragon replied as it leaped from the table to Cassie's shoulder and curled its tail around her neck.

"Oh!" Cassie yelped in surprise, but the creature was so light that she wasn't thrown off balance. "Warn me next time?"

"My apologies... if that frightened you, this next part is going to absolutely terrify." And with a click of its tongue, the world went dark, or, more appropriately, Cassie and the creature blinked out of existence.

Ludo frantically stabbed at the keys in front of him, trying one sequence after another to no avail. The appearance of Janice at the door had only stalled his effort momentarily, before he turned back to the computer, the swirling vortex growing minute by minute as it consumed what remained of the computer lab below.

He thrust raised voices behind him to the periphery of his thoughts, trying to remain focused on the impossible task at hand. It wasn't until a hand was laid on his shoulder that he paused again and craned his neck back to see Janice staring down on him with a quiet intensity that seemed oddly out of place with the chaos that was being unleashed in the floor below.

"Hey, Ludo." Her voice was soothing and warm in the way a girl's can be when her eyes are lowered in a candlelit room. It was the kind of tone that Ludo had no experience with and in the given context was certain he should ignore. "Can you show me what you're doing over here?" Unfortunately, like most other budding teen men, Ludo had built no defenses against such a voice.

"Well... uh... Janice... I'm trying to trace the server process... find some way around the program that is doing... that," he pointed without looking through the observation glass to the room below and the spinning vortex that had begun to cut into the ceiling, sending brilliant cascades of electricity in arcing showers to the floor.

"No, you aren't, Ludo." Again, that voice crawled slowly up his shoulders to tickle the back of his neck.

"I'm not?"

"No... you're going to leave what you're doing and come with me." A light hand caressed his cheek, and Ludo knew that he would do whatever she asked.

"Yeah, sure, you probably know what's best... umm... where are we going?"

"Shhhh..." her face was next to his, her breath soft and warm as it tickled his ear. Ludo couldn't move quickly enough as he abandoned his screen, spun around in the seat, and stood. He had never met Janice before she had walked back out of the Vortex. He'd certainly never been this close to her before, and now he was seeing why Willem was so crazy about her.

Janice's smile pulled Ludo forward. He saw her reach a hand to Whittle, steadying her on her feet as the three walked slowly out the door, down the stairs, and into the open laboratory door.

"Ati Me Peta Babka," commanded Janice as she stretched a hand, palm open toward the swirling vortex, and to Ludo's surprise the Vortex slowed and resolved into a shimmering veil, on the other side of which stood the tall walls of a darkened cavern. While it was much larger than what he had been able to conjure with his device, it was essentially the same effect. He had created a portal to the other world and couldn't help but take a little pride in that.

"Yes... it is a marvel, my little prince." Ludo turned to Janice, who had turned her back to the shimmering portal veil. Her slender arm was stretched toward him, welcoming him to take her hand. "Do you know how many cycles we have waited... How often we have tried to accomplish what you have just done? You must be a very powerful Kispum. I have use for someone with your talents."

Had Ludo held doubts before, those all dissolved. This was not Janice. "Who are you?" His voice was tinged with awe as he gazed at her, the brilliant portal light framing her lithe figure like a glowing angel.

"I am the Ningalix, the chosen vessel of the Ancient Ones of Eridul. Together there are four, each with their chosen vessel. Parci, Azilix, Lananna... and I. I am the first of your kind to have been chosen as Bel Ade, but I need not be the last." Janice, or whatever this creature was, still held her hand toward Ludo.

"Doesn't that mean slave? Or vassal or something?" Ludo couldn't help himself but noted how closely the word resembled the same in the Sumerian he had been studying.

"You're such a nerd, Ludo."

Ludo turned back to see that sanity had apparently returned to Whittle, who was standing uneasily on her own. "Whittle... are you..."

"Back among the living? Yes. Catch me up real quick here... I've been in kind of a fog."

"Well, Willem is missing. I've opened a gigantic portal to another world. This Janice look-a-like is someone's slave from the other world and thinks I should join her. I mean... she's kinda pretty, so the deal isn't sounding too terrible." Whittle smacked him hard on the arm, eliciting an, "Ouch! Yeah, I deserved that."

A sudden clap of air, like a vacuum collapsing in on itself, pulled at Ludo's ears painfully but effectively drew his eyes to a spot deeper in the room where none other than Cassie had arrived, with his missing little friend curled around her neck.

"Now it's a party..." quipped Whittle as she smiled toward Cassie and turned her eyes back to the Ningalix, whose hand had dropped to its side as its mouth split in a fierce grin.

Twenty-Six

"What a quaint reunion... and I see you have managed to win one of my counterparts to your side. But this is fine... We will accept these terms." The Ningalix had not moved, remaining framed a few paces in front of the shimmering veil and in appearance looking very much like a distorted version of the Janice they had known. The features on the Ningalix's face had lengthened, and its proportions changed in such a manner as to slip into the uncanny valley, which is to say that the Ningalix looked human enough to be frightening.

"Wait a minute... no one here agreed to any terms." It was Whittle who spoke up first as the small group of friends squared off against the otherworld creature.

"Oh, but your emissaries sealed the pact... you should consider yourselves fortunate to be counted among the chosen of your kind. I would advise you to cooperate... you have nothing to fear." The Ningalix swept a welcoming arm back toward the shimmering portal as if to invite them to enter.

"Okay, this is starting to sound like some author's lazy plot device." Whittle replied just as Cassie took a step forward and lifted the brush she had retrieved from Mistress Zeltrix.

"We're not going anywhere. And as long as we're making suggestions, I suggest that you tell us what you've done with the other scholars," Cassie leveled a hard stare at the creature as Lananna lashed the air with its tongue and let out a hiss as if to punctuate her sentiment.

"You brought a brush to a magic fight?" Whittle observed with a lofted brow.

Cassie blushed as she turned toward her friend. "I think it's a little more dangerous than that, and also, I'm so sorry about what I said in the field house..."

"Girlfriend, we've all been on a wild chase with this one." Whittle flashed a smile and a wink in return, and Cassie sighed contentedly, at least one thing was heading in a better direction.

A deep echoing roar filled the room, followed by a booming laugh that sent even Lananna skittering to the other side of Cassie's shoulder.

"Oh, it seems that you may all be too late. But since you were not privy to the agreement, let me spell things out for you children in a manner that you will understand."

"Please... enlighten us." Cassie remarked as she scanned the opening behind the Ningalix. Lightly, she whispered from the corner of her mouth to Lananna, "how exactly do I use this thing?"

The little dragon flicked its tongue and replied lightly, "You paint with it, of course..."

"I paint what?" Cassie whispered back in frustration.

"Having trouble with your dragon?" This time it was Whittle who whispered to Cassie, though her eyes remained trained on the Ningalix, whose hands had begun to weave a pattern in the air, the trailing lines of which hung in golden threads.

"That's my dragon..." whispered Ludo, who Cassie had yet to acknowledge. "And... uh... hi, Cassie... I'm sorry, too, about the other day..."

"Wait... what did you two do?" inserted Whittle.

"It's fine, Ludo. Like Whittle said, we've all been under the influence of that thing..." Cassie nodded toward the Ningalix, whose gesticulations were yielding an intricate and nearly three dimensional symbol that hung in the air. "And nothing happened..."

"I tried to kiss her..." Ludo corrected.

"Oh my... and you were just giving eyes to Not-Janice over there..." Whittle commented with a sly look in her eyes.

"You what!" Cassie demanded, her voice no longer in a whisper. Immediately she reddened and looked back to the Ningalix, who was staring at the three of them malevolently.

"This is the symbol of our agreement. I'm sure you all will recognize it." An intricate circular image floated in the air, but made little sense to Cassie, who had never seen anything like it before. In the center was an oddly shaped face with stunted hands pointing out to either side and four equally strange symbols arranged around it. Several concentric circles emanated from the center and were split by eight equally distanced arrows. A far outer ring was formed by a series of symbols all along the edge that Cassie had never encountered before. To her, it was beautiful and precise but utterly meaningless.

"It's a lunar calendar." Ludo spoke up quickly, like he was answering a teacher in class.

"Nerd... you are a total nerd," Whittle remarked with a chuckle and a shake of her head. She was standing tall and firm now, appearing to have recovered fully, though she was drenched in sweat, as though she had been playing a full game of Jalaw, Cassie noted.

"You have a remarkable mind, young one..." responded the Ningalix as it smiled toward Ludo in a way that made Cassie want very badly to hit it.

"What on earth do you see in that thing... it doesn't even look human anymore." Cassie couldn't help herself as the remark burst out of its own accord.

The Ningalix, ignored her as it continued in an odd sing-song tone.

Twelve cycles of the moon transcribed,
Both in your world and in ours.
Twelve keys were forged from three
One each to set another free

Twelve gifts shall we impart
And in return twelve fervent hearts
An exchange is made, a vow is given
Peace at stake is our provision

"So... basically some time long ago you agreed to terms of peace and made an exchange of... gifts to ensure the peace would be held." It was Ludo again, his face crinkled in thought as he linked the cryptic words together.

"Seriously, Ludo..." added Whittle once again, but this time she took a step forward. "But if I'm reading between the lines, we owe you twelve... slaves? Apparently, children from this school, which makes no sense at all, though I'm sure there's a reason. You took six already, and Willem is seven, two guards, and the three of us makes an even twelve?"

The Ningalix laughed loudly, which Cassie thought sounded not unlike the cackling bark of a wild animal. "You are sharp as well, but while in principle you are correct, the deal has already been broken... numerous times over the centuries. And we've... accepted many more than just six of your... children. But should the three of you come willingly, we are willing to hold the truce... for now."

"You'll not be taking these three or any others, witch."

Cassie looked back toward the door as another small group was piling through the doorway. Mistress Maude had arrived... and much to her surprise, she was followed by Trevor and a disheveled looking Sarah.

"I told you to go for Bentley, child." Mistress Maude did not look amused, neither did she look at Cassie as she trained her eyes on the Ningalix that stood between them and the veil.

"Well... well... look what we have here. Stand aside, Sippa, you understand the agreement, and I am claiming these three... now four, as part of the agreement. You know well what will happen if you interfere."

"Oh... so you have a true name... Sippa?" Cassie directed her words toward Mistress Maude but like the mistress kept her eyes warily framed on the imposter as she held the brush in front of her like a talisman.

"That is an insult... not a name," replied Mistress Maude, who stepped forward and spread her arms wide as if to shield the others behind her. The Ningalix tilted her head back and laughed.

"Enough! I will have what is mine!" the Ningalix screamed in frustration as her hands swept forward and closed in a clap that thundered toward the party, a somatic bubble of shimmering light and energy that exploded as it contacted Mistress Maude, incinerating the teacher in a flash of flares and motes that dissipated the remainder of the attack, though a wall of sound continued past, hitting the small group like a fist and pushing them to the ground.

The air rang in Cassie's ears as she tried to mouth a question to Lananna, who had leaped free and held its ground with claws digging into the tile floor, leaving deep gouges. She was certain that she was screaming her question, but the ringing in her ears drowned out any sound she might have been making. Quickly looking toward her friends, she saw them all scattered to the floor, holding their heads in their hands.

As Cassie lay on the tile, she could see the brush she had dropped lying just beyond her reach, but that was not what caught her eye. Instead, as the ringing subsided, she heard a guttural growl as Whittle pushed herself to her feet, eyes locked on the Ningalix. A quick check back to the veil, and Cassie could see that the dangerous creature had turned back toward the shimmering wall of light and was waving her hands along the outer edge. As she did, the shimmering veil began to drop as small snowflakes flittered into the room.

"That's not how you treat my friends..." The voice was Whittle's, and it was a lion's roar as the athletic woman sprinted toward the unwary back of the creature, colliding with her and spinning both of them into the unopened curtain of shimmering light.

Cassie screamed, her hand reaching toward the thin brush, her fingers closing on it too late.

Whittle hit the Non-Janice with a shoulder to the lower hanging rib, which crunched on impact as she wrapped the other in powerful arms and swung her around with vicious force. The pair of them, tangled as they were, twirled directly into the cascade of light, which did not give way immediately; instead, it expanded around them in a crackle of electrical sparks.

Cassie watched helplessly as her friend and the creature were absorbed into the light and translated into fragments of flashing memories. She saw the image of a young girl who looked very much like Whittle riding a bicycle for the first time, then standing under the scolding heat of an adult, followed by a stream of images that bounded from point to point along her life's path. She began to know her friend, truly and deeply, as her eyes swam in tears. There was loss and pain, heartache and grief, but through it all a thin, silvery line of hope.

The Ningalix's image shifted and changed as well. Its visions were darker, more complex, and stretched in an ever-branching arc through numerous lives. Cassie could see one line trail through Janice and others stretch along the paths of others that she took to be the missing scholars. This creature was clearly an amalgam of stolen memories. But there was one image that froze her thoughts completely. A face, simple and sweet. It was her sister Charlie... she was certain, and then more certain when she saw her own face, staring up within the swirling vision. Something tugged at her mind, something screamed in her heart as the last mote of light shimmered and blinked out.

The small corner of the veil that had been opened slammed closed as the outer edge of the portal crackled with fire and began to burn away like embers lifting from a smoldering fire.

"No! No... no! Lananna, we can't let it close! Lananna, do something!" Cassie grabbed the brush fully as she pushed herself to her feet. She made to dive toward the collapsing curtain of light as two pairs of hands grabbed her arms to restrain her.

"You can't go, Cassie, you'll die!" The voice was Ludo's, his timidity gone, his eyes wild and a thin line of blood trickling from an ear.

"Cassie, we need to think, we need to plan... you can't dive into that. We just saw what happened!" This voice came from the opposite side. It was Sarah. Her hair was a disheveled mess, her face was covered with dirt and grime, and she seemed to have gained a red lump just under her left eye.

"LET. ME. GO!" Cassie screamed as she fought her friends' restraining grip. The veil was collapsing rapidly now, and she felt that if she didn't act now she might lose them all... forever. "Lananna! Do something!"

"I cannot. It is true that any action I take here will break the treaty. Doing so would be far more damaging to both of our worlds than you realize. Only you can act, Cassie." The creature's normally happy voice was quiet as it spoke, as though it understood the gravity of the choice that lay before Cassie.

Wrenching her arm free of Ludo, Cassie lofted the brush and began to paint in the air as her heart was torn in two.

Then something magical happened. With each stroke, a glowing filament hung before her, then another and another. In three dimensions, Cassie worked and wove. She let her mind go and wove in new symbols that she had seen or sketched before. Each new runic shape bristled with energy as it was completed and then locked into shape with a sizzling snap. On she wove as the curtain closed.

At last, with barely a pinprick left of light along the curtain, she completed her work and then screamed at Ludo, "Ludo! I need a word! Ludo!"

Hesitantly, the young man replied, "Ag, Kia, Anna, Badur, Zi."

Cassie could hear Lananna hiss from the ground below, but as she shouted the phrase, she looked to it and noticed that it was looking forward and not toward her, as though preparing for a battle to come.

"Ag, Kia, Anna, Badur, Zi!" Cassie shouted into the floating sphere of her design, and as she did so, the pinprick of light snapped open fully once again as the veil between worlds winked brightly and then faded.

Silence filled the room as snowflakes drifted in from the dark chamber that stretched before them. Cassie had opened the gate between worlds.

It was Sarah who spoke first. "Alright... well, I guess we're going to do this then. Not exactly fair that you're the only one with a weapon."

"Here, take this, little sis." Cassie had completely forgotten about Trevor, his tall muscular form towering above all of them. He tossed a long steel pipe to Sarah, who caught it easily and smiled back at him as he gave her a firm nod. "Seems like the Dawson name is going to be part of this story... wherever it leads."

"Hey... what about me?" queried the slimmer Ludo, looking back at Trevor with a hint of hurt in his gaze.

"No offense, but one of these would swing you, and Sarah knows how to use it. Stick to her side... she might need that brain of yours again." Trevor nodded toward Cassie

Cassie opened her mouth to say something further but was cut off immediately by her roommate.

"Don't say it, Cassie. This is about all of us now. I don't know what you saw, but those were friends of ours... and we're going to get them back."

"I was going to say... thank you." Cassie smiled meekly as she looked down toward Lananna. "Can you fight with us now?"

In response, the tiny dragon winked and swirled in a dizzying array of light as it snapped into a monstrous furry shape that towered over even Trevor. "Game on, little soft skin, there are no rules for me in my home."

"I feel like we need a cool phrase or something... feels like we're a team, you know..."

"Shut up, Ludo," Cassie remarked with a smile that pulled a light laugh from all of them.

Ludo shook his head as they stepped into the snow of the other world but whispered all the same,

> "Into the dark they go
> Into the dark they go
> Toward the jaws of death
> With the whisk of life
> On to claim their fate
> Strode the friends of light"

"Such a nerd, Ludo... such a nerd," muttered Sarah with a slim smile. Cassie laughed with the others as they stepped as one into Eridul.

Twenty-Seven

Astorm whipped around them and swirled within the hollow of the towering chasm. Cassie and the others pressed on against the bitter chill of the air, the rubberized soles of their shoes slipping on dark icy patches, making the way forward treacherous as the rising stream bubbled and gurgled with life to their left, leading them inexorably outward into the swirling maelstrom.

Deep groans could be heard, along with strange, muted sounds as flashes of lighting broke the dark sky above, briefly lighting the way forward. A battle was waging, to be certain, but Cassie felt as though they were small pawns on a much larger chess board.

"Something much bigger than us is going on here."

"You think?" chuckled Sarah mirthlessly as she moved forward on unsteady legs, gripping the cold metal in her fingers.

"I see something up ahead," called Trevor as he trekked forward into the blowing snow. Cassie watched as he knelt to the ground near a huddled form, and her heart leaped at his following cry. "It's Whittle! She's alive!"

Cassie and the others surged forward quickly, though cautious of the slick ground lest they be swept into the rushing torrent at their side. As Cassie arrived at last, she tucked the brush she had been holding into her pocket and swept Whittle into a tight embrace, sighing as she held her and whispering softly, "I thought we had lost you... you brave... dumb... knuckleheaded..."

"Wow, you really need to work on your sweet nothings." Whittle croaked, her voice hoarse as she tried to laugh, only to break into a heaving cough. When her coughing subsided, her eyes blinked open as she gazed up to Cassie. "Didn't think to bring a coat... a blanket... you literally walk into a snowstorm with nothing warm at all..."

Cassie's voice caught, a smile overwhelming her face as she hugged Whittle more tightly, tears stinging her cheeks as the biting wind froze them, licking her hair about in a wild, auburn tangle.

"Okay, you two... let's get her up and get her out of here. The longer we sit here, the greater danger we're in." Trevor's voice was one of reason, a calm in the storm as he clamped a hand around Cassie's waist and lifted her easily to her feet. Cassie looked on as Ludo and Sarah knelt to aid Whittle to her feet, the four of them huddled together.

"Willem is out there somewhere. He went looking for the real Janice... we can't just leave him here." Whittle's voice was full of determination.

"We're not impervious... and as you noted, Whittle, we're not even equipped for this." It was Trevor again. He held his tall, steel pole in one hand and looked the veritable warrior as his team jersey whipped in the wind.

"This might be the only chance we get," replied Whittle, her voice solemn. "I... saw things when I hit that monster. Things I'm never going to unsee. But I don't think any of the scholars are lost, I think they're just trapped... I saw a stone bridge."

"I know where that is," added Cassie. "It isn't that far up along the stream. Maybe we just go there and see if there's something we can do. If nothing presents itself, we get back to safety as quickly as we can. Besides, you have me, and we have... whatever this giant furball is." Cassie tilted her head back toward the towering Lananna, whose eyes remained fixed ahead.

"I preferred the little dragon..." Whittle mused as she eyed the bristling fur, the dark inset eyes, and the razor-like teeth of its mouth. The thing looked like a mix between a bear, a lion, and a nightmare.

"We all did... this thing smells," added Cassie. "Let me see if I can conjure up something that can help.

"Hold on there, Picasso..." Ludo shivered in the cold, his lithe frame wasn't made for these kinds of environs, Cassie was certain of that. "I saw what you did last time... and I've had enough time to study these symbols to know that you were a hair away from blowing everything to pieces."

"Well, I'm open to ideas... but make them quick." Cassie's reply was a bit more curt than she intended, but Ludo graciously ignored her as he pulled his slim journal from a backpack that he had managed to snag somewhere along the way out the door. "How did you grab that?"

"It's not mine... but it was sitting in the back of the room... figured something in there might come in handy, and I always keep my personal journal on hand. Don't want that to fall into the wrong hands." His brows lowered meaningfully at that, and Cassie flushed slightly, remembering the moment she had stolen and read from it.

"Here, Whittle... I think this might have been yours." He tossed the backpack to Whittle, who caught it and inspected it briefly before unzipping the back and looking in with satisfaction.

"See, this is someone who comes prepared." She pulled a light jacket from within and slipped her arms into it, zipping it up while the others looked on. "What? It wouldn't fit any of you. Let's see... climbing rope, some carabiners.. And look at this!" she noted triumphantly as she withdrew a signaling flare. With a a practiced hand she removed the end cap, and clipped the striker tip of the flare until a brilliant red plume sizzled to life.

While not as bright as a flashlight would have been, the light from the sputtering flame cut the darkness, highlighting blowing snowflakes as its smoke spilled toward the ground and the roiling surface of the water.

Ludo yelped as a pair of red eyes reflected back at them as the light illuminated the space in an eerie glow. Lananna remained passive behind them, its eyes still locked on something much further ahead. Ludo yelped again at the sound of a sickening crack and scream followed by a splash. Whittle swept the flare back toward the sound of scuffling feet as it lit the slim figure of Sarah, who was wielding her steel pole and shielding her eyes as she glared back at them.

"Put that thing away, Whittle! You're killing our night vision and giving us away."

"What in blazes, Sarah?!" Cassie called out as her mind fought to figure out what had just happened.

It was Trevor who replied. "Nice strike, Sarah, good to see all that training dad put you through wasn't entirely money down the drain." Sarah scowled back at him in reply, though Cassie thought she saw a slight upturn at the corner of her roommate's mouth. With a final rueful look, Whittle tossed the flare into the stream where its sizzling glow slowly faded, plunging them back into darkness.

"Just give your eyes a minute... they'll adjust." It was Sarah's voice again.

"Jeez, girl, when did you suddenly become a ninja commando?" Whittle sounded genuinely impressed.

"Sarah's been a bo staff champion since she joined the family dojo. I thought you were her friends?" Trevor's reply was more than tinted by incredulity.

"I didn't tell anyone about that, Trevor, I'm trying to be an artist, remember... not just a martial artist. I wanted to start fresh, try something new."

"You shouldn't throw your gifts away, Sarah."

"Whatever, Trevor. So, are we heading for this bridge or not?"

"Ludo... you said you had an idea for me... now's the time, and Lananna... couldn't have warned us about that thing earlier, could you?"

"That was nothing to worry about..."

"It had large teeth..." Ludo replied as he stepped to Cassie's side.

"I forget that you are soft skins. Well, there are a few more on the path ahead, but they are not too fast. The Et'La can handle them easily." Lannana remained where it was, watching the way forward but saying nothing further.

"Et'La?" Cassie asked as her eyes finally adjusted enough to make out the stream and the cavern mouth in the distance behind them.

"I think it means 'warrior'" Ludo responded.

"I like it," Sarah noted from her position at the lead. "Okay... I can see again. Trevor, you want to take the right and I'll watch the water's edge here. If there are more, I can't see them yet."

"Ludo... I'm waiting," Cassie urged.

"Right... right. Here... see if you can draw this like you did the other. I think you can just draw it without having to add an incantation to enact it."

Cassie nodded as she looked toward his sketch pad and saw a very poorly scrawled symbol. Fortunately, she had spent a great deal of time in her special project perfecting a series of symbol strokes and elements. "Your drawing skills are lacking..." she noted as she retrieved the brush from her pocket and began to stringing the odd strokes of the design together in the air.

"I'm a writer, not an artist."

"Clearly..." she said with a slight smile as the image finished and snapped into place.

At first, nothing happened, but before long, a ghostly line of footprints began to glow along the ground before them, several stretching away along the water's edge.

"Wow... nicely done, Ludo... Cassie..." Whittle's voice was filled with a hint of awe, having not seen what Cassie had done back in the room.

"That should lead us to the other scholars..." Ludo noted as though he was expecting exactly this result.

"Uh... anything I might be able to use if we get into trouble... a little more offense maybe?" Cassie asked as the group started to move forward.

"Yeah, here's one or two that might be more like a weapon?" Ludo replied as he flipped to a second page in his journal. There were three symbols, each with a single word beneath them.

"Fire, Water, Spirit" she read aloud, nodding as she claimed the shapes to memory.

"This was early on in my exploration. I think technically they mean cinder, geyser, and breath." I have no idea what will happen, but I think you should be careful that none of us are in front of you.

"Don't you dare cook my backside..." remarked Sarah from her lead position. Cassie could see her step easily into a spinning swirl that was followed by a quick crunch and a hiss as something was sent flying into the water with a splash.

"Remember to breathe, sis. That was all arms and legs."

"Yeah, yeah... I got this." Sarah responded, but Cassie could see that she nodded her head toward her elder sibling.

The group followed the trail of glowing footprints, encountering nothing more dangerous along the way than the few small creatures that Trevor and Sarah handled easily with their spinning and slicing maneuvers.

Before long, they reached the dark, stone bridge that spanned the swiftly flowing stream. Its breadth was nearing that of a small river at this point Cassie noted as they huddled together to discuss their next action. She remained alert for the telltale cries of the flying creatures that had attacked her and the security officers the last time she had walked this way.

"You're creeping me out with those looks you're giving the sky." Ludo's comment drew Cassie's eyes back to the group. She hadn't realized that she was staring up into the swirling clouds above.

"She is wise to be wary of the Nergals. They will not try anything as long as they sense that I am here... but eventually they will come, as they can smell soft skins. They have found them to be quite tasty. I cannot disagree with this position." Everyone looked up at Lananna, who grinned back at them with a ferocious row of teeth.

"Okay... I've been thinking about this." Ludo broke the growing silence, giving the others something to take their minds away from the horrific visions that were beginning to manifest in this nightmarish landscape. "I think the bridge is some kind of lock... and I think you can open it, Cassie, but I'm a bit afraid that while it may be what is needed to free Willem and Janice... and maybe the other scholars as well... it might be a lock that is keeping something much worse contained."

"The Samu A'Zu. It will be set free." Once again, the Lananna replied but offered nothing more.

"Super helpful, Lananna..." Cassie replied. "Can we beat the... Sam Ah Zu... whatever?"

"Perhaps." Again, Lananna's reply was blunt and uninformative.

"We got this..." Sarah replied as she turned toward the bridge, her steel pipe held before her in a horizontal blocking position.

"Pretty sure that means thirsty tooth," Ludo added.

"Not helpful, Ludo," Trevor responded as he took position next to his sister.

"Well... this should unlock the bridge. But I would keep one of those other symbols at the ready were I you."

"No kidding, captain obvious." Cassie noted Ludo's crestfallen expression at her rudeness and softened her tone as she settled a hand on his shoulder. "I'm sorry, Ludo, you're being amazing, we're all just... really, really frightened right now."

No one disagreed with Cassie, and Ludo's bright smile was followed by a nod as he stepped back and away from Cassie.

"Alright, everyone... maybe move back from me as I do this, but be ready for... whatever..."

Swiftly, Cassie twirled the brush in the air, the thin filaments lingering as the strokes took shape, glowing as one until the shape was complete. When she finished the final stroke, the golden lines rotated a half turn of their own accord before dissipating into sparkling dust. Again, nothing happened for several heartbeats, until the ground at their feet began to shudder. The bridge in turn rumbled and vibrated, before the many stones from which it had been constructed broke free and fell as one with a splash into the rushing water.

Tensely, they waited, but nothing further happened.

"Did it work?" Sarah was the first to reply, but as she did, a glowing orb of light began to swirl beneath the surface, smoothing away the small, white-flecked face of the water, until bursting like a bubble to reveal seven figures, who all began to cry, yell, and splash at the water.

Swiftly, Sarah and Trevor were at the water's edge, extending their poles into the water and calling for the missing scholars to grab on. Whittle had leaped to action as well, pulling the rope from her backpack and fitting a quick loop to one end that she tossed expertly over the furthest splashing form.

"It's them! I see Janice! Willem! Here! Willem!" It was Trevor's voice that called to his classmates, and in only a few moments, the six missing scholars plus Willem were shivering, gasping, and crying as they lay on the water's edge. Each was trembling, but their faces were lit with relief.

"Now it comes..." The warning came just as the water level began to rise from downstream, displacing water on either side of the wide stream as it moved with speed. It looked as though some massive creature were swimming swiftly toward them from just below the surface.

"Everyone up! Help them... and stay back!" Cassie called as she stepped forward to bar the path, Lananna leaped up beside her, a deep growl in its throat. Already, Cassie was weaving her brush in the air, in moments she had locked one of the symbols in place and flicked it forward with a final stroke as she worked on the second that came to mind.

A roar filled the air as a plume of water erupted below the swimming creature, throwing it into the air and out onto the ground. The thing was massive and scaled, its eyes blood-red and its face distorted, with a long tooth-filled snout. At first, Cassie thought it looked like an alligator... a very large alligator, but a second look eschewed that notion as wings broke free along its back with a sickening cracking sound.

Cassie looked back quickly, noting that the students were all on their feet, Whittle and Trevor supporting two each, but Willem able to stumble forward on his own, an arm slung around the real Janice's shoulders as they all lurched toward the mouth of the waiting cavern.

Familiar screams rent the sky as Cassie clicked the next symbol into shape and flicked it at the massive water creature with a snap of her wrist. Turning her attention to the sky, she began to back away and work on the third shape.

A massive concussive force burst away from her, smashing into the large creature and hurling it back like a dry leaf in the wind.

"Impressive. That will not stop it, but it will buy us time."

"Well, that isn't encouraging," Cassie noted as her first attempt at the third form fizzled. "Drat!"

"Duck!" Lananna cried just in time as it leaped with a roar and snagged a nearly invisible creature from the sky just above Cassie's head. She threw herself to the ground and rolled quickly to her feet as the sound of two large creatures clashing behind her urged her to run.

The others had made it to the cavern entrance, she noted, and so without further thought, Cassie accelerated to a sprint, her feet crunching on the ice and snow along the stony path. Precariously, she made her way toward her friends as the cries in the air above grew in number and ferocity.

"Cassie!!" The shout came almost too late as Cassie dove forward in a hapless sprawl, her hair wrenching back painfully as a taloned foot grabbed at her and nearly yanked a fistful from her skull.

Whittle was at her side in an instant, lifting her free as the group pressed forward into the cave, toward the open portal that loomed far back in the darkness.

The sounds of screams echoed within the stone cavern as huge feet thudded to the ground. Cassie looked back but could only barely make out the near invisible lines of the monstrosities that pursued them.

"Wait... I can do this... we'll never make it otherwise." Cassie called, her breath heaving in her chest as she pushed against Whittle's grip on her arm and turned to face the approaching monsters.

Quickly, she worked, painstakingly ensuring that each line was perfect, each stroke exact as she carved the intricate pattern in shimmering electrical arcs in the air before her. Her hands numb, her mind shaking, Cassie locked the last filament in place and with a shout of fury sent it hurtling forward.

The image flipped from gold to an angry red as it moved away from her in a widening net that expanded rapidly to fill the space from wall to wall and floor to ceiling. The net cut into the creatures as it went, rending them into motes of ash and light, the heat from each deadly contact blowing back at them like a furnace and banishing the chill.

Cassie faltered as her vision blurred. Then strong hands grabbed her, tugging gently, whispering in her ear as she stumbled back, weakness overwhelming her as the brush slipped from her hand to fall forgotten to the cavern floor.

Then light and warmth enveloped her, along with a kaleidoscope of images and faces. The last of which was familiar, its voice tense and precise.

"You did well, child... very well. Unfortunately, you have broken the oath and set us all on the path to war."

As if in a dream, she saw the headmistress's countenance float away, then a flash of light and a booming crash, and all drifted into the sweet embrace of unconsciousness.

Twenty-Eight

"Rise and shine, sleepy head!" Sarah's bright voice chirped from the floor below her bed. As usual, Sarah's bright smile beamed up at Cassie as her roommate stood dressed for the day. Cassie had never been an early riser, and Sarah's early morning habits only highlighted this fact. But as Cassie stretched and yawned, she couldn't think of a roommate she would rather have, even in comparison to her sister Charlie.

Charlie. She hadn't thought of her sister much until the semester had begun to draw to an end and the winter holiday break loomed before her. She hated the thought of having to leave her new friends, and yet, that slight tug for home had pulled at her heart with greater consistency as this final week had arrived. The semester had concluded with a round of final exams that had left Cassie's grades spread between B's and A's… sufficient enough to retain her scholarship and secure her place for the next semester. The time had whisked by so swiftly that she found her memories of the better part of the semester one large blur.

"Come on, Cassie. It's the awards ceremony, and you shouldn't be late for that. Besides, this is supposed to be the best breakfast of the year." Sarah shook her head and laughed lightly as Cassie groaned one last time before slipping from the bed to the floor.

"Yes, Mom," she quipped as Sarah flipped her a look that said a million things but ultimately let her know how much her roommate cared for her. "I'll be along, just save a spot for me, I promise I won't be long."

With a nod, Sarah skipped out of the room, her cheery voice greeting the other women in their hall as she went.

An odd thought niggled at Cassie's mind, as it had on several occasions over the last few weeks. It was as though she was supposed to remember something important but couldn't quiet her mind enough to recall what it was.

Having dressed quickly, Cassie walked out the door to her room, closing it quietly before proceeding down the narrow hallway that led up the winding steps toward the entry to Adicus Lounge above. She nodded politely to the new Dean of Women, who sat stoically at a desk that had been installed at the entryway. Apparently, Mistress Maude had left suddenly. Rumor had it that a family emergency had called her away. In her place, one of the administration staff, Mistress Meredith Prone, had been elevated to the position. It was quite an unfortunate name, but the woman was kind enough, if not even more stoic and severe than the former dean had been.

There at a table, presumably awaiting her arrival, sat Ludo with his ever present notebook. He had been thumbing through it as she arrived and looked up as she approached. "Hey, Cassie! My money is on you for the first year semester award."

Cassie smiled as she shook her head. "I'm a one trick pony, as they say. My grades are garbage. My money is on Sarah, she's well liked and accomplished all the way around."

Ludo tapped the notebook lightly with the eraser end of his pencil, a pensive look crossing his face. "Hey, I've been meaning to ask you. You haven't been having any strange dreams lately, have you?"

Cassie shrugged and shook her head. "I rarely dream, Ludo, certainly nothing that's memorable." She offered her hand to pull him up. "Come on, we're probably late already. Why do you ask, anyway?"

"Oh... I don't know... I've just been going over my notes and nothing makes any sense. Prior to about a month ago, I went on and on about dreams that you were having... but I frankly don't recall any of it. Kinda eerie, really."

"Kinda creepy if you ask me. You shouldn't be dreaming about me at all, weirdo, let alone writing about it." Ludo shrugged before joining her as the pair walked the remaining length of the Lounge and entered the portico that joined the lounge to a common area with a high, vaulted ceiling that led to Bearce Hall on the far side and to the Walter Husch Great Room to the right.

"Hey, first years... let's go!" a friendly voice called from the tall archway leading into the Great Room. A low hum could be heard from within, as most of the students were already gathered for the semester ending ceremony. Cassie and Ludo turned to see Whittle standing to one side of the open doors, apparently having been selected as an usher for the event.

"I was just about to close the doors, let's not have a repeat of your opening performance, Miss Cole," Whittle noted with a wink as she offered them both a printed program. Family members had been invited to attend the day's ceremony, which explained the literature being handed out at the door and the heightened formality.

Ludo broke away to sit with his parents as they entered, giving Cassie a last squeeze of the hand. The two had become fast friends, nothing more than that, but Cassie couldn't have asked for more.

She was as content as could be as she slipped into the back of her society's long table, a little lighter today as many of the student's families had been able to attend the ceremony. She knew that her Aunt Nonie would never be able to attend and so hadn't bothered to inform her of the opportunity.

"Welcome, friends, families, and scholars of the Governor's School for the Arts at Walnut Grove," intoned the headmistress in her smooth and regal tones. "Today, we take a moment to celebrate the accomplishments of our fine community at the midway point in our annual season. As has been the tradition of this institution; today, we wish to highlight the many accomplishments that have already begun to define our new first year class. As we all know, while the accomplishments of our seniors define the school in the eyes of the world, the work of our newest scholars ensures the stability of this institution and hints at what is to come. Allow me to say in all sincerity that this year's class is one of the most promising in the esteemed history of this institution. That is not to say that you are done, that you have even accomplished anything, my dear first year scholars, but to commend you to continue in your work with the same diligence you have shown in these first few months."

Cassie found herself drifting off into her own thoughts as the headmistress continued her address. Casting her eyes across the room, she reflected on how much had changed since she had first arrived those few months ago. It seemed like years had passed. And while warm feelings rose as she looked from face to face, she struggled to recall specific moments. "It's all been such a whirl," she noted softly. A student sitting near her hushed her and pointed to the dais where the headmistress was preparing to announce the first year award.

"Our first year society nominees this year are... Joshua Nettles for the Performing Arts. Maurice Allen for Music..." A smattering of applause followed each. "Staten Danmire for Choreography... Robert Franks for the Digital Arts." A loud whoop followed by boisterous laughter filtered up from the far table. "Apparently young Robert has a fan following."

"Bobby!!" came the enthusiastic response, followed by even more laughter and light applause.

Cassie tensed as Floquet arrived at her society nominee, secretly hoping that she might get the nod, but the result was nearly as satisfying as Floquet called out the winning name, "Sarah Dawson for Visual Arts." Cassie jumped up with her fellow society members to join in what was clearly the loudest applause thus far.

"And while the society for writing has been formally joined with the Digital Arts Society, the Board has decided to extend the award to one deserving student this year who has shown outstanding scholarship and creativity. Your final nominee and the First Year Scholar Gold Award for the first semester is awarded to Ludwig Van Ness."

Cassie was not the only one to realize who had been selected as the room fell silent before an eruption of applause as the few remaining writing society members crowded around their new champion. And there, in the midst of a swarm of praise, beamed Ludo.

"Well, what do you know... a diamond in the rough," Cassie commented to no one in particular as she smiled and applauded along with the rest of the assembly.

The final days swam by in a dream. Cassie conscientiously spent time with each of her closest friends but invested the most time with Sarah, Ludo and Whittle. At long last, she found herself boarding the small white bus, this time alone, as even Ludo had been retrieved by his parents in the wake of his award.

"Hello, Bentley," Cassie called as she boarded the bus and took her familiar seat at the front. The old bus driver smiled as he pulled the doors closed and shifted the little bus with its blue lettering into gear and pulled out onto the lane that would take Cassie home for the holiday break.

"Well, Miss Cole, how was your first semester... everything you hoped it would be?" Bentley's voice drifted back to her as he focused on the road ahead, the scenery swinging by more rapidly as they exited the grounds and turned toward the main road that would take them to the highway.

"It went by so fast. I feel like I learned a lot and yet can't remember anything that happened." Cassie laughed lightly as she watched the trees turn to suburban neighborhoods as the bus made its way toward home.

"Oh, it's not uncommon to leave this place with your mind a bit muddled. So much to learn and do. So much changes, and yet so much stays the same."

Cassie nodded absently at the driver's overly generic remarks. But as the school disappeared in the distance she felt a slight throbbing in her head that she tried to shake away. It was then, as the bus pulled onto the highway that circled the city that a question entered her mind.

"Bentley, you say that it isn't uncommon for people to leave with their mind muddled."

"Oh?" Bentley hedged. "I suppose I did say that. Idle words to fill the quiet. Nothing more."

"But I've had this strange feeling that I'm forgetting something. I can't remember specific things that happened, but it was only a couple of months. Does that seem strange to you?" Cassie hadn't turned to look at Bentley, her eyes continuing to watch the scenery slide by.

"I'm sure it's nothing, my dear. A whole new experience, new people, new friends, and new challenges. They all combine to one large whole. You do feel happy, don't you?"

"Yes, yes, of course. I feel... warm all over." Cassie settled back in her seat, her eyes sliding closed as the rhythm of the bus lulled her to sleep.

The bus jolting to a stop with a high-pitched hiss drew Cassie back to the waking world. She stretched slightly as she sat up. The chill air felt refreshing as Bentley pulled the mechanical lever to open the door, as they had at last returned to building fourteen on South Kettle Lane.

"Welcome home, Miss Cole. I'll be back bright and early in a month to pick you up. Have a wonderful holiday." Bentley's eyes twinkled as he spoke, and Cassie found herself smiling widely back at him as she stepped from the bus and waited for him to bring her bag around. With a slight nod of his head, the old bus driver made his way back to the driver's door before climbing in, closing the passenger side door with a thump, and pulling the bus away.

Cassie sighed as she looked up at the tall tenant building. "This sure doesn't feel like home anymore." And in that moment, a second thought struck her, this one more of a memory. She felt a deep and unsettling truth arise from some far away part of her mind.

"Mom is still alive..." she breathed.

But then the revolving doors to the building spun open and with it a light jingling sound followed by a familiar childish gait and squeals of delight wiped all of her thoughts away like the light dusting of snow that filtered from the sky above.

Cassie embraced her sister, tears cresting at the corners of her eyes as she saw her Aunt Joan approach. She was wrong. This was home.

But she couldn't shake the feeling that everything was about to change.

Acknowledgements

First and always, thank you to my lovely wife Rachael, who has weathered the ups and downs, ins and outs, and all the in-betweens. I love you and cannot imagine a world without you.

Thank you to my children and their spouses Katherine, Hannah, Joshua, Mason, Stetson, Mike and Claire for helping to bring this whole story adventure to life. Thank you, Mom, for being my first beta reader, biggest fan, and for instilling in me a love for creating long ago.

A special thank you to Marni MacRae, who provided the detailed edit that my manuscript so desperately needed, and to Sheryl Soong for the amazing cover and illustrations that help to bring the story to life.

I also owe a deep debt of gratitude to the many voice actors and friends in podcasting I have made along the way. First and foremost my utmost admiration goes to J.D. Rose who voiced Cassie so amazingly well. Her inspirational, emotional and professional performance significantly inspired the character's depth and growth.

My immense gratitude also extends to the entire amazing cast, to list just a few: Mike Atchley, Josh Monroe, Kenneth Eckle, Nikki and Jordache Richardson, Ditrie Marie Bowie, Susannah

Lewis, Storm S. Cone, Rachel Finley, Adam LeGrave, Julie and Corbin Miller, Haley Munoz, Kate Wallinga, Brian Dowling, Joleen Fresquez, and Beth Yadon whose haunting vocals can be heard throughout. A very special thank you to Mike Atchley, my partner in creation at Good Ham Productions. The music, singing, vocal performances, foley and sound effects in the audio version are all original creations of our insanely talented cast at Good Ham Productions. Be sure to follow us on all of the social platforms and check out our extensive world building at goodhamproductions. com

About the Author

Daniel holds a Bachelor of Arts degree from Grove City College, Pennsylvania, a Master of Arts in Counseling, a Master of Divinity from Asbury Theological Seminary, and a Master of Business Administration from the University of Maryland's Robert H. Smith School of Business.

Daniel's story as a Navy Chaplain was featured in a book by author Jane Hampton Cook in 2006, and several of his letters written during his combat experience supporting Operation Iraqi Freedom in 2003 were published in the book titled: *Stories of Faith and Courage from the War in Iraq and Afghanistan.*

Daniel, along with his son Mason, launched HappyGoLukky Productions in 2019, resulting in the creation of the HappyGoLukky family friendly storytelling podcast that reached a peak rank of #21 on Apple Podcasts and has since received numerous nominations and accolades. Their storytelling improv sessions contributed directly to the creation of *Charlie Saves Christmas*, the prologue novella to the *Chronicles of Eridul* series.

Daniel resides in Pittsburgh, Pennsylvania with his wife Rachael and their puppy Penny. His children have begun to fly the nest, as children should.